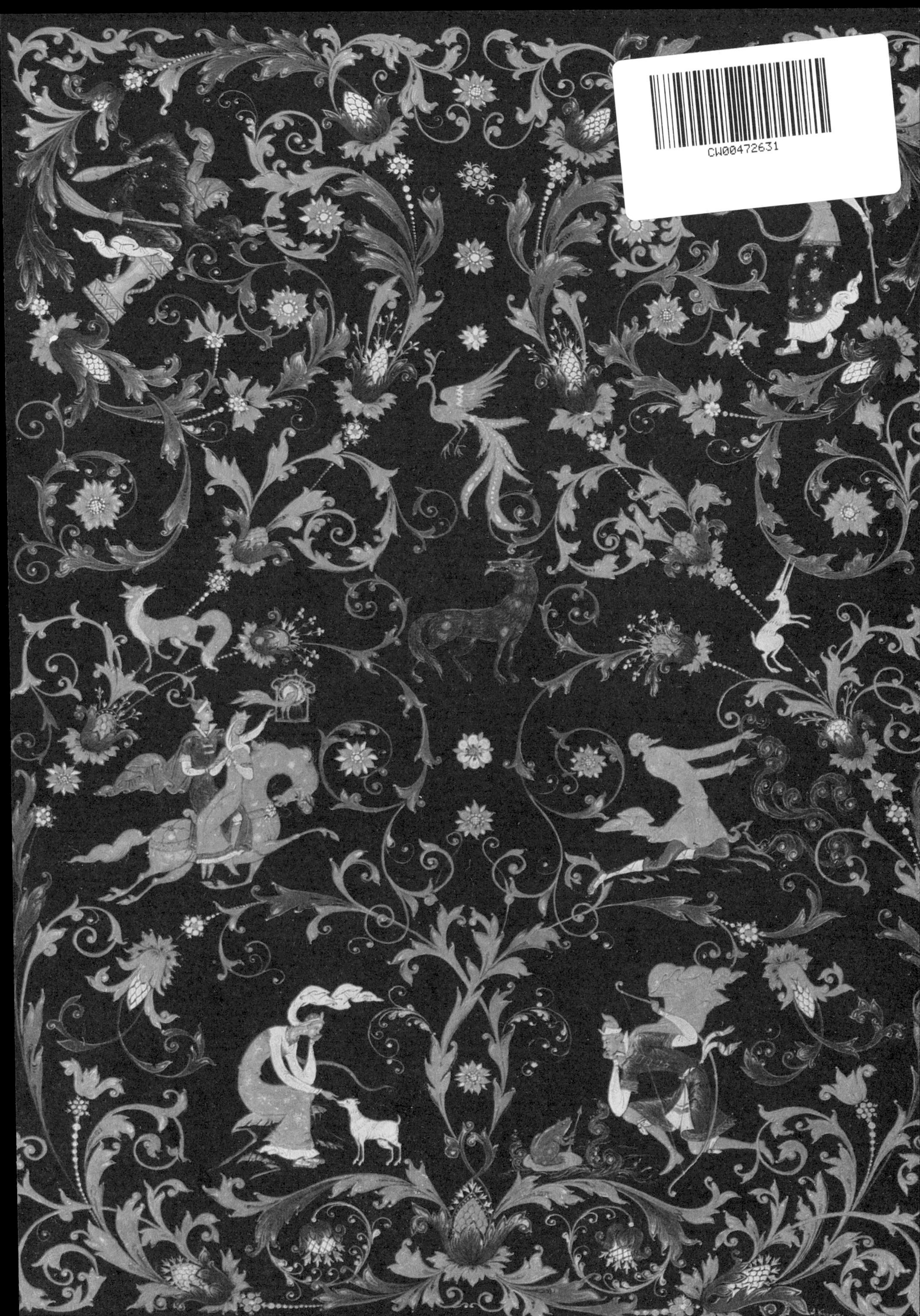

THE MAGIC RING

RUSSIAN FOLK TALES From Alexander Afanasiev's Collection

Illustrated
by Alexander Kurkin

Raduga Publishers
Moscow

Contens

ISBN 5-05-004687-4

Little Sister Fox and Brother Wolf

There was once an old man and woman. One day the old man told his wife, "Bake some pies, old woman, while I go fishing."

He caught his fish and was taking a cartful home. On the way he suddenly spied a fox lying on the path. So he climbed down from the cart and went over to the fox: she was lying there as stiff as the dead. "That'll make my wife a fine present," said the old man, as he took hold of the fox and put her on his cart. Then he walked on in front. The crafty fox seized her chance and began quietly to drop the fish, one by one, from the cart until the cart was empty. Then she jumped down while the cart trundled on. Presently the old man drove into his yard and called to his wife, "Hey, old woman, come and see what a splendid collar I've brought for your winter coat." "Where is it?" she asked. "There, in the cart—fish and a fur collar." The old woman went to the cart: but there was neither collar nor fish, and she began to curse her husband, "Oh, you old nincompoop! Daft so-and-so! You and your stupid tricks!" Then the old man realised that the fox had not been dead after all; he moaned and groaned, but there was nothing to be done.

The fox picked up all the fish she had thrown onto the track and sat down to have a good meal. While she was dining, a wolf chanced by. "Hello, Sister." "Hello, Brother." "Give me some fish." "Go and catch some yourself," said the fox. "If only I knew how," replied the wolf. "Bless me," sighed the fox, "there's nothing to it. Listen, Brother, go down to the river, drop your tail through the ice and the fish will come and hang on it. But be patient or you won't catch anything."

3

So the wolf went down to the river, let his tail through the ice and waited. He squatted like that all night long. By morning his tail was frozen stiff. When he tried to rise, he found he was stuck. "Fancy that," he thought, "I've caught so many fish I cannot pull them all out!" Then he saw some village women coming for water. Catching sight of the grey beast, they began to scream, "Wolf, wolf! Kill him! Kill him!" They set about the wolf with whatever came to hand: pails, yokes, pots and sticks. The wolf tugged himself free and raced off, leaving his tail stuck in the ice. "I'll get even with you, Sister Fox," he thought.

Meanwhile, Sister Fox, full of fish, was up to her tricks again: she crept into a cottage where the women were frying pancakes, fell headlong into the bucket and fled covered with batter. Then she met the wolf. "You and your tricks! I got a good hiding because of you." "Oh, Brother Wolf," said Sister Fox, "they only made you bleed, but I've had the stuffing knocked out of me! I am far worse off than you: I can barely drag myself along." "That's true," said the wolf. "Sit on my back, Sister Fox, and I'll carry you home." The crafty fox mounted the wolf's back and off they went. She sat there saying quietly to herself, "The thrashed is carrying the thrasher; the thrashed is carrying the thrasher." "What's that you said, Sister Fox?" asked the wolf. "Oh, Brother Wolf, I was only saying: the thrashed is carrying the thrashed." "Yes, indeed, Sister Fox."

"Let's build ourselves a house each, Brother Wolf." "All right, Sister Fox," the wolf replied. "I'll build myself a house of wood," she said, "and you build a house of ice." So they set to work, made their houses and lived in them until spring came, when the wolf's house melted right away. "Aha, Sister Fox," said the wolf, "you've tricked me again. I shall eat you for that." "Wait, Brother Wolf, let's have a contest to see who will eat whom." Sister Fox led him into the forest to a deep hole and said, "If you can jump across the hole you'll eat me, but if you can't I'll eat you." The wolf jumped and fell into the hole. "Right," said the fox, "you can sit there and stew." And off she went.

Sister Fox was going along with a rolling-pin in her paws. She came to a peasant's cottage, knocked at the door and said, "Please, let Sister Fox in for the night." "We have no room for ourselves." "I'll be no trouble. I'll lie on the bench with my tail beneath it and my rolling-pin under the stove." So they let her in. She lay down on the bench, tucking her tail beneath it and her rolling-pin under the stove. Early next morning the fox got up, burned her rolling-pin and then asked, "Who's taken my rolling-pin? I wouldn't trade it for a goose!" What could the poor peasant do? He gave her a goose for the rolling-pin and off she went singing:

"Little Sister Fox was going along the road,
Carrying a rolling-pin, hee-hee;
But now she has a goo-oo-sie."

Knock! Knock! Knock! She rapped at the door of another peasant's cottage. "Who's there?" came a voice. "It's me, Sister Fox; please let me in for the night."

4

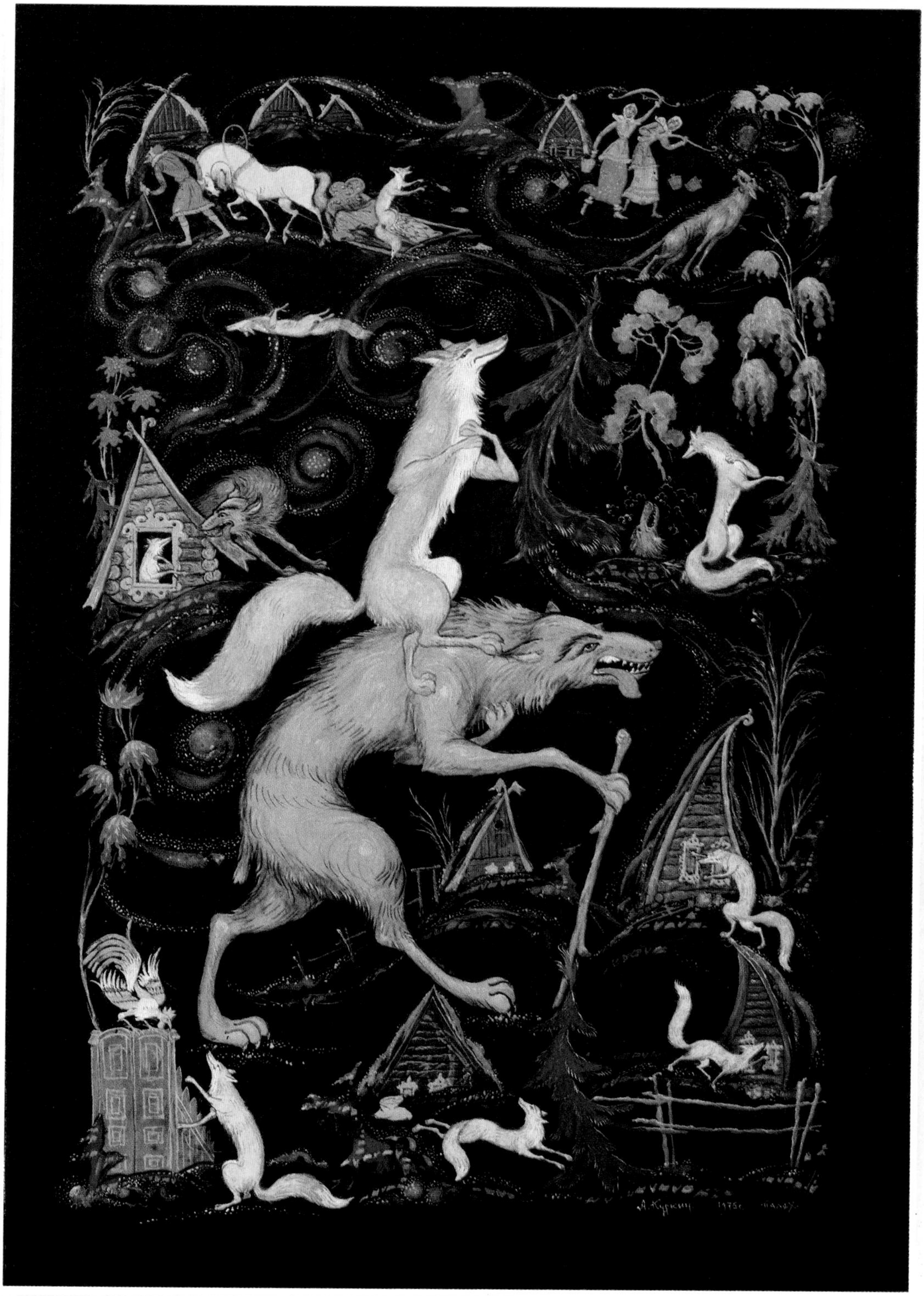
А. Куркин 1975г. Палех

"We have no room for ourselves." "I'll be no trouble," she said, "I'll lie on the bench, with my tail beneath it and my goose under the stove." So they let her in. She lay herself down on the bench, tucking her tail beneath it and her goose under the stove. Early next morning she jumped up, seized the goose, wrung its neck, ate it and said, "Who's taken my goose? I wouldn't trade it for a turkey!" What could the poor peasant do? He gave her a turkey for the goose and off she went singing:

> "Little Sister Fox was going along the road,
> Carrying a rolling-pin, hee-hee;
> Then she had a goo-oo-sie,
> But now she has a tur-ur-key."

Knock. Knock. Knock! She rapped at the door of a third cottage. "Who's there?" came a voice. "It's me, Sister Fox. Please let me in for the night." "We have no room for ourselves." "I'll be no trouble. I'll lie on the bench, with my tail beneath it and my turkey under the stove." So they let her in. And she lay down on the bench, tucking her tail beneath it and her turkey under the stove. Early next morning she leapt up, seized the turkey, wrung its neck, ate it and asked, "Who's taken my turkey? I wouldn't trade it for your son's wife!" What could the poor man do? He gave her his son's wife for the turkey; the fox put her in a sack and went on her way singing:

> "Little Sister Fox was going along the road,
> Carrying a rolling-pin, hee-hee;
> Then she had a goo-oo-sie;
> Then she had a tur-ur-key;
> But now she has a gir-ir-lie!"

Knock. Knock. Knock! She rapped at the door of a fourth cottage. "Who's there?" came a voice. "It's me, Sister Fox. Please let me in for the night." "We have no room for ourselves." "I'll be no trouble. I'll lie on the bench, with my tail beneath it and my sack under the stove." So they let her in. She lay down on the bench, tucking her tail beneath it and her sack under the stove.

But in the night the peasant set the girl free and put his dog in the sack instead. Early next morning Sister Fox woke up and made ready to leave. Picking up her sack she went on her way, and said, "Sing us a song, my dear!" The dog began to growl. The fox took fright, dropped the sack and fled.

Sister Fox was running along, when she saw a cock sitting upon a gate-post. "Good morrow, my son," she said. "You've got seventy wives, yet not once have you been to confession, you sinner. Come down here and I will absolve you."

The cock flew down, and she seized him and gobbled him up.

Fox, Hare and Cock

There was once a fox and a hare. The fox had a house of ice, the hare a house of wood. Fair spring came and melted the fox's house, while the hare's stood firm and strong. So the fox asked the hare if she could come in to warm herself, then drove him out. The hare went down the road crying, and met two dogs, who asked, "Wuff, wuff, wuff! Why are you crying?" "Leave me alone, dogs! Who wouldn't cry? I had a wooden house, while the fox had one of ice. She invited herself into mine and drove me out." "Don't cry, hare," barked the dogs. "We'll chase her out." "No, you won't." "Oh, yes we will." Off they went to the hare's house. "Wuff, wuff, wuff! Come out of there, fox!" "Go away, before I come and tear you to pieces," she shouted back from the stove. The dogs took fright and fled.

Once more the hare went on his way crying. This time he met a bear who asked, "Why are you crying?" "Leave me alone, bear," said the hare. "Who wouldn't cry? I had a wooden house, while the fox had one of ice. She invited herself into mine and drove me out." "Don't cry, hare," said the bear. "I'll chase her out." "No, you won't. The dogs tried and failed; you'll fare no better." "Oh, yes I will." Off they went to chase her out. "Come on out, fox!" roared the bear. But she shouted from the stove: "Go away, before I come and tear you to pieces." The bear took fright and fled.

Once more the hare went on his way crying and met an ox who asked, "Why are you crying?" "Leave me alone, ox! Who wouldn't cry? I had a wooden house,

7

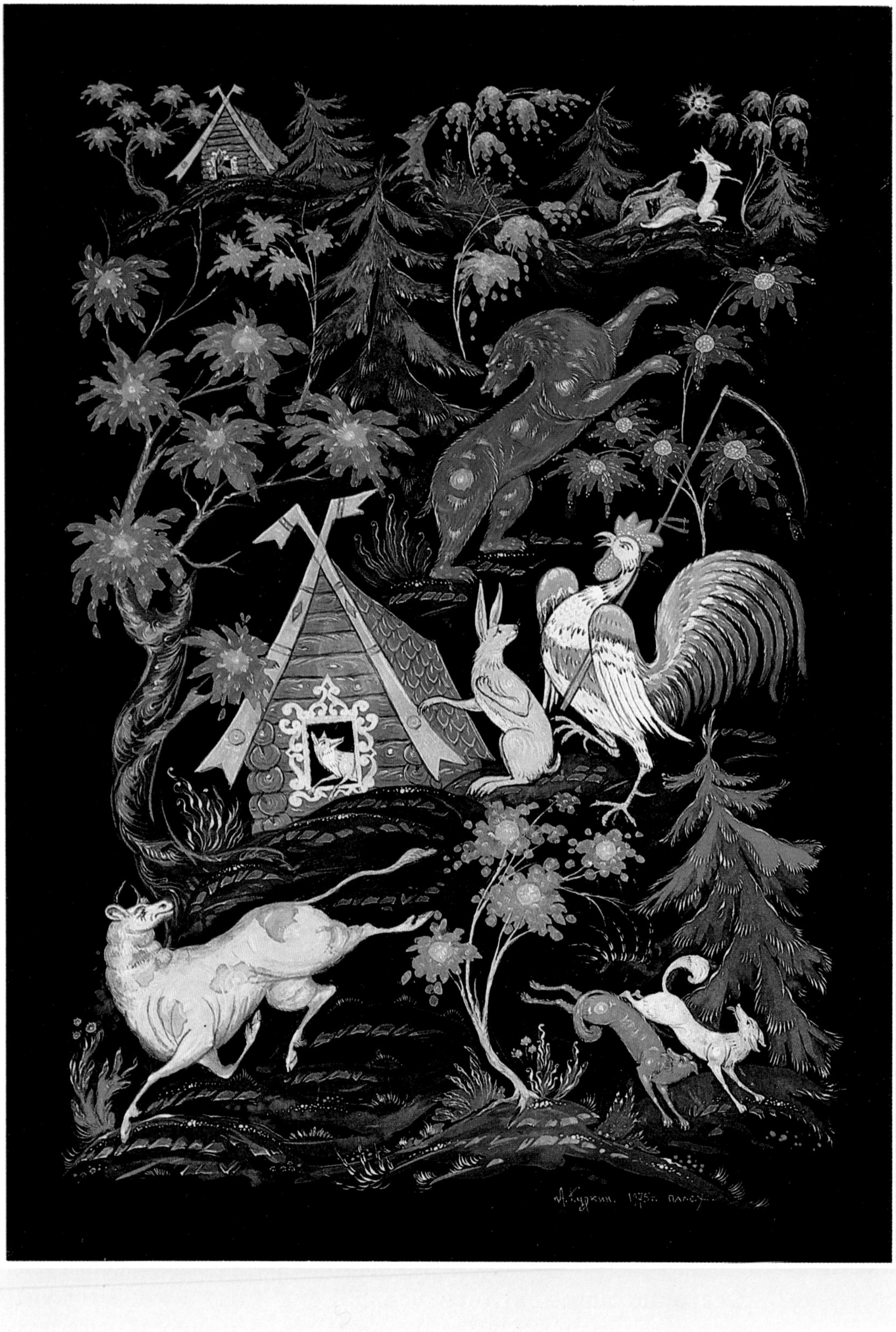
1975г.

while the fox had one of ice. She invited herself into mine and drove me out." "Come with me, I'll chase her out." "No, you won't," said the hare. "The dogs tried and failed, the bear tried and failed; you'll fare no better." "Oh, yes I will." Off they went together to the hare's house. "Come on out, fox!" But she shouted from the stove: "Go away, before I come and tear you to pieces." The ox took fright and fled.

Once more the hare went on his way crying and met a cock with a scythe. "Cock-a-doodle-doo! Why are you crying, hare?" "Leave me alone, cock! Who wouldn't cry? I had a house of wood, while the fox had one of ice. She invited herself into mine and drove me out." "Come along with me, I'll chase her out." "No, you won't," said the hare. "The dogs tried and failed; the bear tried and failed; the ox tried and failed. You'll fare no better." "Oh, yes I will." So they went up to the house. "Cock-a-doodle-doo! I'll cut that fox in two with my scythe so sharp and true!" When the fox heard that, she took fright and called, "I'm getting dressed." Again the cock crowed: "Cock-a-doodle-doo! I'll cut that fox in two with my scythe so sharp and true!" And the fox cried: "I'm putting on my fur coat." A third time the cock crowed: "Cock-a-doodle-doo! I'll cut that fox in two with my scythe so sharp and true!" The fox rushed out of the door and the cock cut off her head. So the hare and the cock lived together happily ever after.

And now a pot of butter for my tale, friend.

The Bun

There once lived an old man and woman.

One day the old man said: "Bake me a bun, old woman." "What shall I bake it with? We've no flour." "Come on, old woman! Sweep round the bin and shake out the tin; maybe there's some in."

Taking up her goose-wing brush, the old woman swept round the bin, shook out the tin and scraped together a few handfuls of flour. She kneaded it with sour cream, baked it in butter and placed the bun on the window-ledge to cool.

By and by the bun got tired of lying there, so he rolled off from the window to the bench, from the bench to the floor, from the floor to the door; there he hopped over the threshold to the porch, from the porch into the yard, from the yard through the gate, and off down the road.

As he rolled along the road he met a hare. "Round bun, round bun, I'm going to eat you." "Oh, please, don't eat me, cross-eyed hare. Let me sing you a song," begged the bun and sang:

> "I was scraped in the bin,
> Ground in the mill,
> Shaken in the tin,
> Baked on the grill,
> Cooled on the sill;
> From grand-dad I then fled,

From grannie I soon fled,
And I'll soon run away from you!"

And off he rolled, so fast the hare could not catch him.

On and on the bun rolled until he met a wolf. "Round bun, round bun, I'm going to eat you." "Oh, please, don't eat me, grey wolf. Let me sing you a song," begged the bun and sang:

"I was scraped in the bin,
Ground in the mill,
Shaken in the tin,
Baked on the grill,
Cooled on the sill;
From grand-dad I then fled,
From grannie I soon fled,
From cross-eyed hare I fled,
And I'll soon run away from you!"

And off he rolled, so fast the wolf could not catch him.

On and on he rolled until he met a bear. "Round bun, round bun, I'm going to eat you." "Oh, you couldn't do that, Bandy-legs!"

"I was scraped in the bin,
Ground in the mill,
Shaken in the tin,
Baked on the grill,
Cooled on the sill;
From grand-dad I then fled,
From grannie I soon fled,
From cross-eyed hare I fled,
From big grey wolf I fled,
And I'll soon run away from you!"

And off he rolled, so fast the bear could not catch him.

On and on rolled the bun, until he met a fox. "Hello there, Master Bun! How handsome you look today."

The bun sang his little song:

"I was scraped in the bin,
Ground in the mill,
Shaken in the tin,
Baked on the grill,
Cooled on the sill;
From grand-dad I then fled,

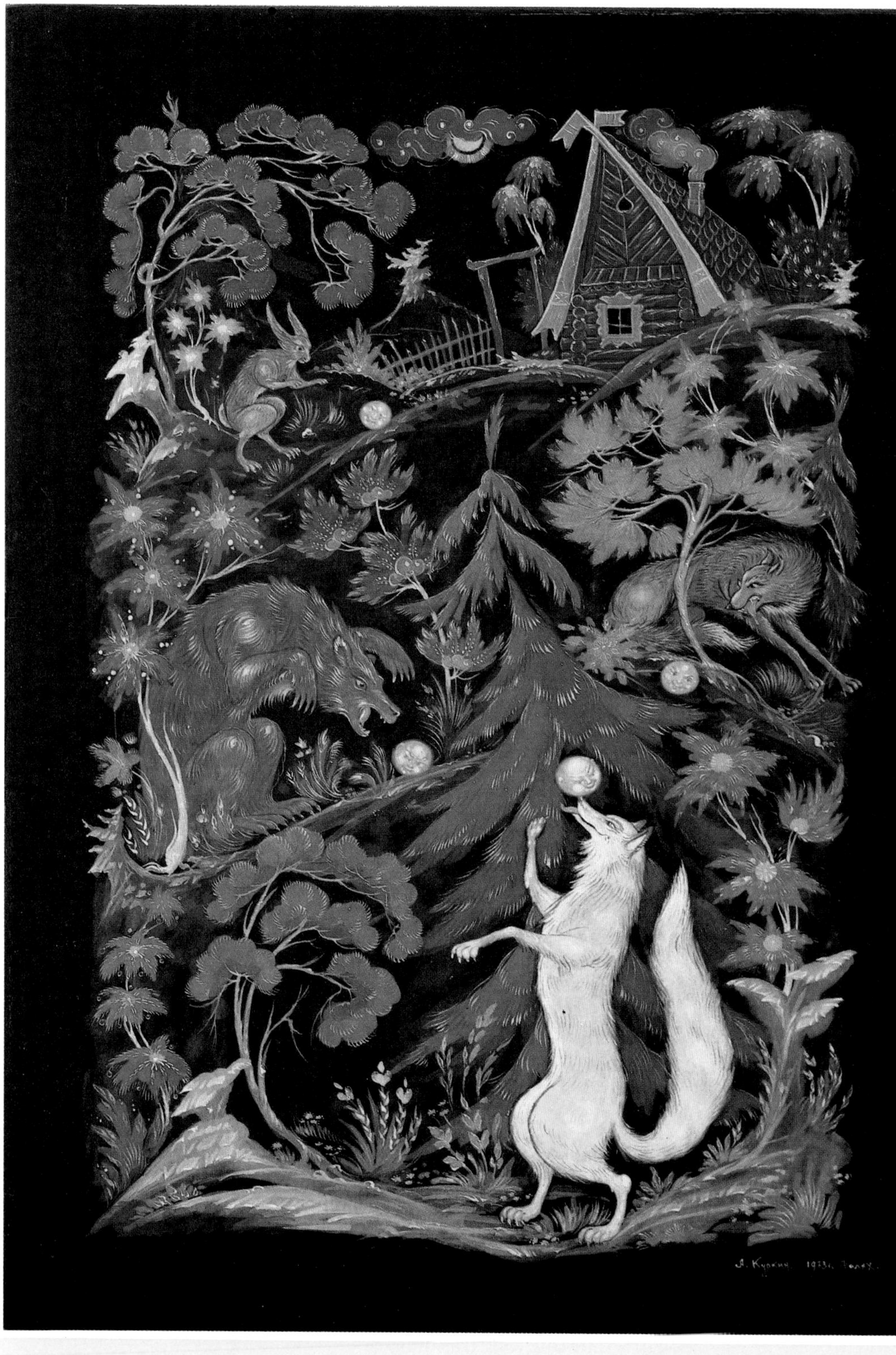
А. Куркин. 1973 г. Палех.

From grannie I soon fled,
From cross-eyed hare I fled,
From big grey wolf I fled,
From bandy bear I fled,
And I'll soon run away from you!"

"What a delightful little song!" said the fox. "The only trouble is, round bun, I'm rather old and don't hear too well. Come, sit on my nose and sing it again."

The bun hopped onto the fox's nose and sang his song again. "Oh, thank you, round bun. What a splendid song; I'd love to hear it just once more. Come, sit on my tongue and sing it one last time." She poked out her tongue. The foolish bun hopped onto her tongue... And the fox —snip-snap —gobbled him up.

Liza the Fox and Catafay the Cat

Once upon a time there was an old peasant. He had a cat who was always getting up to mischief. The old peasant got tired of him. He thought it over, then picked up the cat, put him in a sack, tied it up and took it to the forest. And there he left the cat to fend for himself. The cat wandered about the forest until he came to a woodman's cottage; he climbed into the loft and made himself at home. When he was hungry he would go and catch birds or mice in the woods, eat his fill and come back to the loft. All was fine and dandy!

One day the cat went walking and met a fox who marvelled at the cat: "I've never seen such a beast in all my days." She curtseyed to the cat, asking, "Tell me, kind Sir, who are you, what brings you to these parts and what, pray, might be your name?" Ruffling up his fur, the cat said boldly, "I have been sent from Siberian forests to be your new governor; my name is Catafay Ivanovich." "Ah, Catafay Ivanovich," said the fox, "I had not heard of it. Will you come home with me and be my guest?" So the cat went with the fox; when they arrived at the fox's home, the fox treated her guest to all kinds of game, enquiring: "Tell me, Catafay Ivanovich, are you married or single?" "Single," said the cat. "Ah, so am I. Take me for your wife". The cat agreed. And they began to feast in happy celebration.

Next day the fox set off to get some provisions to feed her new husband; and the cat stayed home. As she ran along a wolf chanced to cross her path and began to banter, "Where have you been, my dear? I looked in all the fox-holes and found no sign of you." "Let me pass, fool! And none of your banter. I'm a married woman now." "Who is your husband, Liza?" "Have you not heard, that we have a new governor sent from the forests of Siberia? His name is Catafay Ivanovich. And I am now the governor's wife." "No, I have not heard, Liza. Please may I take a look at him?" "Oh my! That Catafay Ivanovich of mine is so fierce: if anyone displeases him he eats them up right away! Get a lamb and bring it to pay your respects; then lay it down and make yourself scarce, for if he sees you, brother, you'd better say your prayers!" Off ran the wolf to get a lamb.

On went the fox until she met a bear, who at once began to banter with her. "Hold your tongue, Bandy-legs," she snapped, "I'm a married woman now." "Who is your husband, Liza?" "Our new governor, sent from the forests of Siberia. His name is Catafay Ivanovich and he is my husband." "Please may I take a look at him, Liza?" asked the bear. "Oh my! That Catafay Ivanovich of mine is so fierce: if anyone displeases him he eats them up right away! Get an ox and bring it to pay your respects; the wolf is going to bring a lamb. Be sure you lay the ox down and make yourself scarce for if he sees you, brother, you'd better say your prayers!" The bear ambled off to get an ox.

The wolf got a lamb, skinned it and stood there thinking, when whom should he see but the bear dragging an ox along. "Good-day, Brother Bear," said the wolf. "Good-day, Brother Wolf. Have you seen the fox and her husband?" "No, brother, I want to very much." "Then go and call on them." "No, not me, Brother Bear. You go, you're braver than me." "No, Brother Wolf, I won't go either." All of a sudden a hare came dashing by. The bear shouted at him, "Come here, you cross-eyed devil!" The frightened hare came scurrying up. "Well, now, cross-eyed whipper-snapper, do you know where the fox lives?" "I do, Sir." "Then just you run off and tell her that Brother Bear and Brother Wolf are long ready and waiting to see her and her husband, eager to pay their respects with lamb and ox."

The hare flew off to the fox as fast as his legs would carry him. Meanwhile the bear and the wolf wondered where to hide. Said the bear, "I'll climb up a pine-tree." "But what am I to do?" said the wolf. "Where can I hide? I can't get up a tree! Brother Bear, I beg of you, help me find a place to hide." So the bear hid him in the bushes and covered him with dry leaves. Then he climbed up a pine-tree to the very top, and looked around to see if Catafay the Cat and Liza the Fox were coming. Meanwhile the hare ran to the fox's house, knocked on the door and told the fox, "Brother Bear and Brother Wolf sent me to tell you that they are ready and waiting for you and your husband, eager to pay their respects with lamb and ox." "Go back and tell them we are coming, Cross-eyes."

So the cat and the fox set off together. The bear saw them coming and called down to the wolf, "Brother Wolf, the fox and her husband are on their way; he's

15

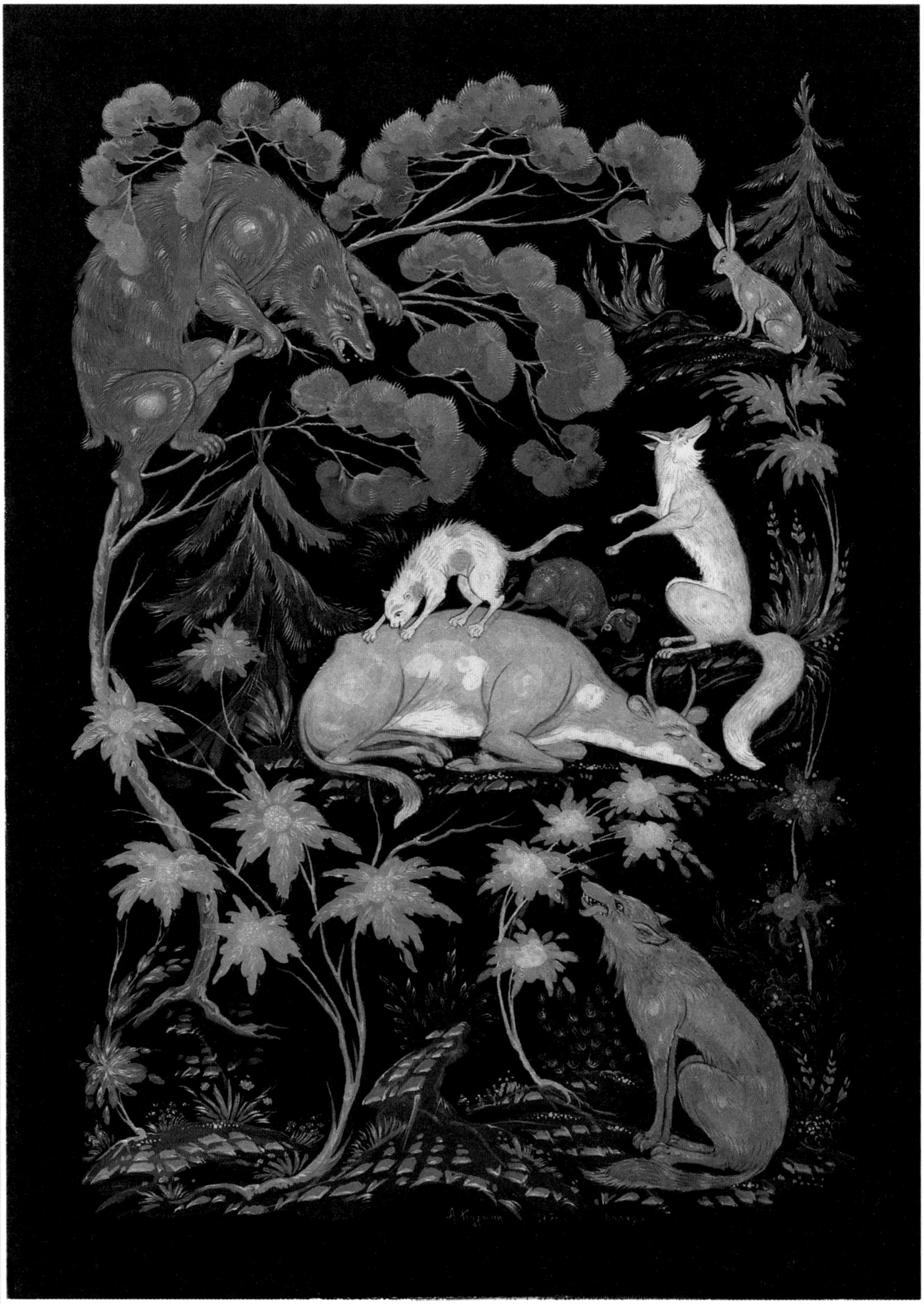

very small." The cat came up and pounced on the ox, his fur bristling, and he began to tear at the meat with his teeth and claws, miaowing all the while as if in anger: "Mo-o-ore, mo-o-ore!" "He may be small, but what a glutton!" said the bear. "There's enough for the four of us, but he wants more; what if he turns on us next!" The wolf wanted to take a look at the fearsome governor, but could not see through the leaves. He began to push them aside. The cat heard the leaves rustle, thought it was a mouse and gave a great bound, his claws landing right on the wolf's nose.

The wolf jumped up and fled in terror. The cat himself also took fright and rushed to the tree in which the bear was sitting. "Oh, my goodness," thought the bear, "he's seen me!" There was no time to climb down, so he gave himself up to God's will and jumped, landing with a great thump that shook his insides up. Then he took to his heels, with the fox shouting after him, "He'll give you what for! Just you wait!" After that all the animals feared the cat; the cat and fox had enough meat for the whole winter and they lived and prospered, and still do to this very day.

The Frightened Wolves
and the Bear

Once upon a time there lived a goat and a ram in the same farmyard. They lived together happily enough, sharing whatever they got; the only thorn in their side was Purrkin the cat. He was such a thief and a rogue, ever on the prowl, ready to gobble anything up.

One day the goat and the ram were lying down and chatting to each other; all of a sudden Purrkin the grey-browed puss came along crying piteously. The goat and the ram asked: "Pussy-cat, pussy-cat, Purrkin! Why are you crying and hopping along on three legs?" "Who wouldn't cry?" replied the cat. "The old woman has beaten me, tweaked my ears, broken my legs and all but wrung my neck." "What did you do to earn such a thrashing?" "Oh dear, goodness knows what came over me: I went and licked up all the cream; that's why I got a thrashing." And once more Purrkin burst into tears. "Pussy-cat, pussy-cat, Purrkin! What are you crying for now?" "Who wouldn't cry? The old woman beat me and said: 'My son-in-law is coming and now there's nothing for him to eat. I'll have to put the goat and the ram in the pot.'"

At that the goat and the ram howled, "Oh, silly Purrkin! You've destroyed us! We'll give you a good butting for that!" Thereupon Purrkin admitted his guilt and

18

begged forgiveness. And they let him be, but all three put their heads together: what were they to do? "Well now, Brother Ram," said Purrkin, "if your head is good and strong why don't you try the gate?" The ram took a run and butted the gate with his head: it shook, but did not open. At that brother goat took a long run and—crash!—the gate flew open.

The dust went up and the grass was trampled underfoot as the goat and the ram fled for their lives, with Purrkin hopping on three legs behind. He soon grew tired and begged his brothers: "Dear Brother Ram, dear Brother Goat! Don't abandon your young brother for wild animals to eat." So the goat picked him up and sat him on his back, and off they rushed again up hill and down dale, and over the drifting sands. On and on they raced, both day and night, as far as their legs would take them.

They had come to a craggy crag, a hilly hill; beneath that crag lay a new-mown field, and in the field were haystacks as big as towns. The goat, the ram and the cat stopped to rest; and the night was dark and chill. "How will we make a fire?" wondered the goat and the ram. Meanwhile Purrkin had been gathering birch bark which he wound round the goat's horns and told him and the ram to butt each other. That they did, so hard that sparks flew from their eyes and the birch bark burst into flame. "Good," said Purrkin, "now we can warm ourselves." So saying he set fire to the haystack.

Hardly had they warmed themselves than who should appear but a most unwelcome guest—Grizzly the Bear. "Let me warm myself and rest awhile; I don't feel well," he said. "Welcome, ant-eater Grizzly," they said. "Whence do you come?" "I have been to the bee-garden and had a tussle with some peasants, that's why I'm feeling rather sore; I'm off to the fox for treatment." The four of them shared the long dark night: the bear under the haystack, Purrkin on top, and the goat and the ram by the smouldering fire. In the night seven grey wolves and a white one made for the haystack. "Fie, foh!" the white wolf said. "It isn't Russian blood I smell. What sort of tribe is this? Let's see what they're made of!"

The goat and the ram began to bleat in fear, while Purrkin opened up his mouth and said, "Hush, white wolf, prince of wolves! Do not anger our elder; heaven help us when he's roused! If you cross him, you'll be sorry. Don't you see his beard? Therein lies his strength; he kills beasts with his beard and skins them with his horns. You had better be wise and seek his favour: say you want to play with his young brother lying beneath the haystack." The wolves bowed to the goat, encircled Grizzly and began to tease him. He put up with it as long as he could, then suddenly grabbed a wolf in each paw. They howled and pleaded for mercy, then crawled away, tails between their legs, and fled into the night for all they were worth.

Meanwhile the goat and the ram picked up Purrkin and rushed off to the forest; but once again they came upon the grey wolves. The cat scampered to the top of a nearby fir-tree, while the goat and the ram hooked their forelegs over a fir branch and hung from it. The wolves stood beneath the fir, baring their teeth and howling as they glared at the goat and the ram. Seeing the goat and the ram wouldn't hold on for long, Purrkin began throwing fir-cones at the wolves, shouting, "One wolf! Two wolves! Three wolves! One wolf for each of us. I, Purrkin, have eaten two wolves, bones and all, so I'm full up; but you went hunting bear and had no luck, big brother, so you take my share of wolf!" No sooner had he uttered these words than the goat slipped and fell, horns first, right on top of a wolf. And Purrkin yelled out: "Grab him! Don't let him escape!" The wolves were terrified and raced off as fast as their legs would carry them. And that was the last they saw of them.

The Fly's Castle

A fly once built himself a castle. Along came a creepy-crawly louse and called, "Who, who, who is in this castle? Who, who, who is in this den?" "I am: I Spy Fly. And who are you?" "I am Creepy-Crawly Louse." Along came an itchy-twitchy flea and called, "Who, who, who is in this castle? Who, who, who is in this den?" "We are. I Spy Fly and Creepy-Crawly Louse." Along came a long-legged midge and called, "Who, who, who is in this castle? Who, who, who is in this den?" "We are," came three voices. "I Spy Fly, Creepy-Crawly Louse and Itchy-Twitchy Flea." Along came a tittle-tattle mouse and called, "Who, who, who is in this castle? Who, who, who is in this den?" "We are," came four voices. "I Spy Fly, Creepy-Crawly Louse, Itchy-Twitchy Flea and Long-Legged Midge."

Along came a busy-lizzie lizard and called, "Who, who, who is in this castle? Who, who, who is in this den?" "We are," came five voices. "I Spy Fly, Creepy-Crawly Louse, Itchy-Twitchy Flea, Long-Legged Midge and Tittle-Tattle Mouse." Along came Liza the fox and called, "Who, who, who is in this castle? Who, who, who is in this den?" "We are," came six voices. "I Spy Fly, Creepy-Crawly Louse, Itchy-Twitchy Flea, Long-Legged Midge, Tittle-Tattle Mouse and Busy-Lizzie Lizard." Along came bob-tabbit rabbit and called, "Who, who, who is in this castle? Who, who, who is in this den?" "We are," came seven voices. "I Spy Fly, Creepy-

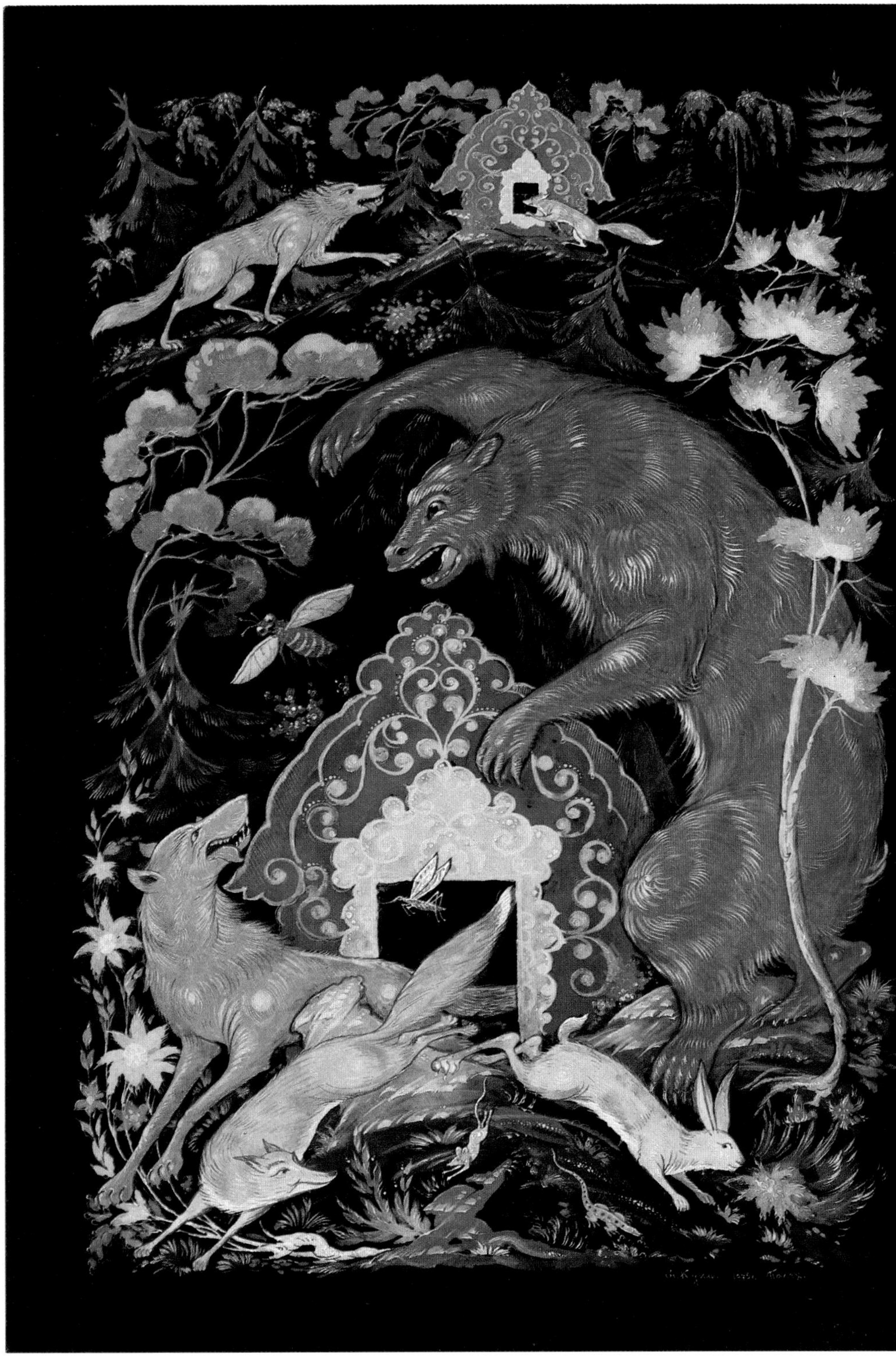

Crawly Louse, Itchy-Twitchy Flea, Long-Legged Midge, Tittle-Tattle Mouse, Busy-Lizzie Lizard and Liza the Fox."

Along came grey-tailed wolf and called, "Who, who, who is in this castle? Who, who, who is in this den?" "We are," came eight voices. "I Spy Fly, Creepy-Crawly Louse, Itchy-Twitchy Flea, Long-Legged Midge, Tittle-Tattle Mouse, Busy-Lizzie Lizard, Liza the Fox and Bob-Tabbit Rabbit." Along came stumpy-legs bear and called, "Who, who, who is in this castle? Who, who, who is in this den?" "We are," came nine voices. "I Spy Fly, Creepy-Crawly Louse, Itchy-Twitchy Flea, Long-Legged Midge, Tittle-Tattle Mouse, Busy-Lizzie Lizard, Liza the Fox, Bob-Tabbit Rabbit and Grey-Tailed Wolf. And who are you?" "I am Crush-'Em-All-Now," said stumpy-legs bear. With that he put his paw on the castle and smashed it to pieces.

The Golden Fish

Once upon a time, on the island of Buyan, there stood a small tumble-down cottage; and in that cottage dwelt an old man and woman. They lived in great poverty. The old man would cast his net and try to catch some fish; but all he caught was barely enough to keep body and soul together each day. One day the old man cast his net, began to haul it in and felt something heavy in it; never had he felt the like before. He could hardly pull it in. Yet when he looked he saw the net was empty: except for a little fish. But it was no ordinary fish—it was golden. And it spoke in a human voice, "Don't take me, old man! Let me go back to the deep blue sea and I'll be useful to you: I'll do whatever you wish." The old man set to thinking, then said, "I need nothing from you: go back and swim in the sea."

He threw the golden fish into the sea and turned for home. The old woman asked him how much he had caught. "Nothing but a single golden fish, and that I threw back into the sea," he said. "It spoke in a human voice: 'Let me go,' it said, 'into the deep blue sea and I'll do whatever you wish.' I was sorry for it, asked for naught and set it free." "Oh, you old devil!" exclaimed his wife. "Good luck falls from the skies and you haven't the sense to grab it." She grew angry and cursed the old man from morn till night, giving him no peace. "You could have asked for bread at least," she yelled at him. "We won't have a dry crust to eat soon, what'll you do then?" In despatir the old man went down to the seashore to ask the golden fish for bread; coming to the sea-edge he shouted in a loud voice: "Fish, oh fish! Stand with your tail on the sea and your head facing me." The fish came swimming to the shore. "What do you need, old man?" it asked. "The old woman is angry with me and has sent me for bread." "Go home, you'll have bread aplenty," said the fish. So he went back home and asked his old woman whether there was any bread. "Bread aplenty," she replied. "But here's the rub: my tub has sprung a leak and I can't do the washing. Go back to your golden fish and ask it for a new wash-tub."

Back went the old man to the sea. "Fish, oh fish!" he shouted. "Stand with your tail on the sea and your head facing me." Up swam the golden fish. "What do you need, old man?" it asked. "The old woman sent me, she wants a new wash-tub." "All right, you'll have a wash-tub too," it said. Back home went the old man; but before he had crossed the threshold, the old woman set on him again. "Go back," she said, "to your golden fish and ask it to build us a new house. We can't live here any more, it's falling about our ears." Off went the old man to the sea, calling, "Fish, oh fish! Stand with your tail on the sea and your head facing me." Up swam the fish, stood its tail on the sea and faced him directly, asking, "What do you need, old man?" "Build us a new house," he said, "the old woman is angry and won't give me any peace. She says she won't live in the old cottage anymore, because it's falling about her ears." "Cheer up, old man," said the fish. "Go on home and say your prayers; all will be done."

So the old man returned and what should he see but a brand new house, made of oak, with carved eaves. And there was his old woman rushing at him, even wilder than before, cursing louder than ever: "Oh, you old fool! You don't know good luck when you stare it in the face. You ask for a house and think that's enough! No, you go back to that golden fish and tell it this: I don't want to be a fisherman's wife, I want to be a fine lady, so that good folk do as I tell them and bow low when they meet me." Back he went to the sea and said in a loud voice, "Fish, oh fish! Stand with your tail on the sea and your head facing me." Up swam the fish, stood its tail on the sea and faced him directly. "What do you need, old man?" it asked. "The old woman gives me no peace," he said. "She's gone raving mad: she's tired of being a fisherman's wife, she wants to be a fine lady." "Very well, cheer up. Go home and say your prayers; all will be done."

So the old man went home and was surprised to see a big stone house in place of his hut, rising up three floors; with servants running about in the yard, cooks banging in the kitchen, and his old woman sitting on a high chair in a rich brocade dress, giving orders. "Hello, wife," the old man said. "What impudence!" the brocaded lady cried. "How dare you address me, a fine lady, as your wife. Servants! Take that silly old dolt to the stables and give him forty lashes till he's sore." Right away the servants came running in, seized the old man by the scruff of the neck and hauled him off to the stables. There he got such a thrashing that he could barely stand. After that the old woman made him her yardman; he was given a broom to sweep the yard and made to eat and drink in the kitchen. What a life the old man led: all day sweeping out the yard, and if he missed a speck of dust he was hauled

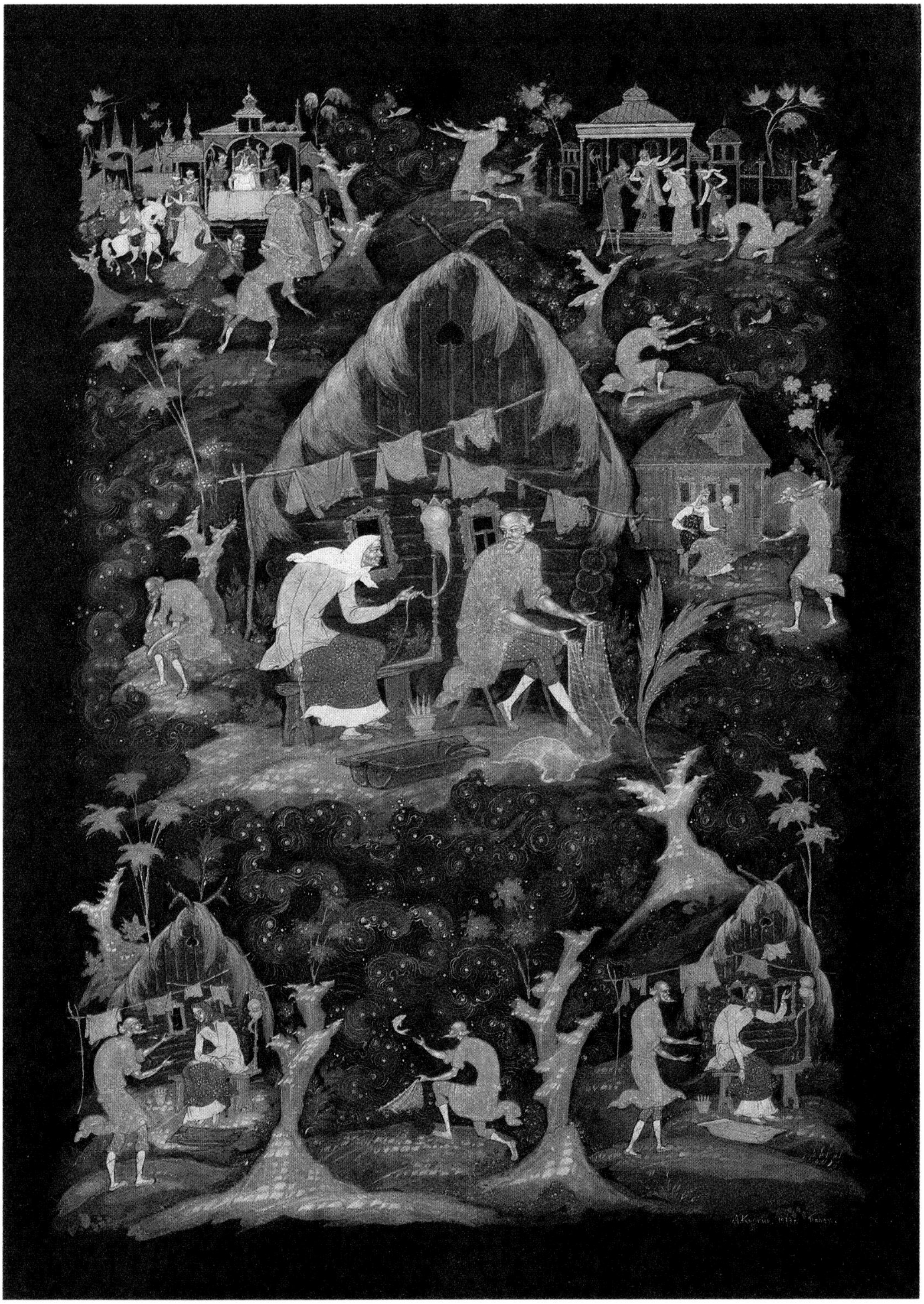

off to the stables for a whipping. "What a witch!" he thought. "I bring her good fortune, and she sticks her nose in the air, doesn't even consider me her husband."

By and by the old woman grew tired of being a fine lady, had the old man brought to her and ordered him, "Go back to the golden fish, you old devil, and tell it this: I don't want to be the Governor's Lady, after all; I want to be the Queen." So the old man went down to the sea and called, "Fish, oh fish! Stand with your tail on the sea, and your head facing me." Up swam the golden fish, asking, "What do you need, old man?" "My old woman has gone even further round the bend; she doesn't want to be a fine lady, she wants to be the Queen." "Cheer up," said the fish. "Go home and say your prayers; all will be done." So the old man returned and instead of his former home saw a towering palace with a roof of gold; guardsmen with rifles marched up and down; behind the palace were elegant gardens, while in front was a big green meadow on which troops were parading. The old woman, all dressed up like a queen, appeared on the balcony with her generals and governors, and began to inspect her troops and take the salute. The drums went bang and the music rang and the soldiers shouted "Hurrah".

By and by the old woman grew tired of being the Queen. She ordered a search for the old man so that she might set eyes on him again. What a fuss there was! The generals buzzed about, the governors huffed and puffed. 'What old man could she mean?' Finally he was found in the back yard and brought before the Queen. "Listen, you old devil," the woman said. "Go to the golden fish and tell it this: I don't want to be the Queen any more, I want to be the Mistress of the Sea, so that all the seas and all the fish obey me." The old man tried to object. But what was the use? If he didn't go he'd lose his head! So, reluctantly he went down to the sea and called, "Fish, oh fish! Stand with your tail on the sea and your head facing me." But this time no golden fish appeared. The old man called it once more—and again no fish. He called it a third time—and suddenly the sea began to murmur and seethe. Where the waters bad been clear and blue, they were now black as pitch. Up swam the fish to the shore, asking, "What do you need, old man?" "The old woman has gone even madder," he said. "She's tired of being the Queen and wants to be the Mistress of the Sea, ruling all the waters, commanding all the fish."

The golden fish said nothing to the old man, just turned tail and vanished into the depths. The old man went back and could scarce believe his eyes: the palace had gone, and in its place stood a small tumble-down cottage. And inside the cottage sat his old woman in a ragged sarafan. They began to live as before. The old man set about his fishing, but no matter how often he cast his net into the sea, never again did he catch the golden fish.

The Sun's Sister and the Witch

In a certain realm in a far-off land, there once lived a king and queen. And they had a son, Prince Ivan, who was born dumb. One day when the boy was twelve years old, he went to the stables to see his friend, a groom; this man was always telling him fairy stories, and now Prince Ivan wanted to listen to a nice fairy tale from him, but what he heard was something quite different. "Prince Ivan," said the groom, "your mother will soon give birth to a daughter, a little sister for you. But in truth she will be a wicked witch who will eat your father and mother and all their subjects. So go and ask your father for the best steed, saying you wish to go for a ride, and flee from here wherever your eyes take you, if you want to escape the evil." Prince Ivan ran quickly to his father and spoke to him for the first time since birth; the king was so delighted he did not even ask why the boy needed a fine steed. Straightway he gave orders for the very best steed from his herds to be saddled for the prince. Prince Ivan mounted and rode off wherever his eyes took him.

On and on he rode until he came to two old seamstresses; and there he asked to be taken in. "Gladly, Prince Ivan," they said, "but we have not long to live. As soon as we break the last needle from our sewing-box and use up the last thread, we shall die!" Prince Ivan wept bitter tears and rode on. On and on he rode until he came to the Oak-Thrower. "Please take me in," he said. "Gladly would I take you in, Prince

29

Ivan," said the man, "but I have not long to live. As soon as I pull up all these oaks, roots and all, I shall die!" The prince shed even more tears than before and rode on. At last he came to the Mountain-Mover and begged to be given shelter. "Gladly would I, Prince Ivan," said the man, "but I haven't long to live. As you see, my job is to move mountains; once I've finished with the last one I shall die!" Prince Ivan wept bitter tears again and rode on across the plain.

On and on he went until, at last, he came to the Sun's Sister. She took him in and gave him food and drink, as if he were her own son. He had all he wanted, and yet sometimes he would suddenly grow sad: he longed to know what was happening in his own home. On such days he would climb a high mountain, look down upon his palace and see that everything had been eaten up, only the walls remained! He would sigh and weep. One day, after he had seen all this and wept, he returned and the Sun's Sister asked him, "Why are there tears on your face, Prince Ivan?" "The wind made my eyes water," he replied. It happened a second time; the Sun's Sister told the wind not to blow. A third time Prince Ivan came home with tears on his face. This time there was no excuse: he had to confess everything and beg the Sun's Sister to let him go to see his native land again. She did not want to, but he pleaded so hard, that finally she gave in and let him go. For the journey she gave him a magic brush, a comb and two apples of youth; no matter how old a person was, if he ate an apple he would regain his youth in an instant!

On his way Prince Ivan came to the Mountain-Mover; only one mountain remained. The lad took his brush and threw it down on the plain: high, lofty mountains shot up out of nowhere, brushing the heavens with their peaks. Range upon range of them. How happy the Mountain-Mover was as he went gaily about his work! By and by, Prince Ivan came to the Oak-Thrower, and saw that he had only three oaks left. He took out his comb and threw it down on the plain: there was a sudden rustling and dense oak forests rose out of the ground, each tree thicker than the next! How happy was the Oak-Thrower, he thanked the prince and set off to uproot the hundred-year-old trees. By and by Prince Ivan came to the two old women and gave them an apple each; they ate the apples, instantly grew young and presented him with a handkerchief: he only had to wave it and a whole lake would appear behind him!

Prince Ivan arrived home. Out rushed his sister to greet him with caressing words. "Come and sit down, dear brother," she said. "Play the psaltery, and I will prepare dinner for you." The prince sat down and began to play, when a little mouse crept out of her hole and spoke to him in a human voice, "Save yourself, Prince, flee quickly. Your sister has gone to sharpen her teeth." Prince Ivan left the palace, mounted his steed and galloped back; meanwhile the mouse scurried to and fro across the strings, twanging the psaltery to make the sister think the prince was still there. Having sharpened her teeth, she rushed back into the chamber—but, lo and

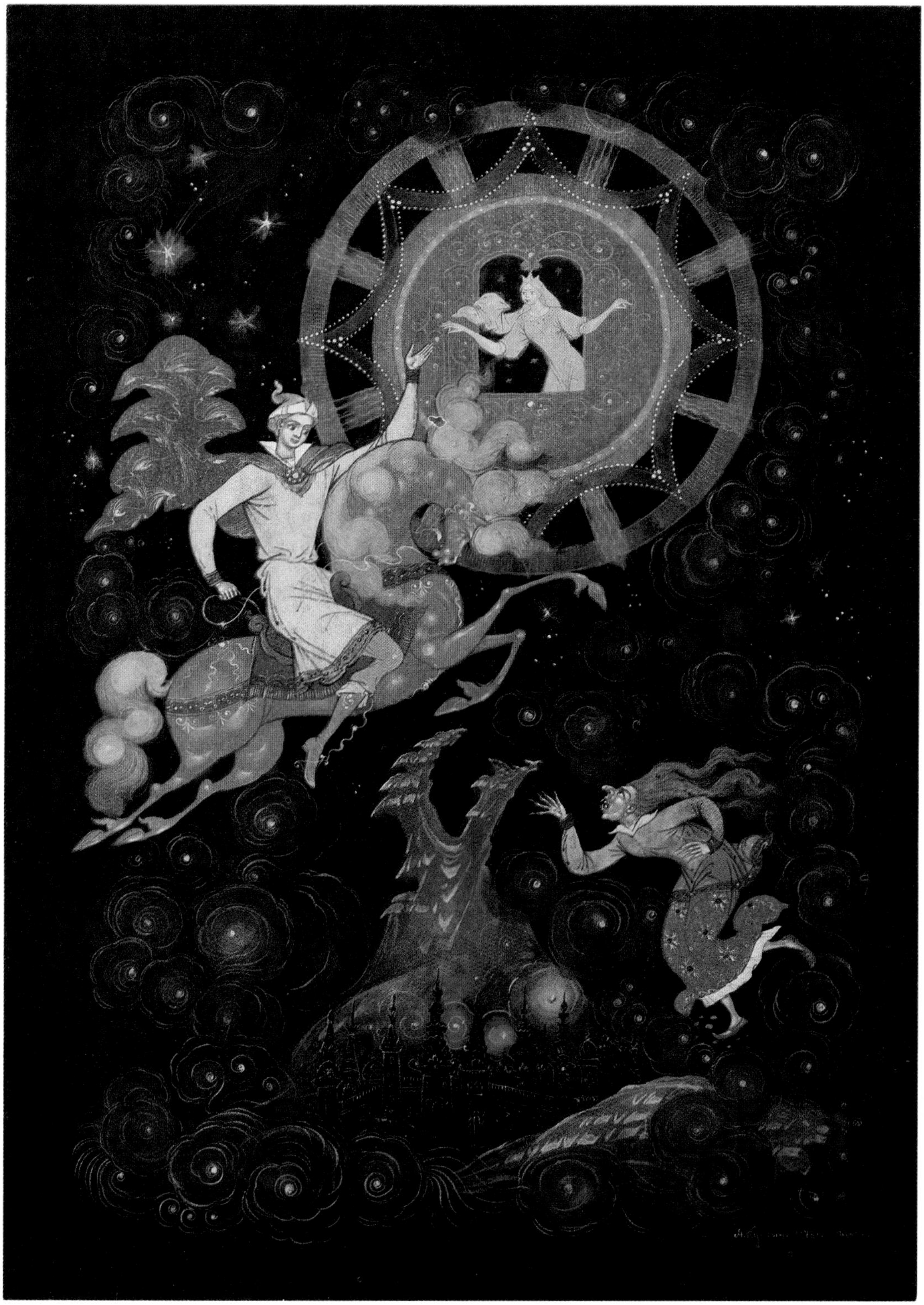

behold, there was not a soul in sight, save a mouse slipping into her hole. The witch flew into a rage, ground her teeth in fury and set off in pursuit.

Prince Ivan heard a noise, glanced round and there was his sister catching him up; he waved the handkerchief and a deep lake appeared. While the witch was swimming across the lake, Prince Ivan rode far on his way. But she flew like the wind and was soon on his heels. This time the Oak-Thrower came to his aid. Seeing the witch gaining on the young prince, he quickly pulled up oak-trees to block the way: a whole mountain of them. The witch could not get past. She set about clearing a way, gnawing through the wood with her sharp teeth, but by the time she got through, Prince Ivan was far away. She took up the chase again, flying like the wind and was soon on his tail once more... There was no escape! But, seeing the witch, the Mountain-Mover seized hold of the highest mountain and flung it down to bar her way; on top of that mountain he set another. While the witch was clambering up the crag, Prince Ivan rode on and on and was soon far away.

At last the witch climbed over the mountains and took up the chase after her brother... This time, when she caught sight of him, she chuckled evilly, "Now you won't escape!" Closer and closer she came! Just in time the prince reached the castle of the Sun's Sister. "Sister, Sister, open the window," he shouted. The Sun's Sister opened the window and the prince leaped through together with his steed. The witch demanded her brother. But the Sun's Sister would not listen or give him up. Then the witch said, "Let Prince Ivan get on the scales with me; we'll see who weighs more. If I am heavier, then I'll devour him; if he is, he may kill me!" The prince agreed. First he got onto the scales, then the witch. But no sooner had she placed her foot upon the scales than Prince Ivan went flying up so high that he landed right in the castle of the Sun's Sister. And the wicked witch remained upon the ground.

Daughter and Stepdaughter

A widowed peasant with a daughter married a widow who also had a daughter: so they each had a stepchild. The stepmother was a wicked woman and constantly nagged the old man, "Take your daughter off to the forest, to a hut. She'll spin more yarn there." What could he do? He did as the woman said, carted his daughter off to the forest hut and gave her steel, flint and tinder, and a bag of millet, saying, "Here is fire; keep the fire burning and the porridge boiling, sit and spin, and let no one in."

Night fell. The maid heated the stove, cooked the porridge, and suddenly heard a little mouse say, "Maid, Maid, give me a spoonful of porridge." "Oh, little mouse," she cried, "stay and talk to me: I'll give you more than a spoonful of porridge, I'll feed you to your heart's content." So the mouse ate his fill and left. In the night a bear broke in, calling, "Come on, girl, put out the light and let's play blindman's buff."

The mouse came scampering up to the maid's shoulder and whispered in her ear, "Don't be afraid. Say yes, then put out the light and crawl under the stove, and I'll run about ringing a little bell." And the game began. The bear started to chase the mouse, but could not catch him; he soon began to holler and hurl logs at him; he hurled one after the other, but kept missing, and he grew tired. "You are good at playing blindman's buff, little girl," he said. "I will send you a drove of horses and a cartload of good things in the morning."

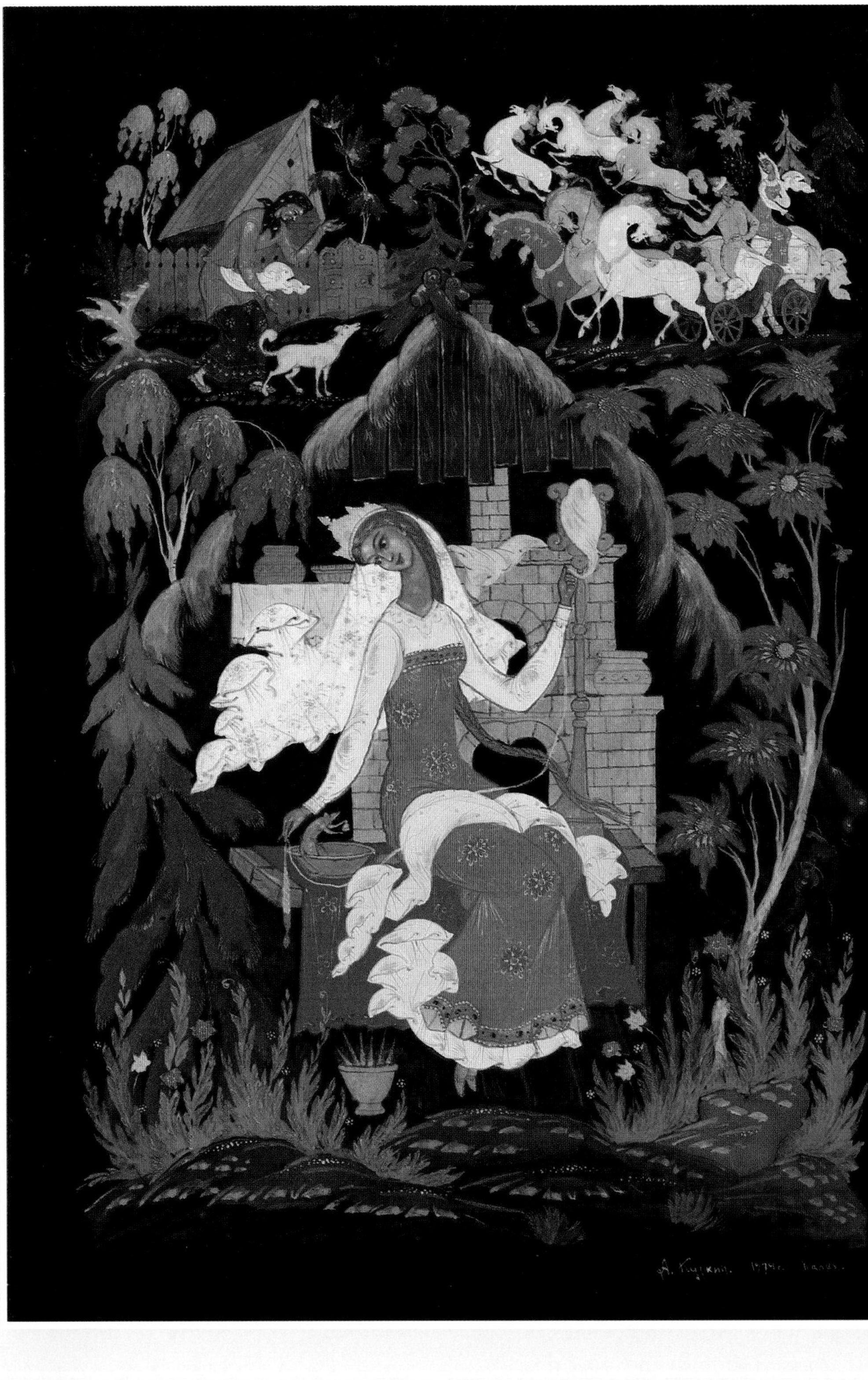

Next morning the old man's wife said, "Go and see how much yarn the girl has spun since yesterday, old man." So off he set, while his wife sat waiting for him to bring back his daughter's bones! By and by the dog began to bark, "Bow-wow-wow! The old man is coming with his daughter driving a drove of horses and bringing a cartload of good things." "You're lying, fleabag!" shouted the step-mother. "Those are her bones rattling and clanking in the cart." The gate creaked, the horses raced into the yard, and there were the old man and his daughter sitting in the cart. With a cartload of good things! The woman's eyes gleamed with greed. "That's a pittance!" she cried. "Take my daughter to the forest for the night; she'll come home driving two droves of horses with two cartloads of good things."

The peasant drove his wife's daughter Natasha to the hut and provided her with food and fire. At nightfall she cooked porridge for herself. Out came the little mouse asking for a spoonful of porridge. But Natasha cried, "Be off, you pest!" And she threw the spoon at him. The mouse ran away. Natasha gobbled up the porridge all by herself, put out the light and lay down in a corner.

At midnight the bear broke in, crying, "Hey, where are you, girl? Let's have a game of blindman's buff." The maid was silent, only her teeth chattering from fear. "Ah, there you are," cried the bear. "Here, take this little bell and run. I'll try to catch you." Her hand trembling, she took the little bell and could not stop it ringing. Out of the darkness came the mouse's voice, "The wicked girl will soon be dead!"

Next morning the woman sent her husband to the forest, saying, "Go and help my daughter drive back two droves of horses with two cartloads of good things." The peasant went off, leaving his wife waiting at the gate. The dog began to bark, "Bow-wow-wow! The mistress's girl is coming: her bones are rattling in the bag, the old man's sitting on the nag!" "You're lying, fleabag," cried the dame. "My daughter's driving droves and bringing loads." But when she looked up, there was the old man at the gate, handing her a bundle. When she opened it and saw the bones, she began to rant and rage so much she died next day from grief and fury. The old man lived out his life in peace with his daughter; and with a wealthy son-in-law, too.

Baba Yaga

Once upon a time there was a man and woman who had an only daughter. When his wife died, the man took another. But the wicked stepmother took a dislike to the girl, beat her hard and wondered how to be rid of her forever. One day the father went off somewhere and the stepmother said to the girl, "Go to your aunt, to my sister, and ask her for a needle and thread to sew you a blouse." The aunt was really Baba Yaga, the bony witch.

Now, the little girl was not stupid and she first went to her own aunt for advice. "Good morrow, Auntie," she said. "Mother has sent me to her sister for a needle and thread to sew me a blouse. What should I do?" The aunt told her what to do. "My dear niece," she said. "You will find a birch-tree there that will lash your face; you must tie it with a ribbon. You will find gates that will creak and bang; you must pour oil on the hinges. You will find dogs that will try to rip you apart; you must throw them fresh rolls. You will find a cat that will try to scratch your eyes out; you must give her some ham." The little girl went off, walked and walked and finally came to the witch's abode.

There stood a hut, and inside sat Baba Yaga, the bony witch, spinning. "Good day, Auntie," said the little girl. "Good day, dearie," the witch replied. "Mother sent me for a needle and thread to sew me a blouse," said the girl. "Very well," Baba Yaga said. "Sit down and weave." The girl sat at the loom, then Baba Yaga went

36

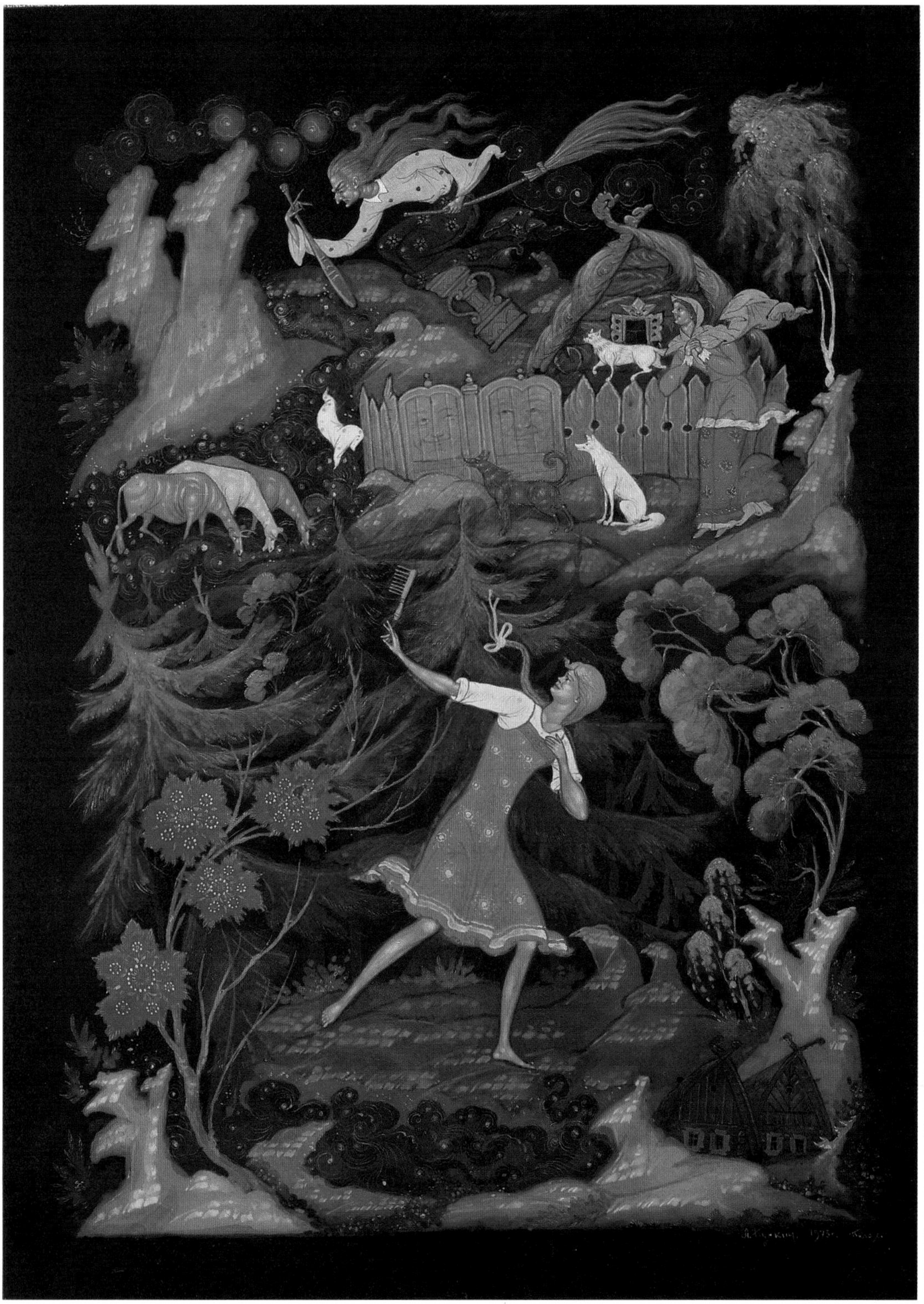

out and told her serving-maid, "Go and heat up the bath-house and give my niece a good wash; I want to eat her for breakfast." The serving-maid did as she was bid; and the poor little girl sat there half dead with fright, begging, "Oh, please, dear serving-maid, don't burn the wood, pour water on instead, and carry the water in a sieve." And she gave the maid a kerchief.

Meanwhile Baba Yaga was waiting; she went to the window and asked, "Are you weaving, dear niece? Are you weaving, my dear?" "I'm weaving, Auntie," the girl replied, "I'm weaving, my dear." When Baba Yaga moved away from the window, the little girl gave some ham to the cat and asked her whether there was any escape. At once the cat replied, "Here is a comb and towel. Take them and run away. Baba Yaga will chase you; put your ear to the ground and, when you hear her coming, throw down the towel—and a wide, wide river will appear. And if she crosses the river and starts to catch you up, put your ear to the ground again and, when you hear her coming close, throw down your comb — and a dense forest will appear. She won't be able to get through that."

The little girl took the towel and comb and ran. As she ran from the house, the dogs tried to tear her to pieces, but she tossed them the fresh rolls and they let her pass. The gates tried to bang shut, but she poured some oil on the hinges, and they let her through. The birch-tree tried to lash her face, but she tied it with a ribbon, and it let her pass. In the meantime, the cat sat down at the loom to weave—though, truth to tell, she tangled it all up instead. Now and then Baba Yaga would come to the window and call, "Are you weaving, dear niece? Are you weaving, my dear?" And the cat would answer in a low voice, "I'm weaving, Auntie. I'm weaving, my dear."

The witch rushed into the hut and saw that the girl was gone. She gave the cat a good beating and scolded her for not scratching out the girl's eyes. But the cat answered her, "I've served you for years, yet you've never even given me a bone, but she gave me some ham." Baba Yaga then turned on the dogs, the gates, the birch-tree and the serving-maid, and set to thrashing and scolding them all. But the dogs said to her, "We've served you for years, yet you've never even thrown us a burnt crust, but she gave us fresh rolls." And the gates said, "We've served you for years, yet you've never even poured water on our hinges, but she oiled them for us." And the birch-tree said, "I've served you for years, yet you've never even tied me up with thread, but she tied me with a ribbon." And the serving-maid said, "I've served you for years, yet you've never even given me a rag, but she gave me a kerchief."

Baba Yaga, the bony witch, leapt into her mortar, drove it along with her pestle, sweeping away her tracks with a besom, and flew off after the girl. The girl put her ear to the ground and heard Baba Yaga coming. At once she threw down her towel—and a wide, wide river appeared. The witch had to stop at the river, gnashing her teeth in fury. She returned home, took her oxen, drove them to the river, and the oxen drank the river clean. Then off she rushed again in pursuit. The girl once more put her ear to the ground and heard the witch getting near. Straightway she threw down her comb—and a dense, dark forest appeared. The witch began to gnaw through it, but it was too much for her and she had to turn back.

Meanwhile the man returned home and asked where his daughter was. "She has gone to her aunt's," said the stepmother. It was not long before the girl herself came home. "Where have you been?" her father asked. "Oh, Father," said the girl, "mother sent me to auntie for a needle and thread to sew me a blouse. But the aunt was Baba-Yaga and she tried to eat me." "But how did you escape, my daughter?" he asked. And she told him the story. When the old man had heard it, he grew so angry with his wife that he took out his gun and shot her. And he and his daughter lived happily ever after. And I was there, drank mead-ale, and yet, scarce did get my whiskers wet.

Vasilissa the Fair

In a certain realm there once lived a merchant. Although he had been married for twelve years, he had only one daughter, Vasilissa the Fair. When the maid was eight years old, her mother died. And as she lay dying, the merchant's wife called her little daughter to her, took a doll from under the coverlet and said, "Listen, dear Vasilissa. Remember and heed my last words. As I die I leave you this little doll with my blessing. Keep it with you always and do not show it to a soul. If you are ever in trouble, give the doll something to eat and ask its advice. It will take your food and tell you what to do." With that the mother kissed the child and died.

After his wife's death, the merchant grieved for a time, as is right and proper, then thought to take another wife. He was a good man and there were many who would gladly have consented, but he was particularly fond of a certain widow. She was no longer young and had two daughters of her own, about the same age as Vasilissa, so he thought she would be an experienced housewife and mother. He married her, but he was wrong, for she did not turn out to be a good mother to Vasilissa. Vasilissa was the fairest maid in the village; her stepmother and stepsisters were jealous of her beauty and were forever tormenting her, giving her all kinds of heavy work to do in the hope that she would grow thin from her toil and rough-skinned from the wind and sun: she had a very hard time.

But she bore it all without complaint and grew lovelier each day, while the stepmother and her daughters grew thin and ugly from spite, even though they were

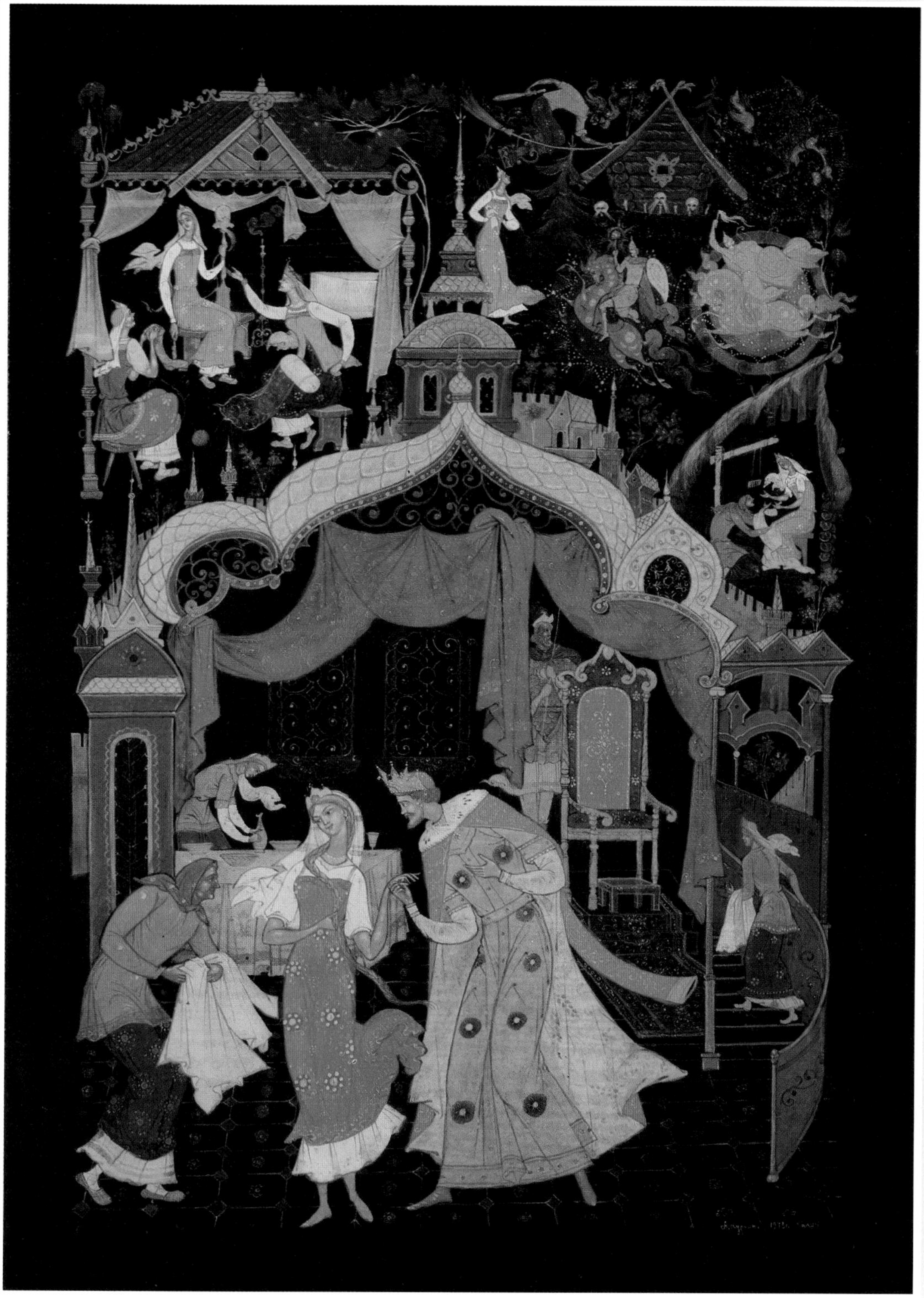

forever sitting idle, like fine ladies. How could this be? Vasilissa was helped by her little doll. She could never have done all her work without it. In return, she sometimes went hungry, keeping the choicest morsels for her doll. And at night, when everyone was asleep, she would lock herself in her little garret and rock her doll, saying, "Come, little doll, eat up, my dear, as I pour all my troubles into your ear." And she told it how unhappy she was in her father's house, how her wicked stepmother was plaguing her to death. The doll would first eat, then give advice and comfort her in her misery. In the morning, the doll would perform all the chores for Vasilissa. As the girl rested in the shade and picked flowers, the vegetable patch was weeded, the cabbages watered, the water fetched, and the stove lit. The doll even showed Vasilissa a herb to protect her from the sun. So she lived happily, thanks to her doll.

Several years went by. Vasilissa grew up and reached the age of marriage. She was wooed by all the young men in the village, yet none would as much as look at the stepmother's daughters. That made the stepmother more spiteful than ever; and her answer to all the suitors was: "I will not allow the youngest girl to wed before the older ones." Every time she despatched a suitor, she vented her rage on Vasilissa in harsh blows.

One day the merchant had to go and trade in distant lands. While he was gone, the stepmother moved with the family to another house. By that house was a dense forest, and in a forest glade stood the hut where Baba Yaga lived. She allowed no one in and gobbled people up like chickens. Once in the new house, the merchant's wife kept sending Vasilissa into the forest on some errand or other. Yet every time the maid came back home safe and sound: her little doll always showed her the way and kept her out of Baba Yaga's clutches.

Autumn came. The stepmother gave jobs to all three girls: the first was to make lace; the second was to knit stockings; and Vasilissa was to sit and spin. Each had to complete her task by nightfall. The stepmother put out all the lights in the house, save one candle in the room where the girls worked, and went to bed. The girls toiled on. The candle began to smoke, and one of the elder girls took up her scissors to trim the wick, but instead, following her mother's instructions, put it out, as if by accident. "What shall we do now!" said the girls. "There's no light in the house and our work is not done. Someone must run to Baba Yaga's for a light." "I can see from my lace pins," said the one making lace, "so I won't go." "Nor will I," said the one knitting stockings, "I can see from my needles." "So you will have to go," they both shouted to their stepsister. "Off you go to Baba Yaga!" And they pushed Vasilissa out of the room.

The poor girl went to her little garret, set the supper she had ready in front of her doll and said, "Come, little doll, eat up, my dear, as I pour all my troubles into your ear." Then she told the doll that they were sending her to Baba Yaga's for a light and the witch would surely gobble her up. The little doll ate the food, and her eyes began to gleam like two candles. "Never fear, Vasilissa," it said, "do as they say, but keep me with you all the time. As long as I am with you Baba Yaga can do you no harm." Vasilissa got ready, put the doll in her pocket and, crossing herself, went off into the dense forest.

On she went, trembling with fear. All of a sudden a horseman galloped past: his face was white, his cloak was white, his steed was white, and his steed's harness was white too. And a new day dawned.

She went on. A second horseman galloped past: his face was red, his cloak was red, and his steed was red too. And the sun rose.

Vasilissa walked through the night and day, and only the next evening did she come to the glade where BabaYaga's hut stood. The fence around the hut was of human bones, and on each stake was a human skull with glaring eyes; the lock on the hut door was a mouth with sharp teeth. Vasilissa stood rooted to the spot with horror. Suddenly another horseman rode by: his face was black, his dress was black, and his steed was black too. He galloped up to Baba Yaga's gate, then vanished as if swallowed up by the earth. Night fell. But it was not dark for long. The eyes in all the skulls on the fence began to gleam, and the clearing grew as light as day. Vasilissa trembled with fear: but not knowing where to run, she stayed where she was.

Soon a terrible noise rushed through the forest: the trees creaked, the dry leaves crackled, and out of the forest came BabaYaga, riding in a mortar, driving herself along with a pestle, sweeping her traces away with a besom. She rode up to the gate, came to a halt and, sniffing the air about her, cried out, "Fie, Foh! I smell the blood of a Russian! Who's there?" Vasilissa went up to the witch in fear, bowed low, and said, "It is I, Grannie. Stepmother's daughters sent me for a light." "Very well," said Baba Yaga, "I know them. You must stay here and work for me, then I'll give you a light. If not, I'll eat you up!" Then she turned to the gate and screeched, "Hey, my strong bolts, unlock! Hey, my wide gates, open up!" The gates opened up and Baba Yaga rode in with a whistle. Vasilissa followed, and all was locked firmly as before. Entering the hut, Baba Yaga stretched herself out on a bench and called to Vasilissa, "Bring me what is in the oven; I'm hungry."

Vasilissa lit a splinter from the skulls on the fence and began to bring the witch food from the oven—enough for ten grown men. From the cellar she brought kvass, mead, beer and wine. And the old witch ate and drank everything, leaving Vasilissa only a spoonful of cabbage soup, a crust of bread and a scrap of pork. Then Baba Yaga got ready for bed, saying, "When I leave tomorrow, see that the yard is swept, the hut cleaned, dinner cooked, and the washing done; take a quarter of wheat from the cornbin and clean the husks off it. See that you do everything, or I'll gobble you up!" That said, Baba Yaga began to snore. Vasilissa put what was left of the old witch's supper before her little doll, wept bitter tears and said, "Come, little doll, eat up, my dear, as I pour all my troubles into your ear." And she told the doll of the hard work Baba Yaga had given her, how she had threatened to eat her if it was not done. "Please help me," she cried. "Never fear, Vasilissa the Fair," the doll replied, "eat your supper, say your prayers and go to bed; morning is wiser than evening."

Vasilissa awoke early, but Baba Yaga was already up. She looked out of the window and saw that the skulls' eyes were growing dim. At that moment the white horseman flashed by. And a new day dawned. Baba Yaga went out into the yard, gave a whistle, and the mortar, the pestle and the besom appeared. The red horseman flashed by. And the sun rose. Baba Yaga got into her mortar and off she went, driving herself along with the pestle and sweeping her traces away with the besom. Vasilissa was now alone. She looked round the witch's hut in amazement at such abundance, then she wondered which other chores she should start first. But—lo and behold!—all the work was done. And there was the little doll separating the last husks from the wheat. "Oh, my rescuer," Vasilissa said to her little doll, "you have saved me from a cruel fate." "All you have to do now," said the doll, slipping back into Vasilissa's pocket, "is to cook the dinner. Cook it with God's help, then rest to your heart's content."

Towards evening Vasilissa laid the table and sat waiting for Baba Yaga. As it grew dark, the black horseman flashed by the gate. And night fell. Only the skulls's eyes were gleaming. The trees began to creak, the leaves to crackle, and Baba Yaga was on her way. As Vasilissa met her, she shouted, "Is it all done?" "Pray see for yourself, Grannie," said Vasilissa. Baba Yaga took a good look, annoyed that there was nothing to complain about, and said, "Very well." Then she cried, "My loyal servants, my faithful friends, grind my wheat." Three pairs of hands appeared, took the wheat and carried it out of sight. Then the witch ate her fill, lay down to sleep and gave orders once again to Vasilissa: "Do the same work tomorrow as today; but as well as that take poppy seed from the bin and dust each grain until it's clean: some spiteful soul threw dust into the bin." That said, the old witch turned her face to the wall and began to snore. At once Vasilissa set to feeding her little doll. The doll ate and repeated what it had said the day before, "Say your prayers and go to sleep; morning is wiser than evening."

Next morning Baba Yaga went off again in her mortar, and Vasilissa and the doll soon had the work done. When the old witch returned, she took a good look and cried, "My loyal servants, my faithful friends, press oil from the poppy seeds." Three pairs of hands appeared, took the poppy seed and carried it out of sight. Then Baba Yaga sat down to eat; as she did so, Vasilissa stood by in silence. "Why don't you say something?" asked Baba Yaga. "Haven't you got a tongue in your head?" "I do not dare," answered Vasilissa, "but, by your leave, I wish to ask you a question." "Go on," the old hag said, "but not every question brings good: those who know too much grow old too soon!" "I only want to ask you about what I have seen, Grannie: as I was coming here a horseman on a white steed rode by, all white himself and dressed in white; whoever can he be?" "He is my day so light," she said. "Then a second horseman overtook me riding a red horse, all red himself and dressed in red: who is he?" "He is my sun so bright," said Baba Yaga. "And the black horseman who overtook me right by your gate, Grannie?" "He is my darkest night: all of them are my loyal servants."

Vasilissa at once recalled the three pairs of hands and fell silent. "Why don't you ask me more questions?" said Baba Yaga. "Let that be all," the girl replied, "you said yourself that those who know too much grow old too soon, Grannie." "It is good that you ask only about what you saw outside, not inside. I don't like gossips in my house; I eat up folk who are too inquisitive," said Baba Yaga. "Now I've a question for you: how do you manage to do all the work I set you?" "My Mother's blessing helps me," answered Vasilissa. "So that's it! Then get you gone, blessed daughter! I want no blessed ones here." With that she quickly dragged Vasilissa out of the hut, pushed her through the gates, took a skull with burning eyes from the fence, stuck it on a stick and gave it to the maid, saying, "Here is a light for your stepsisters. Take it; that is what they sent you here for."

Vasilissa ran home by the light of the skull which did not go out until daybreak; finally, by nightfall next evening, she reached home. As she came near the gate, she was about to throw the skull away, thinking they had no need of a light in the house now. But suddenly a muffled voice came from it, saying: "Don't throw me away, take me to your stepmother!"

She looked up at her stepmother's house and, seeing no light in the windows, decided to enter with the skull. For the first time she was welcomed kindly and told that, ever since she had gone, there had been no light in the house: they had been unable to kindle a spark themselves, and any light brought from their neighbours had gone out as soon as it entered the house. "Perhaps your fire will last," the stepmother said. The skull was brought into the house; but it kept staring at the stepmother and her daughters—and how it burned them! No matter where they tried to hide, the eyes followed them everywhere. By morning they were all burned to cinders. Only Vasilissa remained unharmed.

In the morning Vasilissa buried the skull in the ground, locked and bolted the house, went off to town and asked a lonely old woman to take her in. And there she lived, waiting for her father's return. One day she said to the old woman, "I am tired of sitting here doing nothing, Grannie. Go and buy me some flax, please, the best there is; at least I can be spinning." The old woman bought the best flax, and Vasilissa set to work. She spun quickly and well, and the yarn came out as fine and smooth as the hair on her head. When she had 'spun a lot of yarn the time came to weave it: but no combs fine enough for her yarn could be found, and no one would undertake to make them. So Vasilissa asked her little doll for help, and the doll replied, "Bring me an old comb, an old shuttle and a horse's mane, and I'll fashion one for you."

Vasilissa gathered all that was required and went to bed; during the night the little doll made a splendid loom. By winter's end the linen was woven—and so fine was it that it could pass through the eye of a needle like thread. In spring the linen was bleached, and Vasilissa said to the old woman, "Grannie, go and sell this linen and keep the money for yourself." The old woman looked at the linen and exclaimed: "No, dear child! Such linen may be worn by no one but the king. I'll take it to the palace." So the old woman went to the king's palace, and walked up and down beneath the king's windows until he saw her. "What do you want, old woman?" he called. "Your Majesty," the old woman said, "I have brought some wonderful merchandise; I wish to show it to no one but you." The king ordered her to be brought before him, and when he set eyes on the linen he marvelled greatly. "What do you want for it?" he asked. "It is priceless, Sire," she said, "I offer it to you as a gift." The king thanked her and sent her forth with much reward.

Then he ordered shirts to be made from the linen. But when the cloth was cut, they could not find a seamstress able to do the work. They searched and searched and in the end summoned the old woman. "Since you can spin and weave such cloth," said the king to her, "you must be able to sew shirts from it." "It is not I, Sire," she said, "who spun and wove this cloth. It is the work of a maid who lives with me." "Then let her sew the shirts," the king said.

The old woman returned home and told Vasilissa everything. "I knew all along that my hands would have to do the work," said Vasilissa. So she locked herself in her room and set to work; she sewed ceaselessly and soon had a dozen shirts ready.

The old woman took the shirts to the king. In the meantime, Vasilissa washed her face, combed her hair, dressed and sat by the window, waiting to see what would come to pass. Before long a servant of the king came into the yard. He entered the room and said: "The king wishes to see the seamstress who made his shirts. He wishes to reward her with his own royal hands." So off went Vasilissa to appear before the king. No sooner did the king set eyes upon Vasilissa the Fair than he fell in love with her. "I cannot part with you, my fair maiden. You will be my wife." Taking Vasilissa by her lily-white hands, he sat her down beside him and the wedding was held without more ado. Shortly afterwards, Vasilissa's father returned and was overjoyed by her good fortune. Both he and the old woman went to live in the palace with Vasilissa. And, of course, she carried her little doll in her pocket always, till the end of her days.

Ivashko and the Witch

Once upon a time there was an old man and woman, and they had a little boy whose name was Ivashko. They loved him more than words can tell. One day Ivashko said to his father and mother, "Let me go down to the lake and catch fish." "What? Certainly not! You are too small and will get drowned, God forbid!" "No, I won't, I shall catch you some fish; do let me go!" So in the end his mother dressed him in a white shirt, belted with a red sash, and let him go. So he got into the boat and said,

> "Little skiff, little skiff, sail far away,
> Little skiff, little skiff, sail far away."

The skiff sailed far, far away, and Ivashko began to fish. By and by his mother came running along the bank, calling to her son,

> "Ivashko, Ivashko, my laddie,
> Come back to me and your Daddy.
> I've food and drink for you ready."

And Ivashko called out,

> "Little skiff, little skiff, sail me back o'er,
> For I hear the call of my maw'r."

47

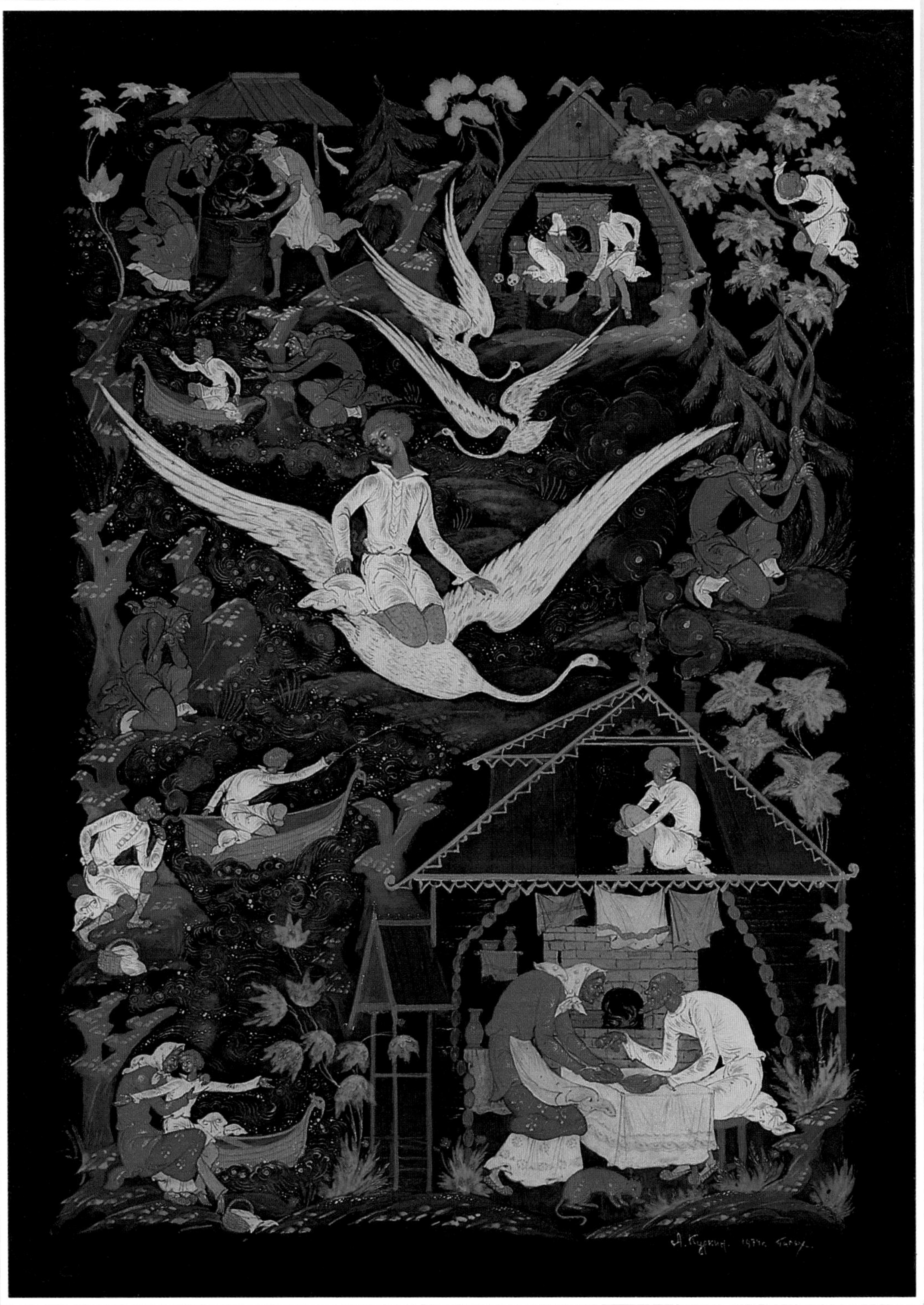

The skiff took him back to the lakeside; his mother collected all his fish, gave her son plenty to eat and drink, changed his shirt and sash and let him return to his fishing.

So he sat in the little skiff and called,

> "Little skiff, little skiff, sail far away,
> Little skiff, little skiff, sail far away."

It sailed far, far away, and Ivashko began to fish. By and by his father came running along the bank, calling to his son,

> "Ivashko, Ivashko, my laddie,
> Come back here to your Daddy,
> I've food and drink for you ready."

Ivashko called out,

> "Little skiff, little skiff, sail me back o'er,
> For I hear the call of my daw'r."

The skiff took him back to the lakeside where his father collected the fish, gave his son plenty to eat and drink, changed his shirt and sash and let him return to his fishing.

A witch had heard Ivashko's mother and father calling him and she wished to get the laddie into her clutches. So she went to the lakeside and called out in her hoarse voice,

> "Ivashko, Ivashko, my laddie,
> Come back to me and your Daddy.
> I've food and drink for you ready".

The boy knew it was not his mother's voice, but that of the witch, so he sang out,

> "Little skiff, little skiff, sail far away,
> Little skiff, little skiff, sail far away;
> It's the witch's call, not maw'r at all."

Seeing that she would have to call Ivashko by the same voice as his mother, the witch ran to the smithy and cried, "Blacksmith, blacksmith! Forge me a sweet voice like Ivashko's mother has, or I'll eat you up!" The blacksmith forged her a voice just like that of Ivashko's mother, and the witch stole along the lakeside at night and sang sweetly,

> "Ivashko, Ivashko, my laddie,
> Come back to me and your Daddy.
> I've food and drink for you ready."

He returned to land, and she collected the fish, seized him too and carried him off. At home, she gave orders to her daughter Alyonka: "Stoke up the stove good and hot and roast Ivashko nice and tender, while I go and invite my friends to the feast." So Alyonka stoked up the stove good and hot, and said to Ivashko, "Come and sit on the end of my spade, so that I can put you in the stove." "I'm too small and silly," replied Ivashko. "I'm no good at doing things like that; would you show me first how to sit on the spade?" "Very well," said Alyonka, "that won't take long." But no sooner had she sat down on the spade than Ivashko pushed her into the oven and shut the fire door; then he left the witch's hut, locked the door and climbed up a lofty oak-tree.

Soon the witch arrived with the guests and knocked upon the door. "Oh, that accursed Alyonka! Gone off to play, I expect." The witch climbed through a window, opened the door and let in the guests. They sat down at the table, while the witch opened the stove door, pulled out the roasted Alyonka and served her up. They ate and drank their fill, then went outside and began to romp about on the grass. "We sport and play, all replete with Ivashko's meat," cried the witch. And she kept repeating, "We sport and play, all replete with Ivashko's meat." But Ivashko took up the refrain from the tree-top, "Sport and play, all replete with Alyonka's meat!" "Did I hear something?" said the witch. "It was only the leaves rustling." Again the witch took up her chant, "We sport and play, all replete with Ivashko's meat!" And back came Ivashko's voice: "Sport and play, all replete with Alyonka's meat!" Thereupon the witch looked up and saw him; straightway she began gnawing the oak—the very one in which Ivashko was sitting. She gnawed and gnawed and had almost gnawed it through when Ivashko leapt across to another oak nearby. Just in time, for the first oak came crashing to the ground. When the witch saw Ivashko sitting in another tree, she gnashed her teeth in rage and began gnawing through the trunk once more. She gnawed and gnawed until her two bottom teeth broke off and she had to run to the smithy. "Blacksmith, blacksmith!" she shouted. "Forge me iron teeth, or I'll gobble you up!" The smith forged her two iron teeth, and the witch returned and began gnawing through the oak once more. This time there was no escape: Ivashko did not know what to do. All of a sudden, he caught sight of swan-geese flying overhead and called to them,

> "Goosie, goosie, goslings,
> Take me upon your wings,
> Carry me to maw'r and Daddy,
> Take them home their poor wee laddie!"

"Let the middle flock take you," said the birds. Ivashko waited until a second flock flew by, then he called,

> "Goosie, goosie, goslings,
> Take me upon your wings,
> Carry me to maw'r and Daddy,
> Take them home their poor wee laddie!"

"Let the back ones take you," called the birds. So Ivashko once more waited until the third flock came flying by.

> "Goosie, goosie, goslings,
> Take me upon your wings,
> Carry me to maw'r and Daddie,
> Take them home their poor wee laddie!"

The swan-geese swooped down, picked him up and carried him home. And there they left him upon the roof.

Early next morning, the old woman was making pancakes and sadly thinking of her little laddie. "Where, Oh where is my Ivashko? If only I could dream of him!" she sighed. And the old man said, "Do you know, I dreamt the swan-geese came flying with our Ivashko on their wings." The old woman fried the pancakes and said, "Come on, old fellow, let's share out the pancakes: one for you, one for me, one for you, one for me..." "And for me?" came Ivashko's voice. "One for you, old fellow, one for me..." "And for me?" came a voice a second time. "Did you hear that, old man? Go and see what it is." The old man climbed up on the roof and brought Ivashko down. How happy the old couple were! Ivashko told them about his adventures. And afterwards they all lived together as happy as can be.

The Prince and His Servant

Once upon a time there was a king who had a handsome son. The prince was good in every way: fair of face and kind of nature. But not his father: he was ever eager to add to his riches, to extort more taxes and rent from his subjects. One day he saw an old man with sable, marten, beaver and fox pelts. "Stay, old man," he cried, "whence come you?" "I hail from these parts, Sire," the old man said, "but now I serve an old wood sprite." "How do you trap the animals?" asked the king. "Well, the wood sprite sets the traps and the stupid animals get caught in them." "Listen here, old fellow," said the king. "I'll pour you wine aplenty and give you money if you show me those traps." The old man gave in to temptation and showed the king. And the king at once ordered the old wood sprite to be seized and shut inside an iron pillar; then he set his own traps in the wood sprite's enchanted forest.

So now the old wood sprite sat inside the iron pillar peering through a grille, in the centre of the gardens. One day the young prince came out to walk in the gardens with his nannies and his nursemaids good and true. And as he passed by the pillar, the wood sprite cried out, "Royal child! Set me free, I shall be of use to you." "But how can I free you?" "Listen closely: go to your mother and tell her this, 'Dear Mama, please look for nits in my hair.' Then place your head on her lap, seize your chance to take the key from her pocket while she's looking in your hair; and set me free." And so he did. The prince slipped the key from his mother's pocket, ran into the gardens, made himself an arrow, fitted it to his bow and loosed it far, far away, shouting for his nannies and nursemaids to find it. And while the nannies and nursemaids scurried off, the young prince opened the iron pillar and set the old wood sprite free.

The wood sprite set about spoiling the royal traps. When the king realised he was catching no more animals he got angry and turned on his wife: why had she given up the key and set the old wood sprite free? And he summoned all his generals, governors and wise men: what was their judgement? Should he chop off her head or send her into exile? The prince felt sorry for his mother and told his father that he was to blame. The king was grief-stricken: what was he to do with his son? He could not execute him, but punish him he must. In the end judgement was pronounced: the prince would be sent into the big wide world, the howling winds, the winter blasts, and the autumn gales. All he could take with him was a knapsack and one servant.

The prince and his servant came to an open plain. They walked near and far, high and low, until at last they reached a well. "Fetch me some water," said the prince to his servant. "No," said the servant. So on they went until they came to a second well. "Bring me some water," said the prince, "I'm thirsty." "No," replied the servant. So they continued on their way until they came to a third well. The servant again refused to fetch water and the prince was so thirsty that he had to go himself. But as he climbed down the well, his servant slammed down the lid, shouting, "I won't let you out unless you become the servant and I the prince." There was nothing for it: the prince signed his agreement with his blood, then they exchanged clothes, and on they went.

They reached another land and made for the king's palace, the servant in front, the real prince behind. Before long the servant was living in comfort as the king's guest, eating and drinking with him at the same table. He said to the king, "Your Royal Majesty, kindly give my servant a job in the kitchens." So the prince was taken into the kitchens, made to fetch wood and clean the pots and pans. Before long he learned to prepare meals better than the royal cooks. So pleased was the monarch that he began to reward him with gold. That made the other cooks jealous and they waited for a chance to get rid of him.

One day the prince made a pie and put it in the oven; the other cooks got hold of some poison and sprinkled it on the pie. The king sat down to dine. The pie was served, and he was just about to pick up his knife when the head cook came rushing in. "Your Majesty," he cried, "pray do not eat!" And he told all manner of tales about the young prince. The king did not spare his favourite dog; he cut a piece of pie and tossed it on the floor. The dog ate it, curled up and died on the spot. The

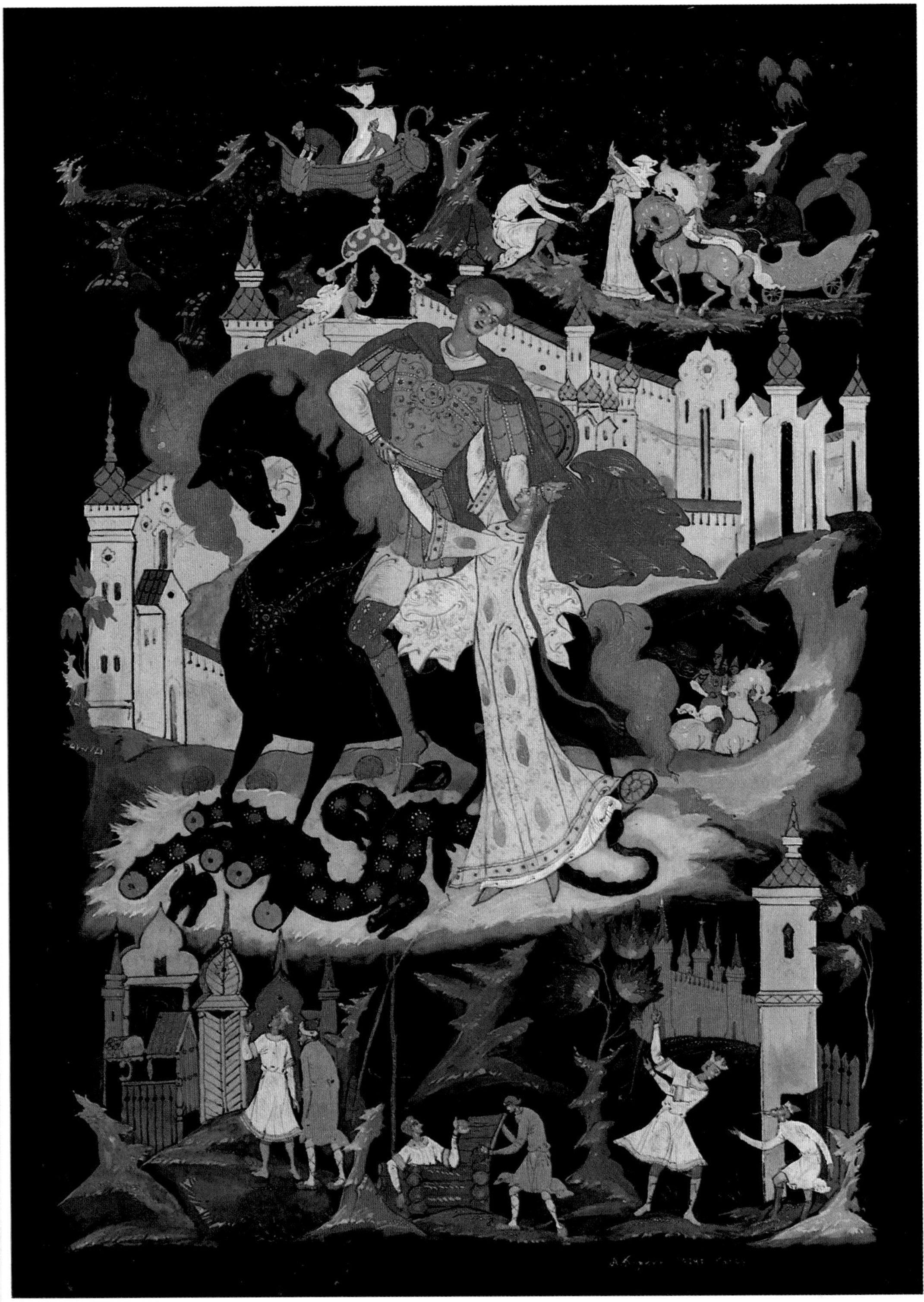

king summoned the prince and shouted at him in a terrible voice, "How dare you bake a poisoned pie? You will die a dreadful death for this!" "I know nothing about it, Your Majesty," replied the poor prince. "Perhaps the cooks took offence at your favours to me and tried to pay me back." The king pardoned the lad and made him his groom.

One day the prince was taking the horses to water when he met the old wood sprite. "Hail, royal son, come and sup with me." "I'm afraid of losing my horses." "Never mind, come with me." His hut was close by. Now, the old wood sprite had three daughters and of the first he asked, "What will you give the king's son for freeing me from the iron pillar?" "A magic table-cloth," she said.

The prince took his gift, left the old wood sprite, and saw the horses waiting; he unfolded his table-cloth and—lo and behold—whatever he wished for appeared: food and drink aplenty!

Next day he was driving the royal horses to water when he came upon the old wood sprite once again. "Come and sup with me," he said. And he led him home and asked of his second daughter, "What will you give the king's son?" "I'll give him a magic mirror: he'll see whatever he wishes in it." On the third day the prince again came upon the old wood sprite, was taken home and heard him ask his youngest daughter, "What will you give the king's son?" "I'll give him a magic flute; he has only to put it to his lips for musicians and singers to appear at once." A merry life began for the king's son: he ate and drank his fill, and harkened to music all day long. What could be better? As for the horses and steeds, they were well-fed, fine-looking and fleet of foot.

The king began to praise the lad to his beloved daughter, how the good Lord had sent him a splendid groom. The lovely princess had long since noticed the groom herself: and how can a fair maid fail to notice a handsome lad! She was curious: why were the new groom's horses fleeter and finer than all the others? "I'll go to his chamber and see how he is getting on, poor lad." Well, everybody knows that a woman gets what she wants. So one day, when the prince had gone to water the horses, she went to his chamber and, when she looked into the mirror, she understood all and slipped away with the mirror, flute and table-cloth.

Now misfortune befell the king about that time: the Seven-Headed Demon attacked his realm and demanded the princess as his bride. "If you do not give her up freely, I shall take her by force," he warned, lining up his troops which number no one could count. The poor king was in a torment. He issued a proclamation throughout the realm, summoning all his dukes and knights: whoever defeated the Seven-Headed Demon could have half his kingdom and the princess as well. So the dukes and knights gathered together and went off to do battle with the Demon, as, too, did the prince's servant with the king's men. And our groom saddled a poor old mare and rode in their wake. On the way he met the wood sprite. "Where are you off to, royal son?" "To battle." "You won't get far on that old nag. And you a groom! Come home and sup with me." He led the lad to his hut and poured him a glass of vodka. The prince drank it down. "Do you feel strong now?" asked the old wood sprite. "If I had a fifty-pood club I'd toss it up, let it fall on my head and not feel the blow." Another glass was set before him. "And now how strong do you feel?" "If I had a hundred-pood club, I'd toss it higher than the clouds." A third glass was poured. "How strong are you now?" "If a pillar were erected from earth to the heavens I'd topple the universe!" The old wood sprite poured vodka from another jar and handed it to the prince, who drank it down and felt his strength diminish by about a seventh.

Thereupon the old wood sprite led him out onto the porch and gave a piercing whistle, and from out of nowhere a jet-black steed came racing, the ground trembled, flames spurted from his nostrils, clouds of smoke curled up from his ears, and sparks showered from under his hoofs. Arriving at the porch, he knelt before the prince. "Now there's a steed for you!" He also gave the lad a silken lash and a mighty club. Off rode the prince on his jet-black steed to face the enemy host. On the way he saw that his old servant had clambered up a birch-tree and was sitting there shaking in terror. The prince gave him a couple of lashes with his silken whip and galloped on to meet the foe. Many a warrior did he fell with his club, and many more did he trample down with his steed, and he slashed off the Demon's seven heads. Meanwhile the princess saw it all. Impatient to learn whose bride she was to be, she watched everything in the magic mirror. Riding out to meet the prince, she asked him, "How can I thank you?" "Give me a kiss, fair maiden," was his reply. The princess was not shy: she kissed him so loudly that the whole army heard.

Spurring on his steed, the prince flew off like the wind, and was soon sitting at home in his little room as if he had never been to war. Meanwhile his old servant was busy boasting: "It was I who slayed the Demon." The king showered him with praise, promised him his daughter and ordered a grand celebration. But the princess was no fool, and she told her father that she was unwell—her head ached and her heart too. What was her betrothed to do? "Sire," he said, "grant me a ship; I'll go for medicine to cure my bride-to-be. And, with your leave, I'll take your young groom along with me, I have grown so used to him." The king consented, giving him a ship and the groom as well.

So off they sailed. After a while the servant ordered a sack to be sewn and had the groom put in it and dropped into the water. The princess looked into the magic mirror and saw the wicked deed. At once she jumped into a carriage and drove quickly to the sea; there on the shore sat the old wood sprite, making a net. "Please, old man," she cried, "aid me in my hour of need: the evil servant has drowned the prince." "Pray do not grieve, fair maid," said the wood sprite calmly. "See, the net is ready. Take it with your own fair hands." So the princess cast the net into the deep blue sea, pulled out the prince and took him home with her. There she told her father all.

In next to no time a merry feast was prepared to celebrate the wedding of the prince and princess. The king had so much mead and beer in his cellars that there was no need to brew more. Meanwhile the servant had purchased various salves and came hurrying back; but the moment he set foot in the palace he was seized and bound. Though he begged forgiveness, it was too late: he was shot outside the palace gates. The wedding of the prince is remembered to this day. All the inns and taverns were open a whole week to the common folk, and the beer ran free. It was at the feast I heard this tale. There it was I drank mead-ale. Though it flowed down my beard, my mouth stayed dry, for nary a drop passed my lips swear I.

The Flying Ship

There once lived an old peasant and his wife with their three sons. The two eldest were clever, but the youngest was a fool. The mother loved the two eldest and gave them nice, clean clothes to wear, but the youngest was always poorly dressed in a dirty smock. One day news came of the king's proclamation: whoever could build a flying ship would receive the hand of his daughter. The two eldest brothers decided to try their luck and asked their parents for their blessing. Their mother gave them provisions for the journey, filled their saddle-bags with fresh white rolls, sweetmeats and a flagon of wine, and sent them on their way with a tender farewell. Seeing this, the fool also begged to go. But his mother tried to stop him, "Don't be stupid; the wolves will get you!" But the fool had it in his stubborn head to go; and go he would! The woman saw there was no reasoning with him, so she gave him black rusks and a flask of water and saw him off.

On his way the fool met an old man who asked whither he was bound. He told the man that the king had promised his daughter to the builder of a flying ship. "Can you really build such a ship?" "No, I cannot," replied the fool. "Then why are you going?" "Goodness only knows." "Well, if that's so," said the man, "let's rest together and have a bite to eat. What have you got in your bag?" "I am ashamed to show my poor fare." "Never mind; we'll eat what the Lord has given." So the fool untied his bundle—and could hardly believe his eyes: instead of black rusks he found fresh white buns and all kinds of sweetmeats. These he shared with his companion. "You see how God has mercy on a fool," said the old man. "You are not forsaken, even if your own mother doesn't love you. Come now, let us have a drink." The fool was even more amazed to find the water in his flask had turned to wine. So they ate and drank, and the old man told the fool, "Listen well: enter the forest, approach the first tree you see, cross yourself thrice and strike the tree with an axe. Then throw yourself face downwards on the ground, and sleep until you are woken. You will see before you a splendid ship; sit in it and fly where you please. But take on board every wayfarer that you meet."

Thanking the man and bidding him farewell, the fool went into the forest. Coming to the first tree, he did all that he had been told: crossed himself thrice, struck the tree with his axe, fell face downwards on the ground, and went to sleep. He was woken some time later. He opened his eyes and there before him stood a magnificent ship! Without further ado, he climbed into it and the ship soared off into the sky.

On and on he sailed, when suddenly the fool saw a man below lying with his ear pressed to the ground. "Ahoy there, fellow!" shouted the fool. "Hello there!" "What are you doing?" "I'm listening to what is happening in the underworld." "Come and join me," invited the fool. Not wishing to argue, the man climbed into the ship and off they went. On and on they sailed, when suddenly they saw a man hopping on one leg with the other tied to his ear. "Ahoy there, fellow! Why are you hopping on one foot?" "Because if I untied the other, I would cover the world in one bound." "Come and join us!" Giantsteps hopped into the ship and off they went again. On and on they sailed, when suddenly they saw a man aiming his gun at goodness knows what—there was nothing to be seen. "Ahoy there, fellow! What are you shooting at? There's not a bird in sight." "It's no fun shooting at close range. I only like aiming at birds and beasts a thousand versts away." "Then come and join us!" The Marksman climbed into the ship, and off they went.

On and on they sailed, when suddenly they saw a man below carrying a sackful of loaves on his back. "Ahoy there, fellow! Where are you going?" "To get some bread for my dinner," replied the man. "But you have a whole sackful of loaves on your back!" "That's nothing, I could swallow that at one go and still be hungry." "Then come and join us!" The Gorger climbed into the ship, and off they went. On and on they sailed, when suddenly they saw a man walking round and round a lake. "Ahoy there, fellow! What are you looking for?" "I'm mighty thirsty, but I can find no water." "But there's a whole lake right in front of you! Why don't you drink that?" "Alas, I could swallow this lake in one gulp and still go thirsty." "Then come and join us!" The Swiller climbed into the ship, and off they went. On and on they sailed, when suddenly they saw a man walking into a forest with a bundle of brushwood on his back. "Ahoy there, fellow! Why are you taking brushwood into the

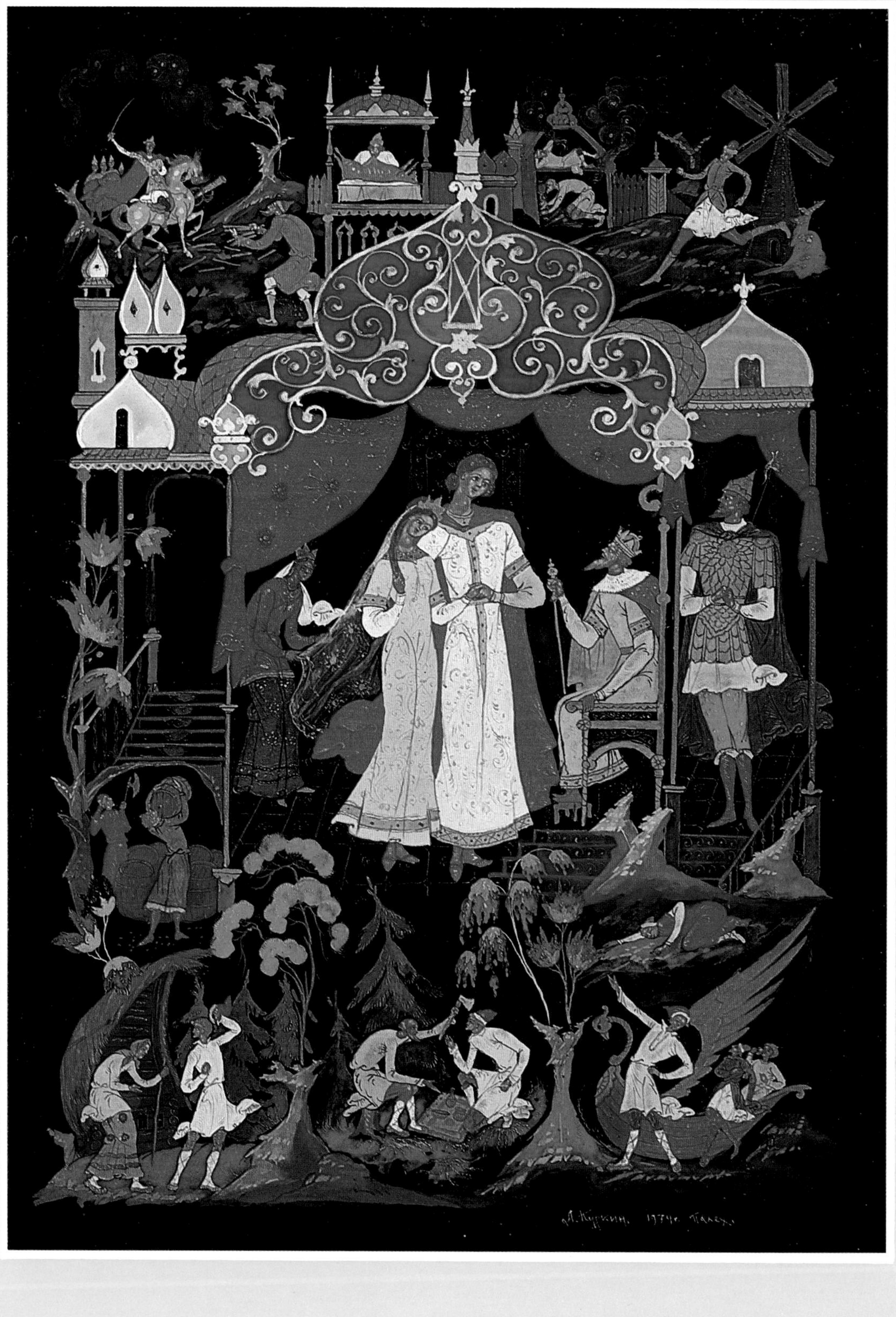
А. Куркин. 1974г. Палех.

forest?" "This is no ordinary brushwood." "What is it then?" "If you scatter it over the ground a whole army will spring up." "Come and join us!" He climbed into the ship and off they went. On and on they sailed, when suddenly they saw a man carrying a bale of straw. "Ahoy there, fellow! Where are you taking that straw?" "To the village." "Isn't there enough straw there already?" "This is no ordinary straw. No matter how hot the summer, if you strew this about, it will get freezing cold, with snow and ice!" "Come and join us!" "Perhaps I will." This was the last wayfarer they met. Soon they reached the king's palace.

The king was having breakfast. Seeing the flying ship, he instantly despatched a servant to discover who the visitors were. On learning that not a single one was of noble blood—they were all common peasants—the king was extremely displeased: he could not wed his daughter to a simple peasant. "I shall set them some impossible tasks," he decided. So the king sent an order to the fool to get him a flask of the water of life—before his meal was over!

While the king was giving the order to his servant, the first wayfarer (the one who had listened to what was happening in the underworld) heard what the king was saying and told the fool. "What shall I do? I could not find such water in a year or even in a lifetime!" "Don't worry," said Giantsteps. "I'll see to it in a trice." The servant came with the king's command. "If you bid me, I will bring it," the fool replied. Giantsteps unhitched his leg from his ear, sped off and found the water of life in no time at all. "There's no hurry," he thought to himself. He sat down to rest by a windmill and dozed off. The king had nearly finished his breakfast, but there was no sign of the fool. The flying sailors were getting uneasy. The first wayfarer put his ear to the ground and heard the snores by the windmill; the Marksman took his gun, fired it at the windmill and woke up Giantsteps, who brought the water of life in the nick of time—just as the king was about to leave the table.

There was nothing for it, the king would have to set a second task. He bade them tell the fool, "If you are so cunning, show your mettle: you and your companions eat a dozen roast oxen and a dozen sacks of bread at a single sitting." The first wayfarer heard this and told the fool. The fool took fright and said: "I couldn't eat one ox at a go." "Don't worry," said the Gorger. "That's only enough to whet my appetite!" The servant came and announced the king's command. "Very well," said the fool, "bring it in." They carried in twelve roast oxen and twelve sacks of bread. The Gorger devoured it all by himself. "What a pity that's all," he said, "I could do with some more." The king bade them tell the fool to drink forty barrels of wine each holding forty bucketfuls. The first wayfarer heard what the king said and told the fool as before. The fool took fright and said: "But I could not even drink one bucketful." "Don't worry," said the Swiller, "I can drain them all in one draught—and still have room for more." And so it was. Forty barrels were filled with wine, and the Swiller drained them dry and asked for more.

Whereupon the king ordered the fool to prepare for the wedding, to go to the bath-house and have a good wash; but the bath-house was made of iron, and the king bade them heat it until it was red-hot—so that the fool would suffocate in it straightaway. They heated the bath-house red-hot and the fool went in with the Straw Man, who scattered so much of his straw over the iron floor that the fool barely had time to wash himself before the water turned to ice. He climbed onto the stove and stayed there all night. When they unlocked the bath-house next morning, there was the fool, hale and hearty, singing merrily. When they told the king, he grew sad and knew not how to get rid of the fool. He pondered hard, then commanded the fool to assemble a whole regiment, thinking to himself: "How can a simple peasant raise an army? That will fox him for sure!"

As soon as the fool learned of the task, he took fright and said: "This is the end. You have got me out of trouble many a time, friends; but nothing can help me now." "Come now. Have you forgotten about me?" cried the Brushwood Man. "Remember, that's just what I can do, and don't worry!" The servant came and gave the fool the king's orders: "If you want to marry the princess, you must raise a whole regiment by tomorrow." "Very well! But if the king refuses to give up his daughter after that, I will conquer his kingdom and take her by force!" That night, the Brushwood Man went into the meadow, spread his brushwood over the grass and there sprang up a vast army of cavalry, infantry and artillery. When the king saw this next morning, he took fright and sent rich velvet robes to the fool, begging him to take the princess with his royal blessing. When the fool put on this splendid attire, he became as handsome as can be. He appeared before the king, wedded the fair princess, received a handsome dowry and became clever and astute. He was dearly loved by the king and queen, but most of all by the fair princess.

Nikita the Dragonslayer

Near the city of Kiev there once appeared a dragon who exacted a terrible tribute from the townsfolk: a fair maid from each household. He would take the maid and eat her up. Eventually it was the turn of the king's daughter. The dragon seized her in his claws and dragged her into his cave. But he did not eat her. So lovely was she that he made her his wife. When he went about his business he would block up the entrance to his cave with logs so that she could not escape. Now the princess had a dog which had followed her from home. She would write a note to her father and mother, tie it round the dog's neck and the dog would deliver it and bring her a reply. One day the king and queen wrote to their daughter: "Find out who is stronger than the dragon." The princess now pretended to be more kindly to the dragon, trying to wheedle out of him who was stronger than he. For a long time he would not tell, but one day he let slip that there was a certain Nikita, a tanner, in the city of Kiev, who was stronger than he. As soon as the princess heard that she wrote to the king: "Search for Nikita the tanner in the city of Kiev and send him to set me free."

When the king received the news he found out where Nikita was and went himself to beg the tanner deliver his land from the evil dragon and rescue his daughter. At that time Nikita was curing hides, holding twelve skins in his hands. When he saw the king himself coming, he trembled in fear and his hands shook so much

63

that he tore all twelve skins. No matter how hard the king and the queen begged him to go and fight the dragon, he refused. So then they decided to assemble five thousand little children and make them beseech Nikita: perhaps their tears would soften his heart! The little children came to Nikita and begged him with tears in their eyes to go and fight the dragon. Tears came to the eyes of Nikita himself as he saw the children weeping. He collected three hundred poods of hemp, soaked it in pitch, wrapped it round his body, and went forth to do battle with the dragon.

As Nikita approached the dragon's cave, the evil beast shut himself in and would not come out. "Come out into the open plain or I'll smash your cave too!" Nikita called and began to break down the door. Seeing no escape the dragon went to Nikita in the open plain. How long Nikita fought the dragon I cannot say, but he beat him in the end, and the dragon began to beg, "Spare me, Nikita! No one is stronger than us two in the whole world; let us divide the world between us: you live in one half and I in the other." "Very well," said Nikita. "We'll have to mark the boundary." So Nikita made a plough weighing three hundred poods, harnessed the dragon to it and drove a furrow all the way from Kiev to the Caustrian Sea. "Well," said the dragon, "we've divided up the land." "Yes," said Nikita, "but now let's divide up the sea or else you'll say people are using your water." The dragon went out into the middle of the sea and Nikita slew him and drowned his body in the water. Nikita's furrow can still be seen; it is ten feet high. Folk till the soil around it, but never touch the furrow. Those who do not know from whence it came call it a rampart. As for Nikita, having done his brave deed, he refused to take anything for his pains and returned to curing hides.

Old Bones the Deathless

Once upon a time there was a king who had an only son. When the prince was small, his nannies and nursemaids would sing him a lullaby: "Hush-a-bye, hush-a-bye, Prince Ivan. When you are big, you'll take a wife: Princess Vasilissa who sits in a tower beyond the Thrice-Nine Land in the Thrice-Ten Kingdom." When the prince was fifteen years old he asked his father's leave to seek his bride. "Seek your bride? You are still too young." "No, Sire, when I was little, my nannies and nursemaids sang me a lullaby, telling me where my true love lives; so now I am going to seek her." In the end his father gave him his blessing and spread the news throughout the land that his son Prince Ivan was looking for his bride.

One day the prince arrived at a city, left his horse to be groomed and went off alone about the town. As he came to a square he saw a man being lashed. "Why are you whipping him?" he asked. "Because he fell into debt to a wealthy merchant and did not pay back the ten thousand in time: whoever pays his debt will lose his own wife to Old Bones the Deathless." Puzzled and perplexed, the prince passed on but when he came back to the square, he saw the man was still being beaten. So sorry was Prince Ivan for him that he resolved to pay the man's debts. "I have no wife," he thought, "so she can't be carried off." He paid the ten thousand and went off; suddenly the man he had saved came running after him, crying, "Thank you, Prince Ivan. If you had not saved me, you would never have found your bride. Now I shall help you: purchase a horse and saddle for me." The prince bought him a horse and saddle and asked him his name. "I am Bulat the Brave," said the man.

They mounted their horses and set off on their journey. As soon as they arrived at the Thrice-Ten Kingdom, Bulat the Brave said to the prince, "Listen, Prince Ivan, have them buy and roast chickens, ducks and geese aplenty. In the meantime I'll go and bring your bride. But mark my words: each time I come running to you, cut the right wing off a bird and give it to me on a plate." Off went Bulat the Brave towards the high tower where Princess Vasilissa was sitting. Tossing a stone high into the air he knocked down the gilded top of the tower. Then he ran back to Prince Ivan and said, "Why are you sleeping? Give me the chicken!" Straightway the prince cut off the right wing and handed it over on a plate. Bulat the Brave took the plate, ran to the tower and shouted, "Good morrow, Princess Vasilissa! Prince Ivan sent me with his compliments and asked me to give you this chicken." The maid was frightened; she sat there saying nothing. So he answered for her: "Good morrow, Bulat the Brave. Is Prince Ivan well?" "He is, thank the Lord." "Well, don't just stand there, Bulat the Brave; take the key, unlock the chest, pour yourself a glass of vodka and go on your way with God's blessing."

Away went Bulat the Brave to Prince Ivan. "Why are you sitting there? Give me the duck," he cried. The prince cut off the right wing and handed it over on a plate. Bulat took the plate and carried it to the tower. "Good morrow, Princess Vasilissa! Prince Ivan sent me with his compliments and asked me to give you this duck." She sat there saying nothing; so he answered for her: "Good morrow, Bulat the Brave. Is the prince well?" "He is, thank the Lord." "Well, don't just stand there, Bulat the Brave; take the key, unlock the chest, pour yourself a glass and go on your way with God's blessing." Away went Bulat the Brave back home and again told Prince Ivan: "Why are you sitting there? Give me the goose." The prince cut him the right wing, put it on a plate and handed it over. Bulat the Brave took it and hastened to the tower. "Good morrow, Vasilissa! Prince Ivan sent me with his compliments and asked me to give you this goose." Right away Princess Vasilissa took the key, opened up the chest for him and handed him a glass of vodka. Without touching the glass, he quickly seized the maiden by her right hand, dragged her out of the tower, sat her on Prince Ivan's horse and they rode off together like the wind, the two bold young men and the fair maiden.

Next morning King Kirbit woke up to find the top of his tower broken off and his daughter stolen away. Sorely angered, he sent guards down all the roads and tracks in pursuit of the thieves. After a while Bulat the Brave took off his ring, hid it and said, "You go on, Prince Ivan; I have to turn back to look for my ring." Vasilissa began to beg him, "Do not leave us, Bulat the Brave. Here, take my ring." "Oh no, Princess Vasilissa!" he replied. "My ring is priceless; my dear mother gave it to me saying: 'Keep this ring in memory of me.'" Back rode Bulat the Brave and met the pursuing guards on the road: in no time at all he had slain them all, save a single man to take news back to the king. He hurried to catch up Prince Ivan.

Some time later Bulat the Brave hid his handkerchief and said, "Oh dear, Prince Ivan, I have lost my handkerchief. Go on your way, I'll soon catch you up." Turning back he rode for a couple of versts and met the pursuing guards, twice as many as before; but he slew them all and returned to Prince Ivan, telling him he had found his handkerchief.

Dark night overtook them, and they put up a tent. Bulat the Brave lay down to sleep leaving Prince Ivan to stand guard and to wake him if need be. As time past, the prince became drowsy, sank down beside the tent and fell asleep. While they all slept, Old Bones the Deathless swooped down from out of nowhere and carried off the lovely Princess Vasilissa. When the prince awoke at dawn, he saw his bride had gone and wept bitter tears. Bulat the Brave woke up and asked: "Why are you crying?" "How can I help it? Someone has carried off Princess Vasilissa." "I told you to stand guard! This is the work of Old Bones the Deathless. We must go in search of him."

For a long, long time they journeyed until, at last, they came upon two shepherds tending their flocks. "Whose flocks are these?" they asked. "They belong to Old Bones the Deathless," replied the shepherds. Whereupon Bulat the Brave and Prince Ivan found out from the men where Old Bones lived, how they could get there, when the shepherds would return home with the flocks, and where they would put them. Then they dismounted, slew the shepherds, dressed in their smocks, drove the flocks home, and stood outside the gates of Old Bones' castle.

Now Prince Ivan was wearing a golden ring given him by Princess Vasilissa. And Princess Vasilissa had a goat in whose milk she washed her face morning and evening. A servant girl came running with her bowl, milked the goat and was carrying off the milk when Bulat took the ring from the prince and dropped it into the bowl. The servant girl scolded them: "Don't play tricks with me, you two rogues." When she came to Princess Vasilissa she complained, "Those two shepherds are playing tricks on us; today they have dropped a ring into the milk." "Leave it here," said Princess Vasilissa. "I'll strain the milk myself." As she did so, she found her own ring and told the girl to bring the shepherds before her. The shepherds came. "Hail, Princess Vasilissa!" said Bulat the Brave. "Hail, Bulat the Brave! Hail, Prince! What miracle brings you here?" "We have come for you, Princess Vasilissa. You cannot hide from us; we would find you even at the bottom of the sea." She sat them at the table, and put all manner of sweetmeats and wines before them. Bulat the Brave told her, "As soon as Old Bones returns from hunting, be sure to ask him where bis death is to be found, Princess Vasilissa. Now we must hide."

Hardly had the guests had time to hide than Old Bones the Deathless came flying back from hunting. "Fie, Foh!" he said. "Before there was neither scent nor sign of Russian blood here; but now I can see and smell it everywhere." But Princess Vasilissa answered, "You've been flying through the lands of Rus, tasting Russian blood, and the smell has stayed with you." Old Bones had his supper and lay down to rest. Vasilissa came and sat beside him, bent her fair head over him, kissed

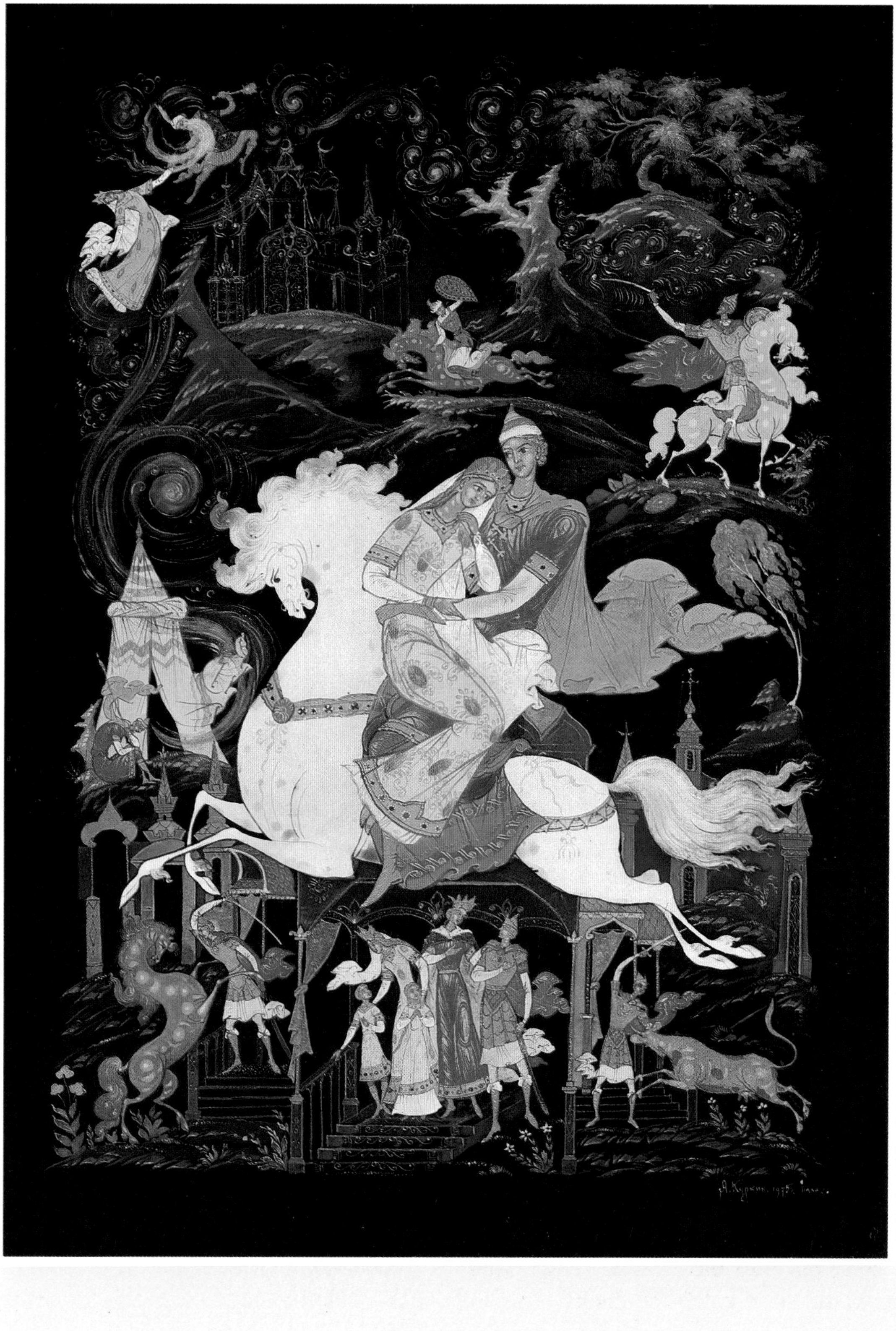

and caressed him, breathing in his ear, "My dearest friend, I have missed you greatly; I was sore afraid I would not see you alive again. I thought the wild beasts had eaten you." Old Bones laughed. "Foolish woman! Long hair, short mind. How could wild beasts devour me?" "Where, then, is your death to be found?" "My death lies in a besom under the doorway," he replied.

As soon as Old Bones had flown away, Princess Vasilissa ran to Prince Ivan and told him that Old Bones' death lay in a besom under the doorway. "No, he is lying," said Bulat. "You must question him more cunningly." Princess Vasilissa had an idea: taking a besom, she gilded it, hung it with different coloured ribbons and laid it on the table. Old Bones the Deathless flew home, saw the gilded, beribboned besom upon the table and asked why it was there. "Why should your death lie rotting beneath the doorway," said Vasilissa, "let it lie on the table." "Foolish woman! Long hair, short mind. Did you really think my death was there?" "Where is it then?" "It is concealed inside a goat," he said. As soon as Old Bones had gone hunting, she decked out a goat in ribbons and little bells and gilded its horns. When Old Bones saw it he roared with laughter again. "Oh my! Foolish woman! Long hair, short mind. My death is farther off: in the middle of the deep blue sea there is an island; on that island stands an oak, under the oak a chest is buried, and in that chest there is a hare, in the hare a duck, in the duck an egg, and in the egg is my death!" and he flew off. Vasilissa told all she had heard to Bulat the Brave and Prince Ivan; and the two companions made ready for the journey and went in search of Old Bones' death.

By and by they ate all their provisions and were very hungry. On the way they came upon a dog with puppies. "I shall kill it," said Bulat the Brave, "we have nothing else to eat." "Do not kill me and make orphans of my children," begged the dog. "Spare me and I will be of use to you." So they let her be and went on their way. After a while they came upon an eagle sitting in an oak with her eaglets. "I shall kill the eagle," said Bulat the Brave. "Do not kill me and make orphans of my children; spare me and I will be of use to you," said the eagle. So they let her be and went on their way. They came to the shores of a wide ocean and saw a crab crawling along the sand. "I shall kill the crab," said Bulat the Brave. "Do not kill me, bold young man," said the crab. "You will gain little from it. Spare me and I will be of use to you." So they let her be. Bulat the Brave called to a fisherman sailing on the sea, "Pull into the shore!" The fisherman did so. The two companions got into the boat and rowed towards the island. They reached it and walked to the oak-tree.

Bulat the Brave took hold of the oak and pulled it up by the roots; then he dug up the chest from beneath the oak, opened it and out skipped a hare that scampered off for all it was worth. "Ah," sighed Prince Ivan, "if only the dog was here, she would soon catch the hare!" All of a sudden the dog came running along with the hare in her mouth! Bulat the Brave cut open the hare and out jumped a duck and soared high into the clouds. "Ah," sighed Prince Ivan, "if only the eagle was here, she would soon catch the duck!" Suddenly there was the eagle swooping down with the duck in her talons! Bulat cut open the duck—out dropped an egg and rolled right into the sea. "Ah," sighed Prince Ivan, "if only the crab was here to fetch it for us!" Whereupon the crab came crawling from the sea with the egg safely in her pincers. They took the egg, went to Old Bones the Deathless, struck him on the forehead with it, and he dropped dead. Prince Ivan took the fair Princess Vasilissa and they set off with her once again.

On and on they rode until dark night descended; they put up a tent, and Princess Vasilissa lay down to sleep. Bulat the Brave told the prince, "You rest too, Prince; I'll keep watch this time." Deep in the night twelve doves came flying down, flapped their wings and turned into twelve maidens. "Bulat the Brave and Prince Ivan, beware! You have killed our brother Old Bones the Deathless and carried off our dear sister-in-law Vasilissa; no good will come of it: as soon as Prince Ivan reaches home and calls his favourite dog, it will break its leash and tear the prince to pieces. And whoever hears this and tells him will be turned to stone from foot to knee!" Next morning Bulat the Brave woke the prince and Vasilissa and set off with them further.

When the second night descended, they put up their tent in the open plain. Once more Bulat the Brave told his companion to lie down to sleep while he stood guard. Deep in the night the twelve doves came flying down, flapped their wings and turned into twelve maidens. "Bulat the Brave and Prince Ivan, beware! You have killed our brother Old Bones the Deathless and caried off our dear sister-in-law Vasilissa; no good will come of it: as soon as Prince Ivan reaches home and asks for his favourite horse which he has ridden since childhood, the steed will tear free of the groom and trample the prince to death. And whoever hears this and tells him will be turned to stone from foot to waist!" At dawn's first light they continued their journey.

When the third night descended they put up their tent in the open plain. As before Bulat told the prince to lie down to sleep while he stood guard. And once again, in the middle of the night, the twelve doves flew down, flapped their wings and became twelve maidens. "Bulat the Brave and Prince Ivan, beware! You have killed our brother Old Bones the Deathless and carried off our dear sister-in-law Vasilissa; no good will come of it: as soon as Prince Ivan reaches home and calls for his favourite cow whose milk he has drunk since childhood, it will break free of the cowman and toss the prince with its horns. And whoever hears this and tells him will be turned to stone from top to toe." Whereupon they turned back into doves and flew away.

Next morning Prince Ivan and Princess Vasilissa awoke and the three continued their journey. The prince reached home, married Princess Vasilissa and said to her a few days later, "I would like to show you my favourite dog. When I was a lad we had such fun together." Bulat the Brave took his sabre, made it razor-sharp and stood by the porch. When the dog was brought, it broke free of its keeper and rushed straight towards the porch; in a flash Bulat raised his sabre and brought it down hard on the dog, cutting it in two. Prince Ivan was very angry, but kept silent because of his friend's past service. Next day he called for his favourite horse to be brought. As he stood in the courtyard, the horse tore free of its halter, knocked over the groom and galloped straight at the prince. In an instant Bulat the Brave dashed forward and cut off the horse's head. At that Prince Ivan was even angrier than before and he would have had him seized and hung there and then had not Princess Vasilissa pleaded with him. "Were it not for him," she said, "you would never have got me." On the third day Prince Ivan called for his favourite cow, but as it was being led into the yard it tore free from the cowman and headed straight for the prince. Bulat the Brave cut off its head, too.

Whereupon Prince Ivan flew into such a rage that no words could appease him: he ordered him to be executed there and then.

"Listen, Prince Ivan. Since you intend to have me put to death, I would rather die by my own hand. But before I die permit me to tell you three things..." And Bulat the Brave told of the first night: how the twelve doves had flown down to the open plain and what they had said—and at once he was turned to stone up to his knees. Then he told of the second night—and he was turned to stone up to the waist. At that Prince Ivan begged him not to continue his story. But Bulat the Brave answered, "It doesn't matter any more—half of me is stone, so what is life to me now." And he told the story of the third night and was turned completely into stone. Prince Ivan had him placed in a special chamber and visited him each day with Princess Vasilissa; and they both shed bitter tears over him.

Many years passed. One day Prince Ivan was weeping over the stone figure of Bulat the Brave when he heard a voice from the stone body: "Do not cry. My heart is heavy enough already." "How can I help crying? It was I who destroyed you." "You can save me if you wish," the voice went on. "You have two children—a son and a daughter: take them and kill them, pour off their blood and daub it over the stone." Prince Ivan told this to his wife. They sorrowed and grieved, but decided to do as the voice had said. Taking their little ones, they killed them, poured their blood into a bowl and daubed the stone with it. No sooner had they done so than Bulat the Brave came to life, and he asked Prince Ivan and his wife: "Do you not grieve about your children?" "Yes, we grieve sorely, Bulat the Brave." "Then come with me to their room." They went and found their children alive and well! How happy were the father and mother; in their happiness they held a feast to which all the world was invited. And I was there, drank mead and wine. Though it flowed down my beard, my mouth stayed dry. For never a drop passed my lips, swear I. My soul was drunk and so was my mind.

Kozma Quick-To-Be-Rich

Once upon a time there was a lad called Kozma who lived alone in the middle of a dark forest. All he had was a tumble-down hut, one rooster and five hens. But a cunning fox had her eye on Kozma's chickens. One day he went off hunting and she straightway ran in, seized a hen, roasted it and ate it up. Kozma got home and found a hen missing. A kite must have taken it, he thought. Next day he went hunting again and met the fox. "Whither are you bound, Kozma?" she asked. "I am going hunting, Mistress Fox." "Farewell then!" and off she went to his hut, straightway killed another hen, roasted it and ate it up. When Kozma came home he found another hen gone. "Aha!" he thought, "could it be the fox who is eating my hens?"

So on the third day he locked the doors and windows of his hut as tightly as he could and went off hunting. Out sprang the fox from nowhere and asked him, "Whither are you bound, Kozma?" "I am going hunting, Mistress Fox." Thereupon the fox ran straight to Kozma's house, and he turned back and followed her.

When she arrived, she walked round the hut and saw that all the windows and doors were shut tightly. How was she to get inside? She climbed up to the roof and went down the chimney. Kozma caught her and said: "Haha! Now I see who the thief is. Just wait, my fine lady, I'll flay you alive!"

The fox began to beg Kozma, "Don't kill me. I'll make you Kozma Quick-To-Be-Rich if you let me go; only roast me one hen in a lot of butter." Kozma agreed,

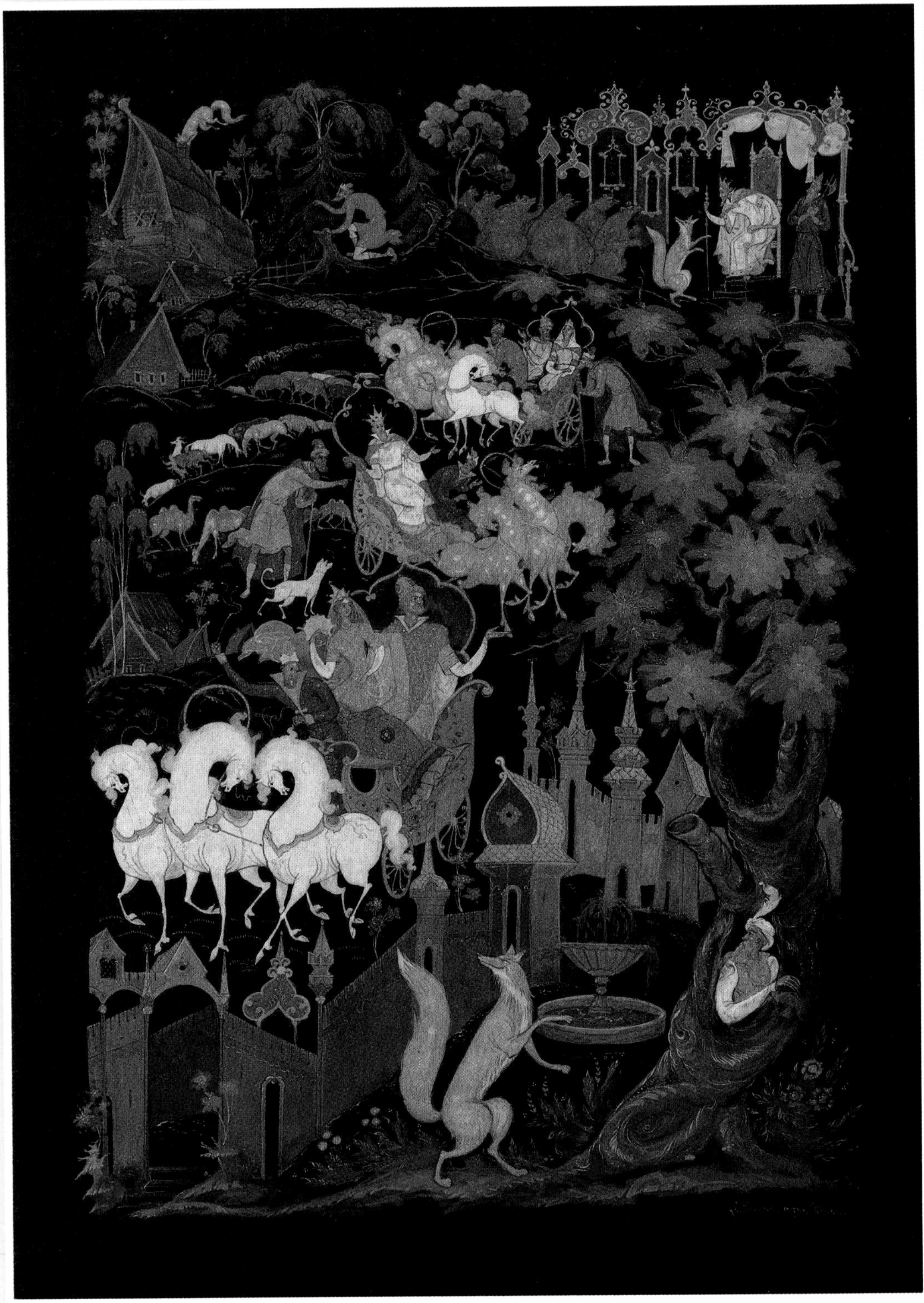

and after eating her fill of the rich fat meat, the fox hurried off to the royal meadows and began to romp about on the grass.

Just then a wolf ran by and said: "Hey, cursed fox, how did you get so fat?" "Ah, dear Brother Wolf," she replied, "I have been dining with the king. Weren't you invited too? All the animals under the sun were there: martens and sables, hundreds of them!" "Dear Sister Fox, do take me with you to dine with the king," begged the wolf. The fox promised she would and told him to get together forty times forty grey wolves and bring them with him. The wolf got together forty times forty grey wolves and the fox took them to the king's palace. Then she entered the king's white-stone chamber, and presented him with forty times forty grey wolves from Kozma Quick-To-Be-Rich. The king was very pleased and ordered the wolves to be driven into a pen and locked safely away. Off ran the fox back to Kozma and told him to roast her one more hen, ate her fill and hurried off once more for the royal meadows to romp about in the green grass.

Just then a bear ambled by. Seeing the fox he called out, "Hey, cursed tailbrush, how did you get so fat and greasy?" "I've just been dining with the king," the fox replied. "All the animals under the sun were there: martens and sables, hundreds of them. And the wolves are still stuffing themselves there. You know how greedy they are, brother. They are still guzzling away." "Dear Sister Fox, do take me with you to dine with the king," begged the bear. The fox promised she would and told him to get together forty times forty big black bears. "The king would not care to entertain you alone," she said. The bear got together forty times forty big black bears and the fox led them to the king. She presented the monarch with forty times forty big black bears from Kozma Quick-To-Be-Rich. The king was pleased with that, too, and ordered all the bears to be rounded up and locked safely away. Off scampered the fox to Kozma and told him to roast the last hen and the rooster for her. He did as she bade him, the fox ate her fill and went off to the royal meadows to frisk about in the green grass.

Just then a sable and marten ran by. "Hey there, crafty fox," they called. "How did you get so fat and greasy?" "Ah, brothers, I have been honoured by the king. He is holding a feast and supper for all kinds of animals. I had a wonderful time eating all that tasty food! And you should have seen all the beasts there—hundreds of them! What a shame you couldn't come. You know what guzzlers those wolves are, as if they haven't eaten in a month of Sundays; well, they are still stuffing themselves at the palace now. As for Bandy-legs the bear—he has eaten so much he's fit to burst!" The sable and marten begged the fox: "Please take us to the king, so that we can see it for ourselves." The fox agreed and told them to get together forty times forty sables and martens. This they did, and the fox took them to the palace and presented the king with forty times forty sables and martens from Kozma

Quick-To-Be-Rich. The king marvelled at the wealth of Kozma Quick-To-Be-Rich, gladly accepted his gift and ordered the animals to be slain and skinned.

Next day the fox again ran to the king, exclaiming, "Your Royal Highness! Kozma Quick-To-Be-Rich has told me to pay you his deep respects and ask if he may borrow a weight: he has to weigh his silver coins. His own weights are caked with gold." The king readily gave her a weight. Off scurried the fox to Kozma and told him to weigh sand with it to make it shine. When this was done, she took it back to the king, and asked him to give his fair daughter's hand in marriage to Kozma Quick-To-Be-Rich. The king agreed and bade Kozma make ready and come to the palace. Kozma set off, and the fox ran ahead and told some workmen to set fire to the bridge. When Kozma rode onto the bridge, it collapsed and fell with him into the water. "Help, help!" cried tbe fox. "My master Kozma Quick-To-Be-Rich is drowning. Help, help!" Now the king heard the cries and straightway sent his men to rescue Kozma. They pulled him out, clothed him in royal attire and led him to the king.

He married the fair princess and lived in the palace for a week or two, when one day the king said to him, "Now, dear son-in-law, take me to your land." There was nothing for it but to do as the king requested. Horses were harnessed and off they went. But the fox ran on ahead. On the way she met some shepherds tending a flock of sheep. "Pray, shepherds," she asked, "whose flock is this?" "King Serpent's," came back the reply. The fox cautioned them: "You had better tell everyone that this flock belongs to Kozma Quick-To-Be-Rich, and not King Serpent, because King Fire and Queen Brimstone are soon to pass by. And they will scorch and burn you and your sheep if you don't tell them it is Kozma Quick-To-Be-Rich's flock." The shepherds saw there was nothing for it but to do as she said, and promised to mention Kozma Quick-To-Be-Rich's name to everyone.

The fox ran on ahead and came to some swineherds tending pigs. "Pray, swineherds," she asked, "whose pigs are these?" "King Serpent's," came back the answer. "You had better say they belong to Kozma Quick-To-Be-Rich," she warned, "for King Fire and Queen Brimstone are soon to pass by. And they will scorch and burn you all if you mention King Serpent's name." The swineherds consented. Once more the fox ran on ahead until she came to King Serpent's herd of cows, then his herd of horses, each time commanding the tenders to keep silent about King Serpent and to say all the animals belonged to Kozma Quick-To-Be-Rich. Finally she came to a herd of camels. "Camel drovers, camel drovers," she shouted. "Whose herd is this?" "King Serpent's." The fox forbade them strictly to mention that name again: they were to say the camels belonged to Kozma Quick-To-Be-Rich. If they did not, King Fire and Queen Brimstone would scorch and burn them with all their camels!

The fox ran off again until she reached the realm of King Serpent himself and went straight to his white-stone chambers. "What tidings do you bring, Mistress Fox?" asked the king. "Hide as fast as you can, King Serpent," panted the fox. "For the dreaded King Fire and Queen Brimstone are coming, scorching and burning everything on their way. They have set fire to your herds and shepherds; first the sheep and pigs, then the cows and horses. I made haste to warn you and all but choked from the smoke!" King Serpent began to moan and groan. "Oh dear, Mistress Fox, where am I to hide?" "There's an old oak-tree in your gardens, rotten in the middle; go and hide inside it until they ride by." Straightway King Serpent did as the fox bade him.

Meanwhile Kozma Quick-To-Be-Rich rode along with his wife and father-in-law. As they passed the flock of sheep, the young princess called out, "Shepherds, shepherds, tell me: whose flocks are these?" "Kozma Quick-To-Be-Rich's," they replied. The king was pleased. "Well, well, son-in-law," he said, "what a lot of sheep you own." On they travelled in their coach until they reached the swineherds. "Swineherds, swineherds," called the young princess, "whose pigs are these?" "Kozma Quick-To-Be-Rich's," came the response. "Well, well, son-in-law, what a lot of pigs you have." On and on they rode, passing in turn by the cows and horses and the camels. Each time they asked whose animals they were, the answer was always the same: "Kozma Quick-To-Be-Rich's."

At last they came to the royal palace; there they were welcomed by Mistress Fox who led them into the white-stone chambers. The king entered and gazed about him in wonder: so richly was the palace furnished. So they began to feast, eat, drink and be merry. They stayed for a whole week. "Now, Kozma," said the fox, "no more merry-making. There's work to be done. Take your father-in-law into the gardens to the old oak-tree. Inside the oak sits King Serpent hiding from you. Shoot the oak to pieces!" No sooner said than done. Kozma went with his father-in-law into the gardens and they began to shoot at the oak-tree and killed King Serpent good and dead. Kozma Quick-To-Be-Rich reigned over his land and lived happily with his fair princess. And as far as I know they still prosper. As for Mistress Fox, she was given hens every day and stayed there until there were no more hens left.

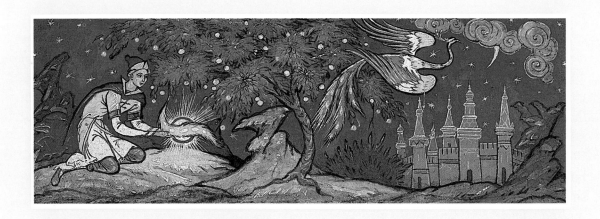

The Tale of Prince Ivan,
the Firebird
and the Big Grey Wolf

In a certain realm, in a certain land there once was a king by the name of Vyslav. And he had three sons: Prince Dmitri, Prince Vassily and Prince Ivan. The king also had an orchard, the best in the whole world; and in the orchard grew many rare trees, some with fruit, some without. And the king had a favourite apple-tree, which bore golden apples. But a Firebird took to visiting the king's orchard: it had wings of gold and eyes like crystal. Each night it came to the orchard and settled in King Vyslav's favourite apple-tree, plucked some golden apples and flew away again.

King Vyslav was deeply grieved that the Firebird should steal so many apples from his tree. So he called his sons to him, saying, "My dear children, which of you will catch the Firebird in my orchard? Whoever catches it alive shall have half of my kingdom while I live, and the rest when I die." Whereupon his princes cried out

78

in unison: "Gracious Lord and Sire, Your Royal Highness! With the greatest joy we will try to catch the Firebird alive."

On the first night Prince Dmitri went into the orchard and, settling down beneath the tree from which the Firebird had taken apples, soon fell asleep and did not hear the Firebird come and pluck many apples. In the morning King Vyslav summoned Prince Dmitri and asked, "Well, my dear son, did you see the Firebird or not?" "No, gracious Lord and Sire, it did not appear the whole night through." On the following night Prince Vassily went to stand guard in the orchard. And he, too, settled beneath the apple-tree and, after an hour or two, fell into such a sound slumber that he did not hear the Firebird fly down and pluck the apples. In the morning King Vyslav called his son and asked, "Well, my dear son, did you see the Firebird or not?" "Gracious Lord and Sire, it did not come the whole night through."

On the third night Prince Ivan went to keep guard and settled down beneath the apple-tree. He sat there for one hour, then a second and a third; and suddenly the whole orchard was ablaze with light, as if lit up by a myriad candles. It was the Firebird: it landed in the tree and began to pluck the apples.

Prince Ivan crept up to it quietly and seized it by the tail. But the Firebird tore free and flew swiftly away, leaving but one golden feather from its tail, to which the prince clung hard. Next morning, as soon as King Vyslav awoke from his slumbers, Prince Ivan went to him with the Firebird's feather. The king was overjoyed that his youngest son had managed to capture at least a feather from the Firebird. It was such a wonderful feather that it lit up all around; if you took it into a dark chamber it illuminated everything as brightly as if a thousand candles were burning there. King Vyslav put the feather away as something to be kept carefully. And the Firebird did not come to the orchard again.

King Vyslav summoned his sons once more and said, "My dear children! Go with my blessing, find the Firebird and bring it back alive. And all that I promised before shall be given to the one who brings me the Firebird." The two eldest princes were jealous of their brother for pulling the feather from the Firebird's tail. Taking their father's blessing they rode off together in search of the Firebird. Meanwhile Prince Ivan also asked for his father's blessing to join the search. But King Vyslav told him, "My dear son, light of my life, you are too young to undertake such a long and arduous journey. Stay here with me; your brothers have gone. What if you leave me too and I see none of you ever again? I'm getting old and will soon go before my Maker. If our dear Lord calls me while you are gone, who will there be to rule my kingdom? There might be a revolt or strife among our people, and no one to quell it; or an enemy could invade our lands, and there'd be no one to lead our army."

But try as he would, King Vyslav could not keep the prince, so insistently did he beg. So Prince Ivan received his father's blessing, chose a fine steed and set off not knowing where he was to go.

Whether he was long on his way I cannot say, whether he went far or near I did not hear—the tale is sooner told than the deed is done. But at last he came to an open plain with green meadows. And there in the open plain was a stone pillar which bore the following inscription: "Straight ahead is hunger and chill. To the right is life and health, though death to your steed. To the left is death, but life and health to your steed." Prince Ivan read the sign and decided to turn right, reasoning that, though he would lose his horse, he would himself stay alive and well and might find another horse sometime. After riding for one day, then a second and a third, he suddenly saw huge Grey Wolf coming towards him. "Hail, Prince Ivan, foolish youth! Did you not read the stone's sign that your steed would die? Why then do you come this way?" So saying the Grey Wolf tore Prince Ivan's horse apart, and ran away.

The prince grieved over his poor horse, wept bitterly and then went on by foot. He walked all day and was more weary than words can tell; he was just about to take a rest when the Grey Wolf overtook him, saying, "I am sorry that you are so weary, Prince Ivan; I am sorry too that I ate your noble steed. So be it. Climb on my back and tell me whither you are bound and why." Prince Ivan told the Grey Wolf whither he was bound.

The Grey Wolf sped off more swiftly than a horse; and some time later, at nightfall, brought the prince to a palace surrounded by a stone wall. There he halted, saying: "Now, Prince Ivan, dismount and climb over the wall. Beyond the wall is a garden and in that garden sits the Firebird in a golden cage. Take the Firebird, but do not touch the golden cage; if you take the cage, you will never leave here alive!"

Prince Ivan climbed over the stone wall into the garden, saw the Firebird in the golden cage, and was sorely tempted. He took the bird out of the cage and was on his way back when he hesitated, saying to himself, "If I take the Firebird without the cage I will have nowhere to put it." So he turned back and the moment he laid hands upon the cage there was a terrible clanging all round the garden, for there were invisible strings running from the cage. The guards woke up, ran into the garden, seized Prince Ivan with the Firebird and took him to their king whose name was Dolmat. King Dolmat was very angry with the prince and shouted at him in a loud and angry voice: "Are you not ashamed to steal, young man? Who are you?

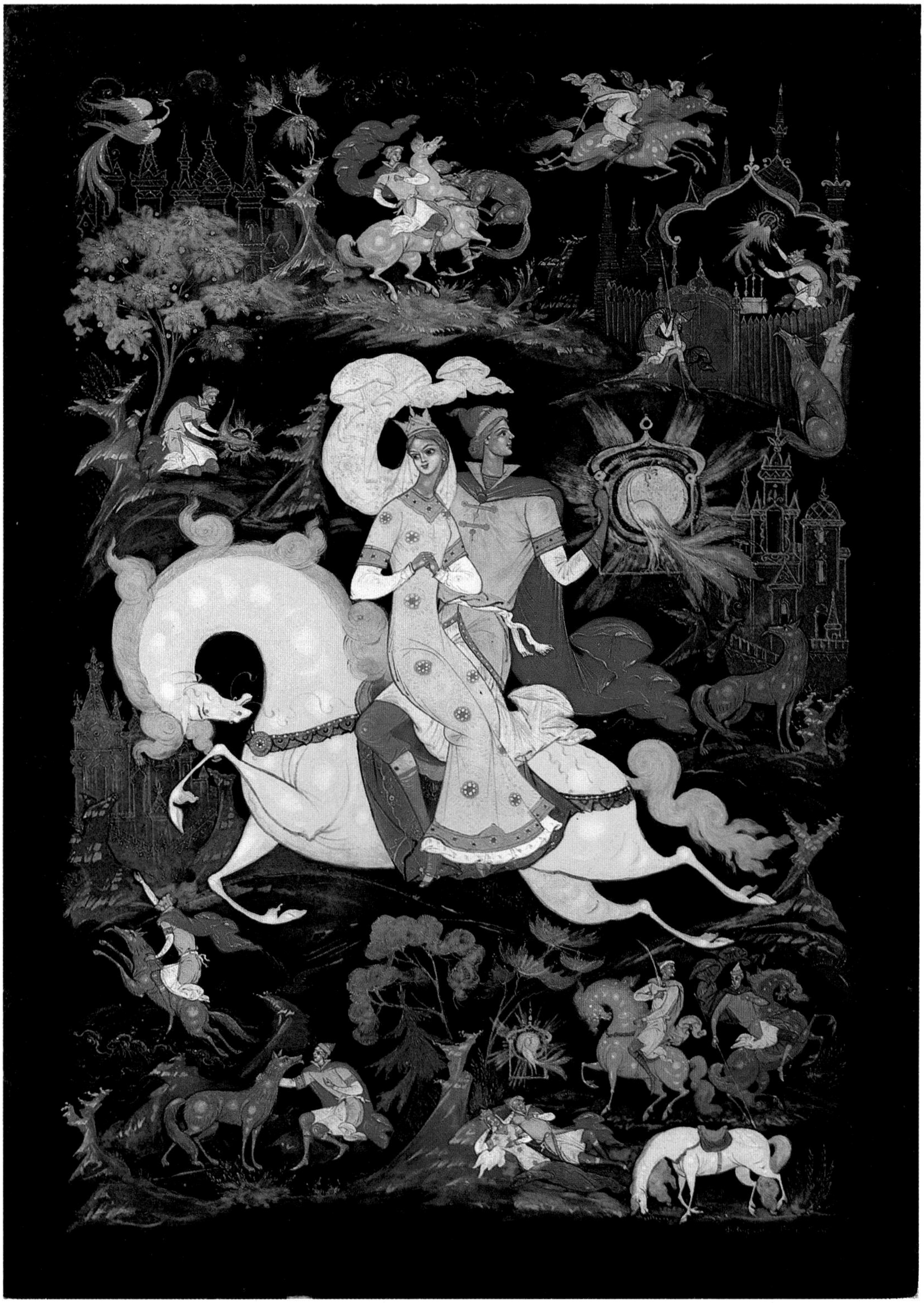

Where are you from, who is your father, and what name do you go by?" "I am from Vyslav's kingdom," Prince Ivan repled, "the son of King Vyslav, and my name is Prince Ivan. Your Firebird came to our orchard every night, stealing golden apples from my father's favourite apple-tree, and spoiled almost the whole tree. So my father sent me to find the Firebird and take it back to him." On hearing that, King Dolmat replied, "Ah, Prince Ivan, foolish youth, is it fitting to act as you have? If you had come to me I would willingly have given you the Firebird. Now what will become of you when I have it proclaimed throughout all the lands how dishonestly you acted here? But listen, Prince Ivan, if you perform a service for me, go to the Thrice-Ten Kingdom, beyond the Thrice-Nine Land and bring me King Afron's Horse with the Golden Mane, I will pardon you and give you the Firebird as a just reward for your services; and if you refuse me this service, I will have it known throughout all the lands that you are a dishonest thief." Sorrowing greatly, Prince Ivan left King Dolmat, having promised to bring him the Horse with the Golden Mane.

He returned to the Grey Wolf and told him all that King Dolmat had said. "Oh, Prince Ivan, foolish youth," said the Grey Wolf. "Why did you not heed my warning and leave the golden cage?" "I am truly sorry," Prince Ivan told the Grey Wolf. "So be it," said the Grey Wolf. "Climb upon my back again, I'll carry you whither you wish." Prince Ivan mounted the Grey Wolf and off they sped like an arrow from a bow. Whether they were long on their way I cannot say, but at last they came at nightfall to the lands of King Afron. Stopping at the white-stone royal stables, the Grey Wolf told the prince, "Go into these white-stone stables, Prince Ivan, while the stable guards are sleeping soundly and take the Horse with the Golden Mane. But mind you leave the golden bridle hanging on the wall; woe to you if you touch it." Prince Ivan entered the white-stone stables, took the horse and was about to leave, when he saw the golden bridle hanging on the wall and was so sorely tempted that he reached out to take it down. No sooner had he touched it, than there was a terrible clanging all round the stables, for there were invisible strings running from the bridle. At once the stable guards woke up, came running, seized the prince and marched him off to King Afron.

"Oh, foolish youth," the king said, "tell me: where are you from, who is your father and what name do you go by?" To that Prince Ivan replied, "I am from Vyslav's kingdom, the son of King Vyslav, and my name is Prince Ivan." "Ah, Prince Ivan," said King Afron, "does an honest knight steal horses? If you had come to me I would willingly have given you the Horse with the Golden Mane. What will become of you when I have it proclaimed throughout all lands how dishonestly you acted here? But listen, Prince Ivan, if you perform a service for me, go to the Thrice-Ten Kingdom beyond the Thrice-Nine Land and bring me back Princess Helen the Fair, whom I have long loved with all my heart and soul, but could not win, I will pardon you and give you the Horse with the Golden Mane. But if you refuse me this service, I will have it known throughout all the lands that you are a dishonest thief, and will tell all how badly you behaved in my land." So Prince Ivan promised the king that he would fetch Princess Helen the Fair, and left the palace crying bitterly.

He returned to the Grey Wolf and told him all that had happened. "Oh, Prince Ivan, foolish youth," the Grey Wolf said. "Why did you not heed my warning and leave the golden bridle?" "I am truly sorry," Prince Ivan said. "So be it. Climb upon my back, and I'll carry you whither you wish." Prince Ivan mounted the Grey Wolf and off they sped like an arrow from a bow, faster than it takes to tell this tale, until they came to the land of Princess Helen the Fair. Halting at the golden railings that surrounded wonderful gardens, the Grey Wolf told Prirce Ivan, "Now, Prince Ivan, climb down and go back along the path by which we came; wait for me in the open plain beneath the green oak-tree." The prince did as he was told. Meanwhile the Grey Wolf sat waiting by the golden railings until Princess Helen the Fair came walking through the gardens.

Towards evening, when the sun began to sink in the west and the air was fresh and cool, Princess Helen the Fair came into the gardens to take a walk with her maids and matrons. When she approached the spot where the Grey Wolf was wait-ing behind the railings, he suddenly sprang into the gardens, seized Princess Helen the Fair, jumped out and sped off with her like the wind. When they came to the green oak-tree in the open plain where Prince Ivan was waiting, the Grey Wolf told the prince to jump on his back quickly and raced off with both of them to the realm of King Afron. All the maids and matrons and ladies-in-waiting who had been walking in the gardens with Princess Helen the Fair ran into the palace and sent guards in pursuit of the Grey Wolf; but no matter how swiftly they rode, they could not catch the fleet-footed wolf and had to return empty-handed.

While Prince Ivan was sitting on the Grey Wolf with Princess Helen the Fair, his heart went out to the lovely maid, and hers to him; so when the Grey Wolf reached the realm of King Afron and Prince Ivan had to take the maid to the old king's palace, he was sorely grieved and wept bitter tears. "Why do you cry, Prince Ivan?" asked the Grey Wolf. To which the prince replied, "How can I help weeping and grieving? I have fallen in love with Princess Helen the Fair, but now I must give her up to King Afron for the Horse with the Golden Mane, and if I do not, he will spread news of my dishonour throughout all the lands." "I have served you truly, Prince Ivan," said the Grey Wolf, "and I will do you one more service too. Listen carefully: I will change myself into the living likeness of Princess Helen the Fair, and you shall lead me to the king instead and trade me for the Horse with the Golden Mane; the king will think I am the real princess. When you mount the Horse with the Golden Mane and are far away, I shall ask King Afron to let me go for a walk in the open plain; and when he gives me leave to go with the maids and matrons and the ladies-in-waiting and I am in the plain with them, think of me and I shall be with you again." So saying, the Grey Wolf struck the earth and turned into a maiden, the very image of Princess Helen the Fair: no one could guess it was not she. Prince Ivan took the wolf-princess to King Afron, and told Princess Helen to wait outside the town gates.

When Prince Ivan came before the king with Helen the Fair, the old king was overjoyed at winning the prize he had coveted for so long. In exchange for the false queen he presented Prince Ivan with the Horse with the Golden Mane. At once the prince mounted the horse and galloped to the town gates; there he sat Helen the Fair behind him and set off for the realm of King Dolmat. Meanwhile, the Grey Wolf spent one day, then a second and a third with King Afron, pretending to be Princess Helen the Fair; but on the fourth day he went to the king and asked leave to take a walk in the open plain to relieve his gloom and grief. King Afron said to him: "Ah, my fair Princess Helen! I will do everything for you and let you walk in the open plain." And he straightway ordered the maids and matrons and all the ladies-in-waiting to accompany her.

Riding along with Helen the Fair and talking with her, Prince Ivan forgot all about the Grey Wolf. Then he remembered: "Oh dear, where is my Grey Wolf?" And immediately the Grey Wolf appeared from out of nowhere and said: "Climb on my back, Prince Ivan, and let the fair princess ride upon the Horse with the Golden Mane." Prince Ivan mounted the Grey Wolf and off they sped to the realm of King Dolmat. Whether they were long on their way I could not say, but finally they reached the realm and halted three versts from the city. Thereupon, the prince began to ask one more favour of his trusty friend, "Dear Grey Wolf, you have done me many favours, will you serve me one last time? I cannot bear to lose the Horse with the Golden Mane." At once the Grey Wolf struck the earth and turned into the Horse with the Golden Mane. Leaving Princess Helen the Fair in a green meadow, Prince Ivan mounted the Grey Wolf and rode to King Dolmat's palace. As soon as he arrived, King Dolmat was overjoyed to see that he was riding the Horse with the Golden Mane and went out to meet the prince in the palace courtyard. He kissed him on his ruby-red lips, took him by the right hand and led him into his white-stone palace. In his joy he ordered a feast to be held, and they sat down at oaken tables laden with food; they ate, drank and made merry for two days, and on the third day the king presented Prince Ivan with the Firebird in its golden cage. The prince took the Firebird, left the city, mounted the Horse with the Golden Mane and set off with Princess Helen the Fair for his homeland, the realm of King Vyslav. Next day King Dolmat decided to take a ride on his wonderful steed; he had it saddled, then mounted and rode off to the open plain. But he had only galloped a short distance, when his steed threw him off, turned back into the Grey Wolf and raced like the wind to catch up Prince Ivan. "Climb on my back," said the Grey Wolf, "and let Princess Helen the Fair ride upon the Horse with the Golden Mane." Prince Ivan climbed upon the Grey Wolf and off they journeyed until they reached the place where the wolf had torn Prince Ivan's horse apart. "Now, Prince Ivan," said the wolf, "I have served you truly. This is the place where I tore your horse apart and to this place I have brought you back. Climb down. Now you have the Horse with the Golden Mane, so mount it and go whither you please. I shall serve you no longer." So saying the Grey Wolf raced off into the trees; Prince Ivan wept bitter tears for his grey friend and journeyed on with the fair princess.

Whether he and the princess were long on their way I could not say, but some twenty versts before his father's lands he halted, dismounted and lay down to rest from the heat of the sun under a tree with the fair princess; he tethered the Horse with the Golden Mane to the tree and placed the Firebird in its cage beside him. They lay upon the soft grass, exchanging lovers' talk and fell into a deep sleep. Just at that time Ivan's two elder brothers, Prince Dmitri and Prince Vassily, having traversed many lands without finding the Firebird, were returning home empty-handed, when they chanced upon their sleeping brother Ivan with Princess Helen the Fair. Seeing the Horse with the Golden Mane and the Firebird in the golden cage, they were sorely tempted and decided to kill their brother, Prince Ivan. Prince Dmitri pulled his sharp sword out of its sheath, struck the sleeping prince and hacked him into small pieces; then he woke Princess Helen the Fair and began to ask her: "Fair Maid, where are you from, who is your father and what name do you go by?" Seeing the dead body of Prince Ivan, Princess Helen the Fair was sore afraid and began to weep bitterly, saying through her tears, "I am Princess Helen the Fair, taken by Prince Ivan whom you have so cruelly put to death. If you had been good knights you would have ridden out with him into the open plain and killed him in fair combat, but you have killed a sleeping man and what praise will you earn for that?" Then Prince Dmitri pointed his sword at the heart of Princess Helen the Fair and said: "Listen, fair Helen, you are in our hands now; we shall take you to our father, King Vyslav, and you will tell him that we rescued you and the Firebird and the Horse with the Golden Mane. If you do not, we shall slay you forthwith!" Seeing no escape the princess agreed and promised to do exactly as they said. With that Prince Dmitri and Prince Vassily drew lots to see who would take Princess Helen the Fair and who the Horse with the Golden Mane. The maid fell to Prince Vassily, the horse to Prince Dmitri. Thereupon Prince Vassily took Princess Helen the Fair and sat her on his horse, while Prince Dmitri mounted the Horse with the Golden Mane with the Firebird to give to their father, King Vyslav, and off they went.

Full thirty days Prince Ivan's body lay on the plain, when the Grey Wolf chanced to pass by and recognised the prince. He wished to help him, to bring him to life, but he knew not how. Then the Grey Wolf saw a Raven and his two young hovering over the body, eager to feast on the dead prince. Hiding behind a bush, the Grey Wolf waited for the young ravens to land and start pecking at Prince Ivan's body, then he sprang out, seized one of them and made as if to tear it apart. At once the Old Raven flew down and said to the Grey Wolf, "Please do not hurt my little child; he has done you no harm." "Listen, Raven," said the Wolf, "I'll not touch your child and will let it go safe and sound if you do me a favour: fly to the Thrice-Ten Kingdom beyond the Thrice-Nine Land and bring me the water of life and the water of death." To that the Raven replied, "I will do you that favour if you do not harm my child."

With that the Raven flew off and soon disappeared from view. At the end of three days he returned with two small flasks: the water of life in one, the water of death in the other. The Wolf took the two flasks, ripped the young raven apart, sprinkled the water of death over it—and two halves joined together. Then he sprinkled the water of life over it—and the young raven flapped its wings and flew off. Next the Grey Wolf sprinkled Prince Ivan's body with the water of death—and the wounds healed. Then he sprinkled the body with the water of life—and Prince Ivan stood up and said: "How long I have slept?" "But for me you would have slept forever," replied the Wolf. "Your brothers slew you and robbed you of Princess Helen, the Horse with the Golden Mane and the Firebird. Now you must hurry to your father's palace, for today your brother Prince Vassily is to marry Princess Helen the Fair. And if you want to get there in time, climb on my back and I will carry you." Prince Ivan leapt upon the Wolf's back and they raced off to the realm of King Vyslav. When they reached the town gates, the young prince took leave of the Grey Wolf and went into the palace, just in time to find that Prince Vassily had returned from the church with Princess Helen and was sitting at the head of the table with her. The moment she saw Prince Ivan, she sprang to her feet and began kissing him on his ruby-red lips, crying: "This is my dear betrothed, Prince Ivan, and not the villain who sits at the table!" King Vyslav rose and asked Princess Helen what her words might mean. Then she told the whole truth: how Prince Ivan had won her, the Horse with the Golden Mane and the Firebird, how his brothers had killed him when he lay sleeping and made her say it was they who had won everything. The king was greatly angered to hear of the cruel misdeeds of his two sons and had them flung into a dungeon, while Prince Ivan married Princess Helen the Fair and they lived together so happily that they could not bear to be parted for a single moment.

Silver Roan

There was once an old man who had three sons, and the youngest, Ivan the Fool, did nothing but sit all day long on the stove blowing his nose. As death approached, the old man called his three sons to him, saying, "When I die, you must take it in turns to sleep by my grave for three nights." The old man died and was buried, and that night it was the turn of the eldest brother to go to his grave. But he was either too lazy or too scared, so he said to his youngest brother: "Ivan the Fool, you go in my place to our father's grave tonight. You're not doing anything anyway." Ivan made ready and went to his father's grave. He lay down, and at the stroke of midnight the grave suddenly opened and the old man rose up saying, "Who is there? Is it you, my first-born?" "No, Father, it is I, Ivan the Fool." Recognising his voice, the old man asked, "Why did my eldest not come?" "He sent me instead, Father." "Well, that is your good fortune," the old man said, gave a loud whistle and cried out: "Silver Roan, all alone!" And a charger came racing up, the earth shaking under his hoofs, sparks flying from his eyes, smoke streaming from his nostrils. "Here is a fine steed for you, my boy; and you, my horse, serve my son as you served me." With that the old man lay down in his grave. Ivan the Fool stroked and caressed Silver Roan, then set him loose and made his way back. At home his brothers asked: "Did the night pass well, Ivan the Fool?" "Very well, brothers," Ivan replied. Another night came. The second brother did not want to go to the grave either, and said: "Ivan the Fool, you go in my place to our father's grave and spend the night there for me." Without a word, Ivan the Fool made ready and went on his way; coming to the grave he lay down beside it to await midnight. At the stroke of midnight, the grave opened as before and the old man rose up, saying, "Is it you, my second-born?" "No, it is I again. Father," said Ivan the Fool. The old man gave a loud whistle and cried out: "Silver Roan, all alone!" And the charger came racing up, the earth shaking under his hoofs, sparks flying from his eyes, smoke streaming from his nostrils. "Now, Silver Roan, serve my son as truly as you served me," the old man said. "Off you go." The charger sped away, the old man lay down in his grave and Ivan went home. His brothers asked again, "How did you pass the night, Ivan the Fool?" "Very well, brothers," he replied. On the third night it was Ivan's turn; he made ready and set off, without waiting to be told. He lay down on top of the grave and, at the stroke of midnight, the old man again rose up; knowing that it would be Ivan the Fool, he gave a loud whistle and cried out: "Silver Roan, all alone!" And the charger came racing up, the earth shaking under his hoofs, sparks flying from his eyes, smoke streaming from his nostrils. "Now, Silver Roan," he said, "serve my son as truly as you served me." So saying he bade his son farewell and lay down in his grave. Ivan patted Silver Roan, and set him loose before returning home. When he reached home his brothers asked once more: "How did you pass the night, Ivan the Fool?" "Very well, brothers."

Time passed with the two eldest working, while Ivan the Fool did nothing. One day the king made it known throughout the land that whoever could snatch the princess's veil at a height of so many logs would receive her hand in marriage. Ivan's brothers made ready to go and see who would try to snatch the veil. Ivan whined from his ledge on the stove: "Give me any old horse, brothers, I want to go and see too." "You stay where you are," they railed at him. "What's the point of you going? You'll only make people laugh." But Ivan the Fool would not take no for an answer. He kept on and on, until his brothers gave in. "All right, Fool, take that three-legged mare."

The brothers rode off. Ivan the Fool rode after them into the green meadows of the open plain; he jumped down from the mare, slaughtered and skinned her, hung up her skin to dry and left the meat where it was; then he gave loud whistle and cried out: "Silver Roan, all alone!" And the charger came racing up, the earth shaking under his hoofs, sparks flying from his eyes, smoke streaming from his nostrils. Ivan climbed into one ear, ate and drank his fill, then climbed out of the other, a finely clad and handsome young man, even his brothers could not recognise him. He climbed onto Silver Roan's back and set off to snatch the veil. He sent Silver Roan leaping into the air, but only reached the ninth row of logs and failed to snatch the veil. Everyone saw him come, but no one saw him go! He set his horse free, returned home and climbed up onto the stove ledge. Soon his brothers came home

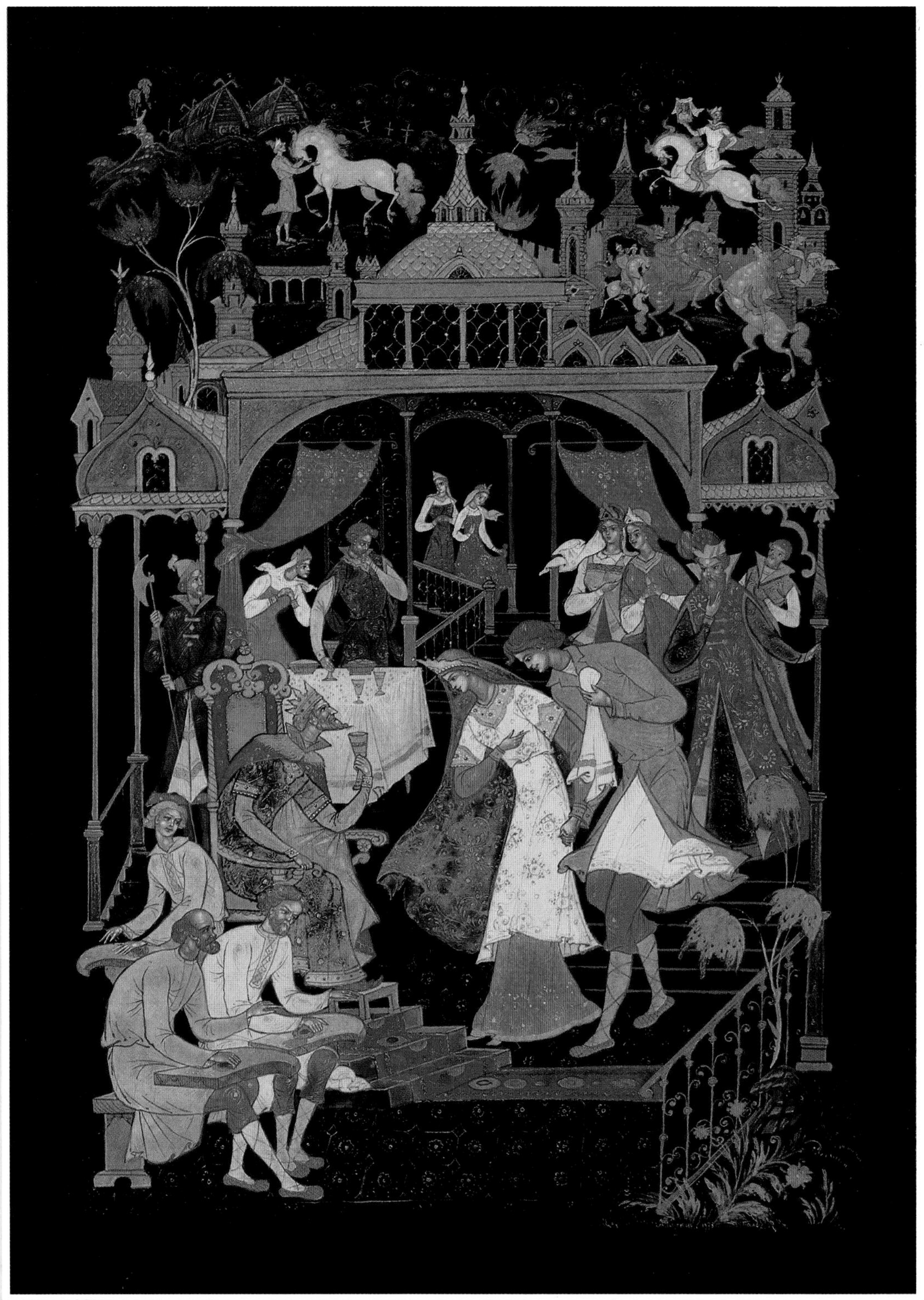

and told their wives, "You should have seen the handsome fellow who failed by only three logs to reach the veil. Everyone saw him come, but no one saw him go. Perhaps he will try again..." Ivan called down from his ledge behind the chimney, "Was it perchance not I, brothers?" "You, stupid dolt! You just sit on the stove and wipe your nose, Fool."

Time passed. The king issued the same challenge again. And again the brothers made ready to go and watch. "Brothers," called Ivan from the stove, "give me any old horse to ride with you." "You stay home, Fool," they said. "Or you'll go losing another of our horses." But the Fool would not take no for an answer, so in the end they gave him a lame mare. Ivan the Fool drove his mount, slaughtered it, hung its hide up to dry and left the meat where it was; then he gave a loud whistle and cried out: "Silver Roan, all alone!" The charter came racing up, the earth shaking under his hoofs, sparks flying from his eyes, smoke streaming from his nostrils. Ivan the Fool climbed into his right ear and out through the left, a finely clad and handsome young man. Then off he rode. This time he leapt as high as the tenth row of logs; but failed to reach the princess. Everyone saw him come, but no one saw him go. He set his horse free, returned home and sat on the stove to await his brothers. The brothers came home and told their wives, "That handsome young fellow came again; this time he was only two logs short." Ivan called down, "Was it perchance not I, brothers?" "You, nincompoop, that's not for the likes of you!"

Some time later yet another challenge came from the king. And the brothers made ready to leave a third time. "Give me any old horse, brothers," begged Ivan the Fool, "I want to take a look." "You stay home, Fool!" they cried. "We don't want you ruining all our horses." But the Fool kept on and on until, finally, they gave him the worst mare there was. And off they rode. Meanwhile, Ivan the Fool slaughtered his nag, skinned it, left the meat where it was, then gave a loud whistle and cried out: "Silver Roan, all alone!" The charger came racing up, the earth shaking under his hoofs, sparks flying from his eyes, smoke streaming from his nostrils. Ivan climbed into one ear, ate and drank his fill, and climbed out of the other, a finely clad and handsome young man; then he leapt on his horse and sped off. As soon as he reached the palace, he took a great leap and snatched off the veil. Everyone saw him come, but no one saw him go. Again he set his horse free, went home and sat on the stove to await his brothers. The brothers came and said: "Well, wives! The same handsome fellow leapt up and snatched off the veil today." Ivan called down from behind the chimney: "Was it perchance not I, brothers?" "Shut up, Fool!" they shouted.

Not long after the king held a ball to which he invited all his lords and knights, princes and counsellors, senators and merchants, burghers and peasants. Ivan's brothers set off; the Fool was not far behind them. He settled down behind the palace chimney, looking on and gaping. The princess attended to the guests, giving each a mug of beer to see if anyone would wipe his whiskers with her veil. But no one did wipe his mouth with it; and she did not notice Ivan the Fool. The guests went home. Next day the king held another ball, and once more the man who had snatched off the veil was not to be found. On the third day the princess again handed each man a mug of beer with her own hands, but no one wiped his lips with her veil. "How can it be that my betrothed is not here?" she thought. She glanced behind the chimney and saw Ivan the Fool there; he was covered in soot, his clothes tattered and his hair all sticking out. She poured a mug of beer and took it to him, as his brothers looked on in amazement: fancy the princess taking beer to the Fool! Ivan the Fool drank it and wiped his lips with the veil. The princess was overjoyed, seized him by the hand and led him to her father, saying: "Here is my betrothed, Sire." The two brothers were thunderstruck. "The princess must be out of her mind to call the Fool her betrothed!" they thought. In no time at all the wedding took place followed by much merry-making. Now our Ivan was no longer Ivan the Fool, but Ivan the King's Son-In-Law; he became such a clean, finely clad, handsome young man that no one recognised him. And so his brothers learned what it meant not to heed their father's last behest.

Treasure

In a certain realm there was once an old man and woman who lived in great poverty. Time passed and the old woman died. It was winter and freezing cold. The old man went out to ask his neighbours and friends to help him dig a grave for the old woman. But his friends and neighbours, knowing his great poverty, all refused. So off he went to the priest. But the village priest was very greedy and dishonest. When the old man asked him to bury his wife, the priest demanded that he pay in advance. "I will not tell you a lie," said the old man. "I haven't a single penny. But wait a bit, I'll earn some money and pay you more than enough, I swear."

But the priest would not hear of it. "If you've no money, don't dare come here again." "What am I to do?" thought the old man. "I'll go to the cemetery, dig some kind of grave and bury the old woman myself." So he took an axe and a spade and went to the cemetery; there he set about digging a grave. First he broke up the frozen soil on top with his axe, then he began to dig with the spade until he unearthed a pot full of gold coins glittering like the sun. The old man was overjoyed. "Thanks be to the Lord!" he exclaimed. "Now I've got enough to have the old woman buried in style." And leaving his grave-digging, he took the pot of gold and carried it home.

Now that he had money, of course, things went smoothly; good folk appeared to dig the grave and make the coffin; the old man sent his son's wife to buy all manner of fancy victuals that befitted a funeral repast, and himself took some coins and went off to the priest again. As soon as he appeared in the doorway the priest started shouting at him: "I told you not to bother me if you have no money, you dolt, yet here you are pestering me again!" "Don't be angry, Father," said the old man humbly. "Here is a gold piece for you—bury my old lady and I'll never forget your kindness." The priest took the money and immediately began to treat the old man like royalty, finding a comfortable seat for him and assuring him: "Yes, yes, of course, leave everything to me, all will be done." The old man bowed low and went home, while the priest began to talk about him to his wife. "The old devil comes here saying he's poor, then hands me a gold piece. I've buried many well-to-do persons in my time, but I've never been given as much as this..."

So the priest and all his deacons gave the old woman a fine funeral. Afterwards the old man invited him home for the funeral repast. The guests arrived, sat down at the table, and there were all sorts of food and drink in abundance. The priest sat guzzling enough for three and marvelling at such plenty. When the guests had supped and gone their different ways, the priest rose to go also. The old man showed him out. As soon as they were outside and the priest saw that no one was about, he began questioning the old man: "Listen, friend. Confide in me and don't leave a single sin on your conscience—it's the same as confessing to God; tell me how you got rich so quickly. You used to be poor, but now you are living in plenty! Come on, friend, who did you do in? Who did you rob?" "Father," exclaimed the old man, "I'll tell you the honest truth: I didn't rob or thieve or do anyone in. The treasure just fell into my hands!" And he told all.

When the priest heard the story, he shivered with greed. He went home and could do nothing day and night but think of the fortune. "That puny old man goes and finds a mint of money! How can I outwit him and get my hands on his pot of gold?" He told his wife about this and they put their heads together. At last the priest hit on a plan. "Listen, Mother. We've got a goat, haven't we?" "We have." "Good. Let's wait for nightfall and do the job properly." Late that evening the priest dragged the goat into the house, killed it, skinned it, horns, beard and all, then pulled the goatskin over his head and said to his wife, "Take out your needle and thread, Mother, and sew it all round so that it doesn't slip off." The priest's wife took a strong needle and thread and sewed up the goatskin.

At dead of night the priest went straight to the old man's cottage, stood beneath his window and began to rap and scratch. Hearing the noise, the old man jumped up and asked, "Who's there?" "The devil." "God be with us!" wailed the peasant, crossing himself and mumbling his prayers. "Listen here, old man," said the priest. "Praying and crossing yourself won't do you any good. You just give back my pot of gold, or that will be the end of you! I took pity on your plight, and showed you my treasure, thinking you would just take a little for the funeral, but you grabbed the

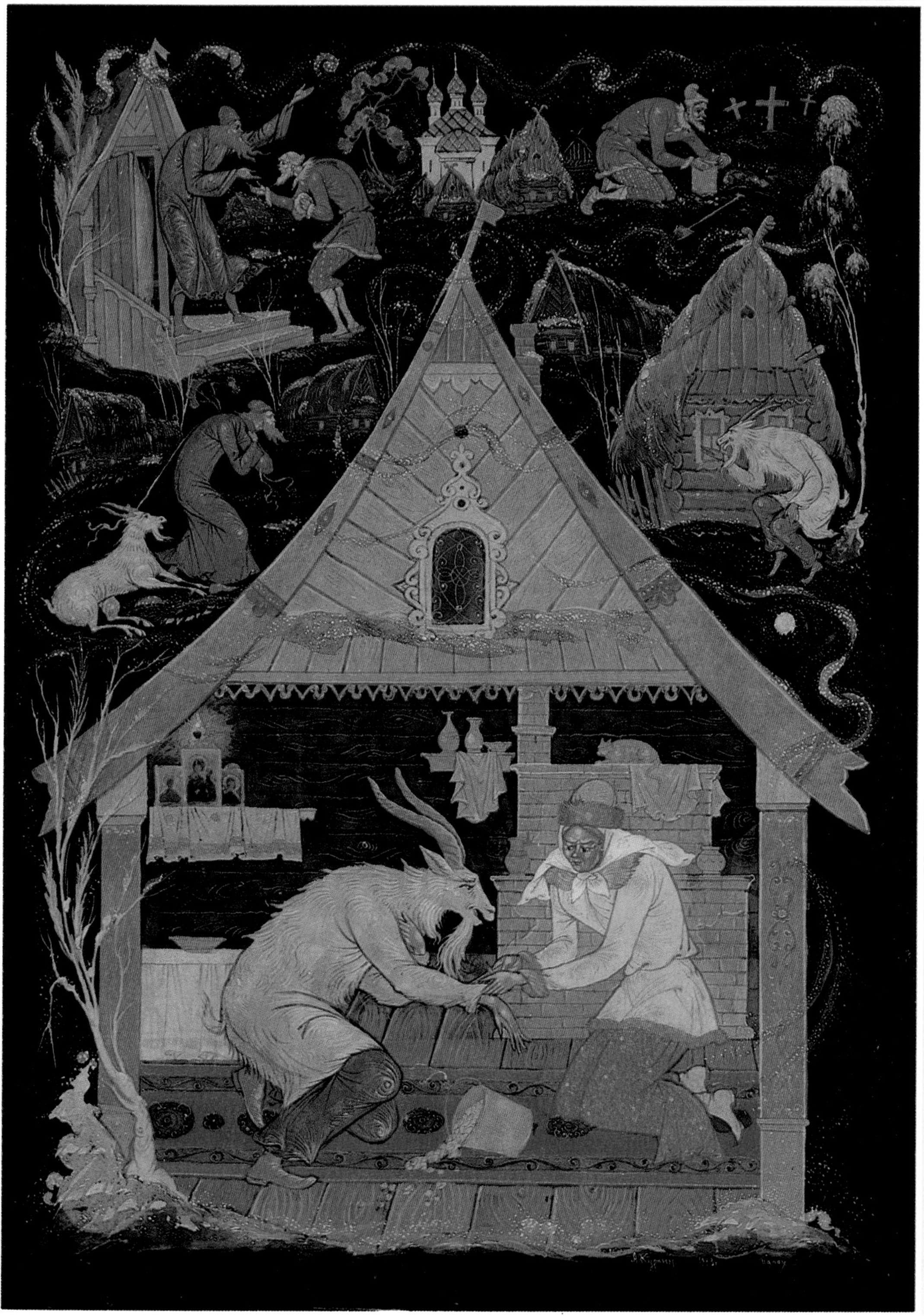

whole lot!" The old man looked out of the window and saw the horns and beard: it was the Devil himself and no mistake. "Never mind about the money," thought the old man, "I got by without it and I'll get by again!" So he took the pot of gold outside, threw it quickly to the ground and ran indoors again. The priest grabbed the pot and made off. Back home he said: "The money's ours now, Mother. Hide it quick and get a sharp knife to cut the thread and take this goatskin off me before somebody sees me."

The priest's wife picked up a knife and began to cut the stitches, when the blood gushed out and he shouted: "That hurts, stop cutting!" She tried to cut in another place, but the same thing happened. The goatskin had grown onto the priest's body. No matter what they did and how they tried—they even took the old man back his money—nothing helped. The priest remained in the goatskin. That must have been God's punishment for being so greedy!

Two from the Sack

There once lived an old man and woman. The old woman was forever nagging and cursing the old man and beating him with the broom or the oven fork. The old man had not a moment's peace. One day he went off to the fields, set his traps and caught a crane. "Be my son," he said to the crane, "I'll take you home to my old woman and perhaps she will stop scolding me." But the crane answered, "Come home with me, Father." So the old man went home with the crane. As they entered the crane's house, the bird took down a sack from the wall, saying, *"Two from the sack!"* Out jumped two strapping lads: they set down oaken tables, spread silk table-cloths and served all manner of good things to eat and drink. Never in his life had the old man seen such abundance and he was overjoyed. Then the crane said to him, "Take this sack home to your old woman." He took it and went on his way. It was a long way home and he dropped in at a neighbour's to spend the night. The woman had three daughters. They gave him the little they had to eat. He tried it and said to the woman, "Your food is poor." "It's all we have," replied the woman. Then he said: "Take it away!" and, picking up the sack that the crane had given him, cried, *"Two from the sack!"* In an instant two strapping lads jumped out of the sack, set down oaken tables, spread silk table-cloths and served all manner of good things to eat and drink.

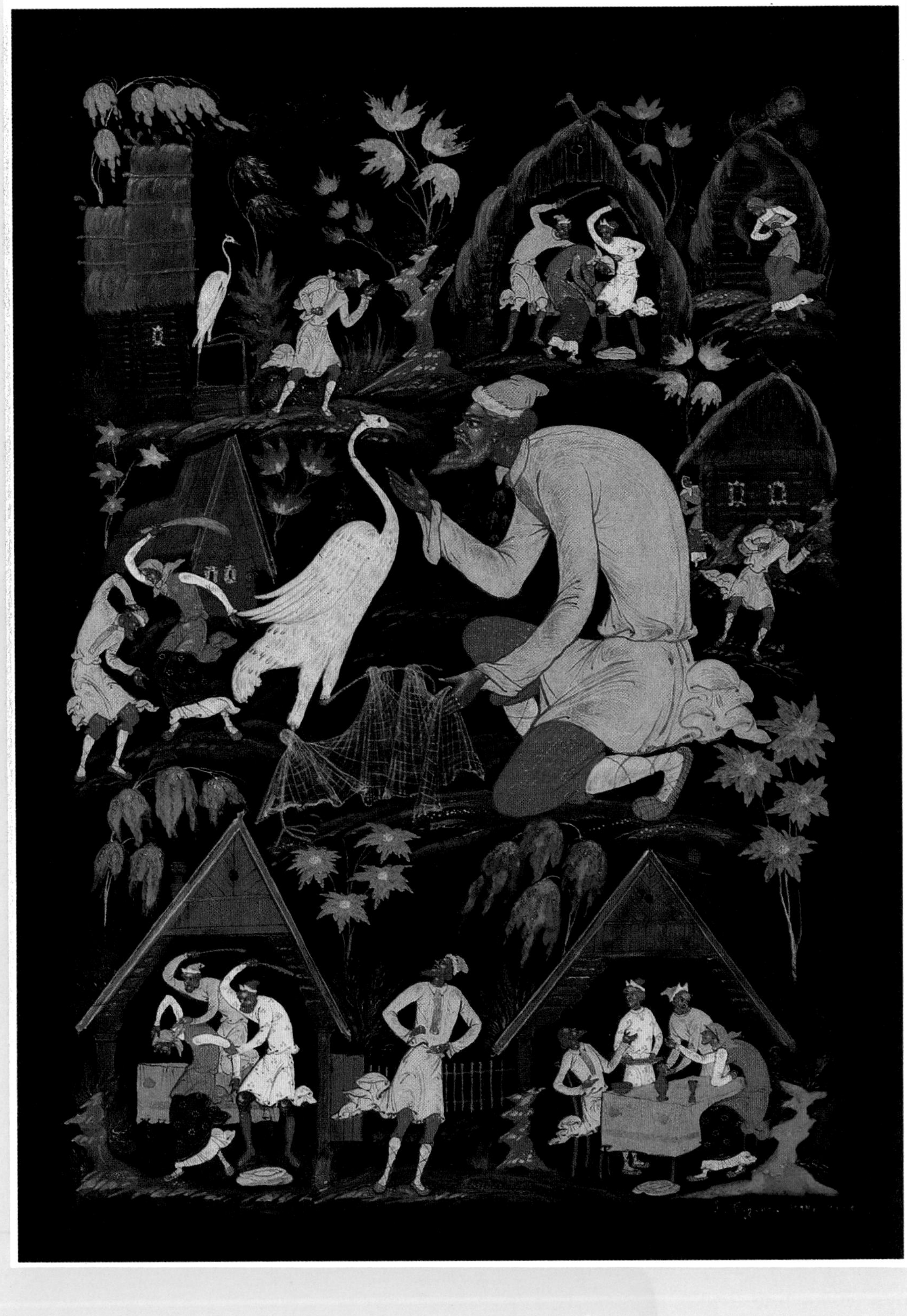

The woman and her daughters were astounded; she resolved to steal the old man's sack and said to her daughters: "Go and heat up the bath-house; perhaps our guest would like a steam bath." No sooner had the old man entered the bath-house than the woman told her daughters to make a sack just like the old one; they sewed one, exchanged it for the old man's sack and put his away. When he came out of the bath-house, he picked up the false sack and went happily home to his old woman. Entering the yard, he called out in a loud voice, "Old woman, old woman, come and greet me and our crane-son." The old woman gave him a quick look and muttered, "Come here, you old goat, and I'll give you a taste of my oven fork." But the old man repeated, "Old woman, come and greet me and our crane-son." Into the house he went, hung the sack on a nail and cried, *"Two from the sack!"* Nothing happened. *"Two from the sack!"* he cried again. Again nothing happened. The old woman thought that he was talking nonsense, snatched up the wet mop and set about him.

The old man took fright, burst into tears and went off again into the fields. Who should he meet there but the crane! Seeing the old man's plight, he said, "Come home with me again, Father," and off they went. There was a sack just like the last one hanging on the wall. *"Two from the sack!"* shouted the crane. And two strapping lads jumped out and served as tasty a meal as before. "Take this sack for yourself," said the crane. Picking up the sack, the old man went on his way. He walked for a long time until he began to feel hungry, then said the words the crane had taught him. *"Two from the sack!"* Out jumped two strapping lads with big cudgels and began to beat the old man, saying, "Do not go to your neighbour or steam in her bath!" They thrashed him so hard that he could barely whisper: *"Two into the sack!"* As soon as he uttered these words the two men jumped back into the sack again.

The old man picked up the sack, went to the same neighbour, hung the sack on a hook and said to the woman, "Heat up the bath-house for me." She did so. He entered the bath-house and pretended to be washing himself, in fact he was just biding his time. The woman called her daughters, sat them down at the table ready to feast, and shouted, *"Two from the sack!"* At once the two strapping lads with big cudgels jumped out of the sack and began to beat the woman, saying, "Give back the old man's sack! Give back the old man's sack!" They thrashed her so hard that she could barely whisper to her eldest daughter: "Tell the old man to come from the bath-house or these two will beat me to death." "I haven't finished steaming yet," replied the old man. The two strapping lads went on beating her and saying, "Give back the old man's sack!" Then the woman sent her second daughter to fetch the old man quickly. But he called back, "I haven't washed my hair yet." So she sent her third daughter. "I haven't washed myself down yet," came the reply. Whereupon the woman could stand it no longer and told her daughters to bring the stolen sack. The old man came out of the bath-house, saw his first sack and called out, *"Two into the sack!"* The two lads with the cudgels jumped back into the sack.

Picking up the two sacks—the good and the bad one—the old man set off home. He came to his yard and called to his old woman, "Come and greet me and our crane-son." The old woman gave him a quick look and said, "Just you come indoors and I'll give you what for!" Entering the house, the old man told his wife: "Sit down at the table," and then cried, *"Two from the sack!"* At once the two strapping lads jumped out and laid a fine meal upon the table. The old woman ate and drank her fill and praised the old man, saying: "Well, old fellow, I'll never thrash you again." After the meal, the old man went into the yard and took the good sack with him, hanging up the bad sack on a hook. Then he paced up and down the yard biding his time.

The old woman wanted some more to drink, so she repeated the old man's words, *"Two from the sack!"* Out jumped the two strapping lads with big cudgels and began to beat her; they thrashed her until she could stand it no longer and cried: "Old man, old man! Come here quickly, they are beating me to death!" But he dawdled in the yard, chuckling to himself and saying, "They'll give you what for!" The two lads thrashed the old woman even harder, repeating all the time, "Don't beat your old man! Don't beat your old man!" At last the old man took pity on his wife, went inside and said, *"Two into the sack!"* And back jumped the two strapping lads. After that the old man and woman lived so happily together that the old man did nothing but praise her, and that is the end of the story.

The Magic Ring

In a certain realm, in a certain land, there once lived an old man and woman with their only son Martin. All his life the old man had been a hunter, catching animals and birds and feeding his family on his catch. With time the old man took sick and died, leaving Martin and his mother alone in the world; they grieved and sorrowed, but there was nothing for it: tears won't bring back the dead. A week passed by and they had eaten all the food in the larder; seeing there was nothing more to eat, the old woman realised she would have to spend some money. The old man had left them two hundred rubles; though she was loath to open the money-box, they had to eat somehow and keep the wolf from the door. So she counted off a hundred rubles and told her son, "Here, Martin, take these hundred notes and borrow the neighbour's horse so that you can ride to town and buy some food. That will see us through the winter and we will look for work come the spring."

Martin borrowed his neighbour's horse and cart and rode off to town; as he was passing butchers' stalls in the market he saw a noisy crowd gathered there. What had happened? The butchers had caught a hound, tied him to a post and were beating him with sticks, and the dog was cowering, whining and yapping with pain. Martin ran over to the butchers and asked, "Why are you beating the poor dog so mercilessly?" "That devil deserves all he gets," the butchers said. "He stole a whole side of beef." "Stop, brothers," Martin cried. "Don't beat him, sell him to me instead." "Buy him if you please, but it will cost you a hundred rubles," said one butcher in jest. Martin pulled out a hundred rubles, paid the butcher, untied the hound and took him along. The dog wagged his tail and licked his new master's hand; he knew the young fellow had saved his life.

When Martin got back home, his mother asked him at once, "What have you bought, my boy?" "My first piece of good fortune," Martin replied. "What are you blathering about? What good fortune?" "Here it is, Blackie," he said pointing at the dog. "Is that all?" "If I'd had any money left I might have bought more; but the whole hundred went on the dog." The old woman scolded him: "We've nothing to eat; I've scraped the last bits of flour to make a roll for today, but tomorrow there'll be nothing at all."

Next day his mother took out the last hundred rubles, gave it to her son and told him: "Go to town and buy some food, son, but don't fritter the money away." Martin arrived at the town, began to walk up and down the streets and take a look around, and saw a boy dragging a cat along on a string towards the river. "Stop," called Martin. "Where are you taking that cat?" "I'm going to drown him; he stole a pie from our table." "Don't drown him," Martin said. "Sell him to me instead." "Buy him if you please, but it will cost you a hundred rubles." Martin did not think twice: he pulled out the money and gave it to the boy; then he put the cat in his bag and turned for home. "What have you bought, my boy?" asked his mother. "Stripey the cat." "Is that all?" "If I'd had any money left, I might have bought more." "Oh, what a fool you are!" she cried. "Leave this house at once and go begging food at someone else's door."

Off went Martin to the next village in search of work, taking with him Blackie the dog and Stripey the cat. On the way he met a priest. "Where are you going, my son?" he asked. "To look for work," the lad replied. "Come and work for me; only I take on workmen without fixing a wage: whoever serves me well for three years gets what he deserves." Martin agreed and toiled away three summers and winters for the priest; when the time came for payment, his master summoned him. "Well, Martin," he said, "come and get your reward." He led him into the barn, pointed at two full sacks and said, "Take whichever you want." Martin saw that there was silver in one sack and sand in the other, and thought: "There's more to this than meets the eye. Come what may, but I will take the sand and see what happens." So he said: "I will take the sack of fine sand, master." "Please yourself, my son. Take the sand if you prefer it to silver."

Martin heaved the sack of sand upon his back and went to look for work again. He walked and walked, until he found himself in a dark, dense forest. In the middle of the forest was a glade, and in the glade a fire burned brightly, and in the fire sat a maiden more fair than tongue can tell or tale can spell. The fair maiden called to him, "Martin, the widow's son, if you wish to win good fortune, rescue me: put out

the flame with the sand for which you laboured three years." "Aha," thought Martin, "it would be better to help someone than drag this load around. Sand is not worth much anyway, there's plenty of it about." He put down his sack, untied it and began to pour out the sand; the fire went out at once, the fair maiden struck the earth with her foot, turned into a snake, leapt upon his chest and wound herself about his neck. Martin took fright. "Do not be afraid," said the snake. "Go to the Thrice-Ten Kingdom beyond the Thrice-Nine Land; my father is king there. When you come to his palace he will offer you gold and silver and precious stones. But do not take anything. Just ask for the ring from his little finger. It is no ordinary ring: when you put it on one hand and then on the other twelve strapping youths will appear to do whatever you order, all in a single night."

Martin went on his way; by and by he reached the Thrice-Ten Kingdom and saw a huge rock. The snake jumped down from his neck, struck the earth and became a fair maiden once more. "Follow me," she said, leading the way under the rock. For a long time they walked along the underground passage until suddenly a light appeared; it got brighter and brighter, and they came out to a wide plain under a clear blue sky; and on the plain was a magnificent castle where the fair maiden's father lived—the king of this underground realm.

As the travellers entered the white-stone castle they were greeted warmly by the king. "Welcome, my dear daughter. Where have you been all these years?" "Father, noble Sire, I would have perished had it not been for this man: he saved me from a cruel death and brought me here to my native land." "Thank you, young man," said the king, "your good deed deserves reward; take all the gold, silver and precious stones that your heart desires." But Martin, the widow's son, answered, "Your Majesty, I want neither gold, nor silver, nor precious stones; all I ask is the ring from the little finger of your royal hand. I am a single fellow: I shall look at the ring, and think of my future bride to drive away my loneliness." At once the king took off the ring and gave it to Martin. "Here, take it and good luck to you. But tell no one of the ring or you will find yourself in dire trouble."

Martin, the widow's son, thanked the king, took the ring and a small sum of money for the road, and set off the way he had come. By and by he returned to his native land, sought out his old mother, and they began to live happily without a care in the world. One day Martin thought to take a wife and sent his mother off as matchmaker. "Go to the king himself," he said, "and ask for his lovely daughter." "Oh, my son," the old woman replied, "don't bite off more than you can chew. If I go to the king, he will get angry and have us both put to death." "Do not worry, Mother," said her son, "since I am sending you, go forth boldly. And bring back the king's reply whatever it is; don't come home without it." The old woman set off sadly for the king's abode: she walked into the courtyard and made straight for the royal staircase, without as much as by your leave. But the guards seized her. "Halt, old hag! Where do you think you're going! Even generals don't dare come here without permission..." "Leave me alone!" cried the old woman. "I've come to do the king a favour; I want his daughter to marry my son, and you are trying to stop me!" She caused such a commotion that you'd have thought the palace was on fire. Hearing the shouts, the king looked out of the window and ordered the woman to be brought to him. She marched straight into the royal chamber, crossed herself before the icons and curtseyed to the king. "What have you to say, old woman?" asked the king. "Well, you see, I have come to Your Majesty; now don't get cross: I have a buyer, you have the wares. The buyer is my son Martin, a very clever fellow; the wares are your daughter, the beautiful princess. Will you let her marry my Martin? They'd make a good pair." "Have you taken leave of your senses, woman?" cried the king. "Not at all, Your Majesty. Pray, give me your reply."

Straightaway the king summoned his ministers and they took counsel as to what the reply should be. And it was decided thus: let Martin build the richest of palaces within a single day and link it to the king's palace by a crystal bridge with gold and silver apple-trees growing on either side. And let him build a church with five domes: so there was a place where the wedding could be held and the marriage celebrated. If the old woman's son could do all that, he would be really clever and would win the princess's hand. But if he failed, he and the old woman would lose their heads for their impudence. Home went the old woman with the reply, weeping bitter tears as she trudged along. "Well, my son," she cried. "I told you not to bite off more than you can chew; but you would have your way. Now our poor heads are for the chop, tomorrow we shall die." "Who knows, mother, we might stay alive. Pray to God and go to bed: morning is wiser than evening."

On the stroke of midnight, Martin got up from his bed, went out into the yard, put the ring on his other hand—and right away twelve strapping youths appeared, all exactly alike. "What is it that you require, Martin, the widow's son?" they asked. "It is this: build me by first light on this very spot a splendid palace, with a crystal bridge leading from my palace to the king's and with gold and silver apple-trees growing on either side, and birds of every kind singing in their branches; build me, too, a church with five domes; so there is a place where my wedding can be held, and my marriage celebrated." "All will be ready by the morrow," replied the twelve strapping youths. With that they set to busily, brought workmen and carpenters from all sides and got down to work. They worked with a will and soon everything was done. In the morning Martin woke up to find himself not in his simple cottage, but in splendid chambers. He stepped onto the high porch and saw that all was ready: the palace, the church, the crystal bridge, and the trees with gold and silver apples. The king also walked onto his balcony, looked through his spy-glass and marvelled to see that all had been done as he had ordered. He summoned the fair princess and told her to get ready for the wedding. "Well," he said, "I never thought I would hand my daughter over to a peasant's son, but there's nothing for it now."

While the princess was dressing herself in her finery, Martin, the widow's son, came into the yard, put the magic ring on his other hand, and saw twelve strapping youths appear as if from out of the ground. "What is it that you require?" they asked. "It is this," Martin said, "dress me in a nobleman's caftan and get ready a golden coach with six fine horses." "Straightway, master." In the twinkling of an eye Martin was brought the caftan; he put it on and it fitted him perfectly. Then he looked round and saw standing at the portals a carriage harnessed to six splendid horses dappled silver and gold. He got into the carriage and drove to the church; the bells were already ringing for mass, and people were flocking by the score! Behind the groom came the bride with her maids and matrons and the king with his ministers. After mass Martin, the widow's son, took the fair princess by the hand and, as right and proper, they were wed. The king gave his daughter a rich dowry, bestowed high office upon his new son-in-law and held a wedding feast to which all the world was invited.

The young couple lived together one month, then two and three; all the while Martin had new palaces and gardens built by the day, if not the hour. But it pained the princess to think that she had been wed not to a prince, a royal heir, but to a simple peasant. So she began wondering how to get rid of him. She pretended to be as sweet and loving as any husband could desire. She saw to her husband's every need, served him in every way she could, trying all the time to wheedle his secret out of him. But Martin was as firm as a rock and would not betray it.

One day, however, after drinking with the king, he came home and lay down to rest; the princess ran to his side, kissing and caressing him, breathing sweet words into his ear; and so oily was her tongue that Martin finally told her about his wonderful ring. "Good," thought the princess, "now I'll finish you off." As soon as he fell asleep, she snatched the ring from his little finger, went into the courtyard and put it on her other hand. At once the twelve strapping youths appeared. "What is it that you require, fair princess?" they asked. "Listen, lads," she said, "make the palace, the church and the crystal bridge vanish by dawn; and bring back the humble cottage as before. Leave my husband as poor as he always was, and carry me off to the Thrice-Ten Kingdom beyond the Thrice-Nine Land, to the Mice's Realm. I am ashamed to live here." "Straightway, Your Highness," they said. In a flash she was swept up by the wind and borne off to the Thrice-Ten Kingdom, the Mice's Realm.

Next morning the king awoke and went out onto his balcony to look through his spy-glass—but there was no palace with a crystal bridge and no five-domed church, just a humble cottage. "What does this mean?" he thought. "Where has it all gone?" And without delay he sent his adjutant to find out what had happened. The adjutant galloped off, inspected everything, then returned to report to the king, "Your Majesty, where the grand palace once stood there is now the humble cottage as before; and inside the cottage lives your son-in-law with his mother; but there is no sign of the fair princess and no one knows where she is." The king called a grand council to pronounce judgement on his son-in-law: they condemned him for sorcery and the wrong he had done to the fair princess. Martin was to be immured in a high stone pillar with neither food nor drink. Let him starve to death. Stonemasons came and put up a tall stone pillar in which Martin was immured, with one small window for light. And there he sat, poor lad, shut in without food or drink one day, then a second and a third, weeping bitterly.

Martin's old friend, Blackie the dog, found out what had happened and came running to the cottage. Stripey the cat lay purring on the stove. "You lazy scoundrel, Stripey," said the dog, "all you can do is lie and stretch on the stove in the warm, while our master is shut up in a stone prison far away. Have you forgotten how he gave his last hundred rubles to save your miserable skin? If it hadn't been for him the worms would have eaten you away long ago. Get up quickly! We must go and help him." Stripey hopped down from the stove and, together with the dog, ran off to search for their master. Coming at last to his stone prison, the cat scrambled up to the window. "Hey, master! Are you still alive?" "Only just," answered Martin, "I'm starving; it must be my fate to die of hunger." "Don't despair; we will bring you food and drink," said Stripey, jumping out of the little window and down to the ground. "Our master's starving to death, Blackie; what can we do to help him?" "Oh, Stripey, you're too stupid to think of anything! I know: let's go to town, and as soon as we meet a pieman with a tray of pies, I'll trip him up and make him drop the tray. Then grab some pies and take them to our master."

So they went to the high street and met a man carrying a tray on his head. The dog darted under his feet, making the man stumble and drop his tray. The pies went flying, and the poor man ran off in a panic, thinking a mad dog was after him. Stripey snatched up a pie and ran off to Martin. He gave him the pie and dashed back for another, then a third. In the same fashion they frightened away a man selling cabbage soup, and thus got many a bowlful for their master. Then Blackie and Stripey decided to set off for the Thrice-Ten Kingdom, the Mice's Realm, to bring back the wonderful ring; the road was long and it would take them some time. Before setting off they brought Martin a good store of rusks, rolls, pies and provisions to last a whole year. "Eat and drink, master, but make sure your supplies last out until we return." They bade him farewell and set off on their long journey.

By and by they came to a deep blue sea. "I think I can swim to the other side, what about you?" said the dog. "I'm no good at swimming," Stripey said, "I'll drown in no time." "Then climb on my back." So Stripey climbed on the dog's back, dug his claws into Blackie's thick fur, and they swam off across the sea. When they reached the other side they came to the Thrice-Ten Kingdom, the Mice's

Realm. There was not a single human being in that land; but there were more mice than you could count—wherever you looked they were scampering about in their thousands. "Now it's your turn, Stripey," said the dog. "You break their necks, while I gather up the bodies and put them in a pile."

Stripey was used to this sort of hunting; off he went to deal with the mice in his way: one pounce and the mouse was finished. The dog could hardly keep up with him and by the end of a week the pile was huge. A terrible grief lay over the entire realm. When the Mouse King found that his subjects were missing, that many had suffered a cruel fate, he crawled out of his hole and begged the dog and the cat: "I bow before you, mighty warriors. Take pity on my poor people, do not kill us all; tell me, instead, what I can do for you. Whatever you say will be done." The dog told him this: "You have a palace in your realm, and within that palace dwells a fair princess; she stole our master's magic ring. Fetch us that ring, or you will die and your kingdom will perish—we will lay it waste!" "Wait," said the Mouse King, "I will summon my subjects and ask them."

Immediately he gathered all the mice, large and small, and asked if one of them would creep into the palace to the fair princess and steal her ring. One little mouse answered, "I often go to that palace. By day the princess wears the ring on her little finger, and by night when she goes to bed she puts it into her mouth." "Go and try to get it," said the Mouse King. "If you succeed I will reward you handsomely." The little mouse waited until nightfall, made his way into the palace and crept on tiptoe into the princess's bed-chamber. She was sleeping soundly. Climbing onto the bed, he poked his tail into the princess's nose and tickled her nostrils. She sneezed, and the ring flew out of her mouth and dropped onto the carpet. The little mouse hopped down from the bed, seized the ring in his teeth and took it to the Mouse King. The Mouse King handed the ring to the mighty warriors, Blackie and Stripey, and they in turn paid him their compliments. Then they held counsel between themselves: who should look after the ring? "Give it to me, I'll never lose it, not for anything," said the cat. "All right," said Blackie. "But see you guard it with your life." The cat took the ring in his mouth and they set off on their return journey.

When they arrived at the deep blue sea, Stripey climbed onto the dog's back, dug his claws into Blackie's thick fur as tightly as he could, and into the water they went, swimming across to the other side. They swam for an hour or two, then out of nowhere a black raven swooped down and started pecking at Stripey's head. The poor cat did not know how to protect himself from the enemy. If he used his claws he would slip into the water and end up at the bottom of the sea; if he used his teeth, he might lose the ring. What was he to do?! He endured it as long as he could, until his head was bloody from the raven's pecking. Then he lost his temper, opened his mouth to seize the raven and ... dropped the ring into the deep blue sea. The black raven flew up and disappeared into a dark forest.

As soon as they reached land, Blackie demanded to see the ring. Stripey hung his head in shame. "Forgive me, Blackie," he said. "I'm sorry. I dropped it into the sea." The dog let fly at him. "You stupid oaf! You're lucky I didn't find out earlier, or I'd have dropped you into the sea, you dolt. What are we going to tell our master? Crawl into the sea at once and find that ring, or I'll tear you to pieces!" "What good will that do?" growled the cat. "We must put our heads together: just as we caught mice before, we'll catch crabs now. Perhaps they will find our ring for us." The dog agreed. So they began to walk along the seashore catching crabs and piling them up. The pile grew and grew. A huge crab crawled out of the sea to take a walk; in a flash Stripey had him in his claws. "Don't kill me, mighty warriors, I am the Crab King. I shall do whatever you order." "We dropped a ring into the sea," said Stripey, "go and look for it if you desire our pardon; or we will put your whole kingdom to waste."

The Crab King called his subjects at once and told them about the ring. Then up spoke a tiny crab: "I know where it is. When the ring fell into the deep blue sea, a sturgeon seized it and swallowed it before my very eyes." All the crabs ran through the sea in search of the sturgeon; when they found it they began pinching and tweaking the poor fish ceaselessly. The fish twisted and turned this way and that, and finally leapt onto the shore. The Crab King again emerged from the water and addressed the cat and the dog: "Here is the sturgeon, mighty warriors. Have no mercy on it, for it has swallowed your ring." The dog pounced on the sturgeon and started eating it up from the tail. But the cunning cat guessed where the ring would be. He gnawed a hole in the sturgeon's belly, tore out its insides and there was the ring. Seizing it in his teeth he scampered off as fast as his legs would carry him, thinking, "I'll run to the master, give him the ring and say I found it all by myself; and the master will love me more than Blackie."

Meanwhile the dog was finishing his meal of fish and wondering where the cat had gone. He soon guessed what the cat was up to, that he was trying to curry favour with their master. "It's no good, Stripey, you rascal! I'll catch you up and tear you to pieces." And off ran Blackie after the cat. He caught Stripey up and threatened him with a terrible fate. Spying a birch-tree in a field, Stripey scampered up it and sat there right at the top. "Very well," said the dog, "you can't sit in a tree forever; you'll want to come down sometime. And I shan't budge until you do." For three days Stripey sat up the tree, and for three days Blackie stood guard, not letting him out of sight for a moment. They both got very hungry and agreed to make it up, then set off together to their master. When they reached the stone prison, Stripey sprang up to the little window and asked, "Are you still alive, Master?" "Hello, dear Stripey! I thought you would never return. I haven't had a bite to eat for three days." Thereupon the cat gave him the magic ring. Martin bided his time till dead of night, put the ring on his other hand and the twelve strapping youths appeared.

"What is it that you require?" "Set up my former palace, lads," said Martin, "and the crystal bridge and the five-domed church; and bring back my unfaithful wife; have it ready by morning."

No sooner said than done. The king awoke next morning, went onto his balcony, and looked through his spy-glass: where the cottage had stood there was now a lofty palace; from the palace stretched a crystal bridge, and on either side of the bridge grew trees with gold and silver apples. The king ordered his coach to be made ready and rode off to see whether it had all really come back or whether he was dreaming. Martin met him at the gates, took him by his fair hands and led him into his splendid palace. "Well, this is how it was, Sire, and all because of the princess", and he told the king the whole story. The king ordered the princess to be executed: the unfaithful wife was tied to the tail of a wild stallion which was set loose upon the open plain. The stallion flew like the wind, dashing her snow-white body against the gullies and steep ravines. But Martin still lives and prospers to this day.

The Magic Mirror

In a certain realm, in a certain land there once lived a merchant. His wife was dead, but he had a son and daughter, and a brother. One day he made ready to travel to foreign lands and purchase merchandise; he was taking his son with him, but leaving his daughter home. Calling his brother to him he said, "I entrust you, dear brother, with all my house and chattels and beg you earnestly to keep a strict eye on my daughter, teach her to read and write, but do not spoil her." Then the merchant bade farewell to his brother and daughter and set off on his way. Now, the merchant's daughter had already come of age and was fairer by far than any other maid in the whole wide world. Her uncle began to think evil thoughts that gave him no peace night or day. And he pestered the fair maid saying, "Give yourself to me, or you'll depart this world; I shall kill myself and you too!"

One day the fair maid went to the bath-house. Her uncle followed, but as he came through the door she took a bowl of boiling water and drenched him from head to toe. It took him three weeks to recover. A terrible hatred gnawed at his heart and he pondered on how to take his revenge. He thought and thought, then wrote a letter to his brother, telling him that his daughter was up to no good, traipsing round other yards, spending her nights away from home and never obeying her uncle. When the merchant received the letter, he read it and flew into a rage. "Your sister, has shamed our whole family!" he told his son. "I will not spare her: go back this minute, chop the hussy into small pieces and bring me her heart stuck on this knife. I will not have decent folk mocking our good name."

The son took the sharp knife and rode home. He came unnoticed to his home town, told no one of his errand, and began to make enquiries: how was a certain merchant's daughter disporting herself? Everyone had nothing but praise for her. She was quiet, modest and pious, and heeded the advice of good folk. On learning this, he went to see his sister. She was overjoyed and ran to embrace and kiss him, saying, "Dear brother, what brings you here? How fares our own dear Father?" "Oh, dear sister, hasten not to rejoice. My journey does not bode well: Father has sent me to cut your white body into small pieces, stick your heart on this knife and take it to him."

She burst into tears. "Dear Lord," she said, "but what for?" Thereupon her brother told her of their uncle's letter. "Oh, brother, I am innocent of all he says." And she recounted all that had happened. At last her brother said, "Do not cry, sister. I myself know you are innocent, and though our Father would allow no excuses I do not want to kill you. Make ready and leave our Father's house; go out into the wide world and the Lord will be with you." Without further ado the merchant's daughter made ready to go, bade farewell to her brother and set off she knew not where. Then her brother killed a stray dog, cut out its heart, stuck it on his sharp knife and took it to his father. Handing over the dog's heart, he said, "I killed my own dear sister on your orders, Father." "Serves her right," his father said. "A dog's death is what she deserved."

The fair maid wandered far and wide and finally entered a dense, dark forest, with the sky barely visible above the tall trees. She began to walk through the forest and came to a big glade. And in the middle of the glade was a white marble palace surrounded by iron railings. "I will enter this palace," thought the girl. "Not all folk are wicked; no harm will come to me!" She went into the palace. There was not a soul to be seen. She was about to turn back when two stalwart young knights came riding into the courtyard, saw the girl, and said: "Hail, fair maiden!" "Hail, honest knights." "Well, brother," said one knight to the other, "we were sad that we had no one to keep house for us; now the Lord has sent us a sister." The knights let the merchant's daughter stay with them, called her their sister, gave her the keys and made her mistress of all the palace. Then they pulled out their sharp sabres, drew blood from each other's breast and took an oath: "If one of us dare harm the maid, the other will cut him down mercilessly with this very sabre."

So the fair maid lived with the two knights. Meanwhile her father purchased foreign wares, returned home and shortly after took another wife. This woman was of untold beauty. She possessed a magic mirror which, when you looked into it, would tell you what you wished to know. One day the two knights made ready to go hunting, and warned their sister, "See that you let no one in before our return." With

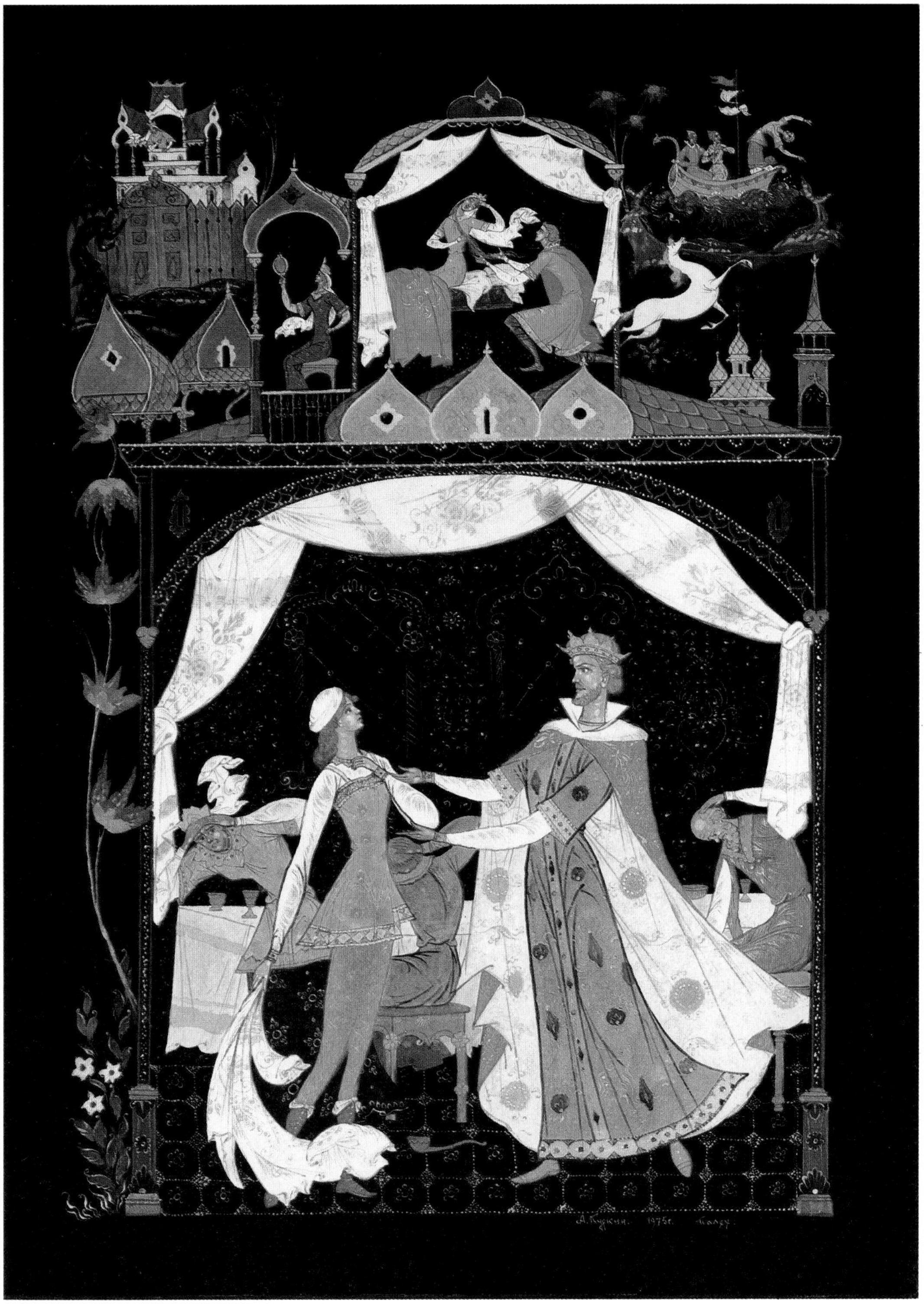
А. Кукин. 1975г. Палех.

that they rode off. At that moment the merchant's new wife glanced into her mirror to admire her own beauty and murmured, "I am the fairest of them all."

But the mirror answered, "You are fair indeed. But you have a step-daughter who lives with two knights in a dense wood. She is fairer still."

Not liking this reply at all, the stepmother summoned an old woman to her, saying, "Take this ring and go into the dense forest; there you will find a white marble palace in which lives my step-daughter. Give her this ring, saying that her brother sends it as a keepsake." The old woman took the ring and went where she was told. She arrived at the white marble palace. The fair young maid saw her and came running to greet her, hoping she had brought tidings from her father's home. "Welcome, Grannie! What brings you here? Is everyone at home alive and well?" "They're all alive and well," replied the old woman. "Your brother asked me to see how you were faring and sent this ring as a present. Here, put it on." The girl was happier than words could tell. She took the old woman into the palace, offered her all manner of tasty food and drink and bade her give her fondest wishes to her brother. Within the hour the old woman set off back. The fair maid admired the ring, put it on her finger, and fell down dead that very instant.

When the two knights came home there was no sister waiting to greet them. What could be the matter? They looked into her bedroom; she was lying there dead, not saying a word. How grieved they were. Sudden death had taken away the fairest of the fair. "We must clad her in new robes and lay her in a coffin," they said. But while they were doing so, one of them noticed the ring on the fair maid's finger and said: "Let's not bury her with that ring. I'll take it off as a keepsake." No sooner had he taken off the ring than the fair maid opened her eyes, sighed and came to life. "What happened to you, sister?" they asked. "Did you let someone in?" "An old woman came from home bringing a ring." "Why did you not heed our words? We had good reason to warn you not to let anyone in. Never do it again."

Some time later the merchant's wife looked into her mirror again and learned that her step-daughter was still alive and fairest of all. She called the old woman to her, gave her a ribbon and said, "Go to the white marble palace where my step-daughter lives and give her this gift. Tell her it is from her brother." Again the old woman came to the fair maid, telling her tales and winning her confidence, and handed her the ribbon. The girl was delighted, tied the ribbon round her neck and fell lifeless upon the bed that very instant. When the two knights returned from hunting, they found their sister lying dead. They began to attire her for burial, untied the ribbon from her neck, and she at once opened her eyes, sighed and came to life. "What happened, sister? Was the old woman here again?" "Yes," she said, "the old woman came from home bringing me a ribbon." "Silly girl. Did we not tell you not to let anyone into the palace?" "Forgive me, dear brothers. I was so eager to have news from home."

114

A few more days passed by. Once again the merchant's wife looked into her mirror and learned that her step-daughter was alive and well. She summoned the old woman. "Now take this strand of hair, go to my step-daughter and make sure you get rid of her this time!" The old woman waited until the knights had gone hunting, then went to the palace. The fair maid saw her from a window and ran out eagerly to meet her. "Hello, Grannie. How do you fare?" "Still alive, my dove," said the woman. "I was roving around and came to see how you are keeping." The fair maid took her into the palace, offered her all manner of tasty food and drink, asked her about her family and bade her give her fondest wishes to her brother. "Very well," the woman said. "Now, my poor dove, you have no one to look for nits in your fair hair, have you? Then, let me do it for you before I go." "Thank you, Grannie." So the old woman began to look through the fair maid's hair, and wound the magic strand into her braid. The girl fell down dead that instant. With an evil cackle, the old woman hurried off before anyone could see and stop her.

When the knights came home and found their sister lying dead, they looked hard for something new on her. But there was nothing to be seen! So they made a crystal coffin—more wonderful than words can tell. And they attired the merchant's daughter in a glittering robe like a bride at her wedding, and laid her in the crystal coffin. They placed the coffin in a hall in the middle of the palace, and above it they put a red velvet canopy with diamond tassels and gold fringes; and hung twelve icon lamps from twelve crystal pillars. Their work done, the two knights wept bitter tears and grieved deeply. "What have we to live for?" they said. "Let us put an end to it all." They embraced, bade each other farewell, went onto a high balcony and jumped down hand-in-hand to death on the sharp stones below.

Many years passed by. One day a prince was out hunting: he rode into the dense forest, sent off his hounds in all directions, left his retinue and rode alone along an overgrown path. On and on he went until he reached a glade—the glade where the white marble palace stood. The prince dismounted from his horse, climbed the stair-case and began to look round the palace. It was so rich and luxurious, yet bore no trace of human care. Everything had been deserted, untended for many a year! In one chamber stood a crystal coffin and in the coffin lay a dead maiden of untold beauty: her cheeks were rosy and her lips bore a smile as if she were alive.

The prince went up and looked at the maid, then stayed rooted to the spot as if held by some invisible force. He stood from dawn to dusk, unable to look away, his heart beating fast. He was captivated by the maiden's incomparable beauty. His huntsmen had long been searching for him, scouring the forest, blowing their horns and shouting—but the prince stood by the crystal coffin hearing nothing. The sun set, darkness fell, and only then did he come to his senses. Kissing the dead maiden he departed. "Where have you been, Your Highness?" the huntsmen enquired. "I was chasing a wild beast and lost my way." Next day at dawn the prince made ready for hunting. He rode into the forest, left the other huntsmen and took the same path to the white marble palace. Again he stood all day by the crystal coffin, unable to take his eyes off the lovely maiden. It was late at night when he returned home. "What has happened to our prince?" the huntsmen said. "We must follow him, lads, and make sure he comes to no harm."

The prince went off hunting next day, sent the hounds off into the forest, left his retinue and set off for the white marble palace. His men followed close behind him, reached the glade and went into the palace. There in a chamber was a crystal coffin, and in the coffin lay a dead maiden, and before the maiden stood the prince. "Ah, Your Highness, small wonder that you have tarried here all week! Now we too shall not leave here until nightfall." They stood in a ring about the crystal coffin, gazing at the maid, admiring her beauty, and stayed there from dawn to dusk. When it was quite dark, the prince turned to his huntsmen, saying, "I want you to do me a great service, brothers: take this coffin with the dead maiden, bring it to my palace, and place it in my bed-chamber, but secretly so that no one learns or hears of it. Do that and I shall reward each of you with gold and other treasure, so that none shall go short." "Reward us if you will," they said. "We are happy to serve you without it, Prince." They lifted up the crystal coffin, carried it into the yard and took it to the prince's palace. There they carried it into the palace and placed it in the prince's bedchamber.

From that day forth the prince gave no more thought to hunting; he would sit at home, never leaving his chamber, gazing upon the maiden. "What has happened to our son?" wondered the queen. "How long is it now that he has stayed home, never leaving his room or letting anyone in? He is pining and grieving, or perhaps he has taken sick. I must go and see him." As soon as the queen entered the prince's chamber she saw the crystal coffin. She learned the story, then straightway gave orders for the girl to be buried in mother earth, as custom befits.

The prince wept, went into the gardens, picked a bunch of fragrant flowers and began to brush the fair maid's hair, plaiting garlands in her braid. All of a sudden, the magic strand of hair fell from the maiden's braid—and she opened her eyes, sighed, rose from the crystal coffin and said, "Oh, how long I have slept!" The prince was overjoyed more than words could tell. Taking her by the hand he led her to his father and mother. "See what God has granted me," he said. "I cannot live a single minute without her. Allow me, dear Father and you, dear Mother, to wed this maid." "Marry, my son. We would not go against God's will; and such beauty cannot be found throughout the big wide world." A royal wish brooks no delay, and that very day they held a merry feast and wedding.

So the prince wed the merchant's daughter, and they lived together happily. Time passed and the young maid desired to visit her father and brother. The prince was not against it, nor, indeed, was the king. "Go," he said, "pay your respects, my dear children. You, Prince, travel on horseback and acquaint yourself with our lands and customs, while your wife shall sail straight home in a ship." So a ship was built for the voyage, sailors were hired and a captain appointed to the vessel. The princess boarded the ship and sailed out to sea, while the prince set off on horseback over land.

The ship's captain, seeing the lovely maid, was taken with her beauty and began to pester her with his attentions. "What is there to fear?" he thought. "She's in my hands now, and I'll do as I wish." "Give your love to me," he told the princess. "If you do not, I'll toss you into the sea." The princess turned away from him, giving him no reply, and burst into tears. Hearing the captain's threatening words, one of the sailors came to the princess in the evening and said, "Do not cry, Princess. Dress up in my sailor's clothes, and I will put on your dress; then go up on deck and I'll stay here in the cabin. Let the captain toss me into the sea—I'm not afraid. With any luck, I'll swim back to shore. Thank goodness land is close at hand." So they changed clothes, the princess went on deck and the sailor lay in her bed. In the night the captain appeared in her cabin, seized the sailor and threw him into the sea. At once the sailor struck out for shore and, by morning, had reached safety. When the boat reached its destination, the sailors went ashore and, with them, the princess; she went straight to the market, bought herself a cook's outfit, put it on and got a job in the kitchens at her father's house.

Not long after, the prince arrived at the merchant's. "Good-day, Father," he said. "Do you not know me? I am married to your daughter. Where is she? Surely she has arrived by now." The ship's captain appeared and gave the following account. "It's like this, Your Highness. An accident occurred: the princess was standing on deck, a storm blew up, the waves rose high, the princess grew dizzy and, before we could move a finger, she had tumbled into the sea and drowned." The prince grieved and pined: she would never return from her watery grave. Such, it seems, was her fate. So the prince stayed with his father-in-law for a while, then ordered his men to prepare for the journey home. The merchant prepared a grand farewell feast and invited other merchants, noblemen and all his relatives—among them was his brother, the evil old woman, his wicked wife and the ship's captain.

They ate, drank and made merry. Then one of the guests caled out, "Harken, you good and honest folk. It's all very well eating and drinking, but let's have a story. Is there no one here who can tell a good tale?" "Here, here!" resounded from all sides. "Who will begin?" One man could not, another would not, a third's memory was blurred by drink. What were they to do? So they turned to the merchant's steward. "We have a new cook in the kitchens," he said. "She's journeyed a lot in foreign parts, seen many wonders and can tell a tale or two. She'll do all right." The merchant called in the cook. "Entertain my guests," he said. And the cook-princess replied, "What shall I tell you? A fairy tale or a true story?" "A true story." "All right, I'll tell you a true story if you like, only on one condition: whoever interrupts will get the soup ladle on their head."

Everyone agreed. And the princess began to recount all that had happened to her. "Well, then," she said. "There was once a merchant's daughter. One day her father went abroad and left her in the charge of his brother. The uncle was led astray by her beauty and would not give her a moment's peace..." Hearing talk of himself, the uncle said, "That's a lie, friends." "A lie, is it? Well, take this." And the cook-princess banged him on the head with the soup ladle. On she went with her story about the stepmother, how she had looked into her magic mirror, and about the old woman, how she had come to the white marble palace of the two knights... And the stepmother and old woman shouted out, "Rubbish! That's impossible." So the princess hit them both on the head with her ladle and continued her story: how she lay in a crystal coffin, how the prince had found her, brought her to life and wed her and how she had set out to see her father.

The sea-captain felt uneasy at this point and asked permission to go home. "I have a headache," he said. "Just wait for a while," said the prince. Then the princess came to the captain's wicked deeds. Of course, he could not stand it: "She's lying," he said. Giving him a good bang on the head with her ladle, she threw off her cook's apron and revealed her princess' robes. "I am not the cook," she cried to the prince, "I am your true wife!" The prince was overjoyed, and the merchant too. Together they rushed to embrace her. And then they held judgement. The old woman and the uncle were stood up against the gates and shot. The evil stepmother was tied to a stallion's tail and set loose across the open plain; her bones were strewn to the winds. As for the ship's captain, he was exiled and replaced by the sailor who had befriended the princess. From that time on the prince, his wife and the merchant lived together, long and happily.

Knee-High in Silver,
Chest-High in Gold

In a certain land there lived a merchant who had two daughters. One day he announced throughout the land that the prince who wed his younger daughter would have three sons: knee-high in silver, chest-high in gold, with the moon on their brows and stars about their sides. And so Prince Ivan came galloping from another land to marry the merchant's daughter. They lived together for a year and the wife gave birth to a son—knee-high in silver, chest-high in gold, with the moon on his brow and stars about his sides. Her elder sister grew envious and bribed the midwife to steal the child, turn him into a dove and set him free. Then she went to the prince and said, "Your wife has given birth to a cat." The prince grew angry, but waited for a second son.

Within a year the merchant's daughter gave birth to another fine son just like the first. But the midwife turned him into a dove, too, set him free and told the prince that his wife had given birth to a dog. The prince was enraged but decided to wait until a third son was born. The same thing happened a third time: the midwife turned the boy into a dove and told the prince that instead of a son he had a block of wood. All three dove-brothers flew off together to the Thrice-Ten Kingdom, beyond the Thrice-Nine Land. The prince, meanwhile, awaited a fourth son. When the boy

119

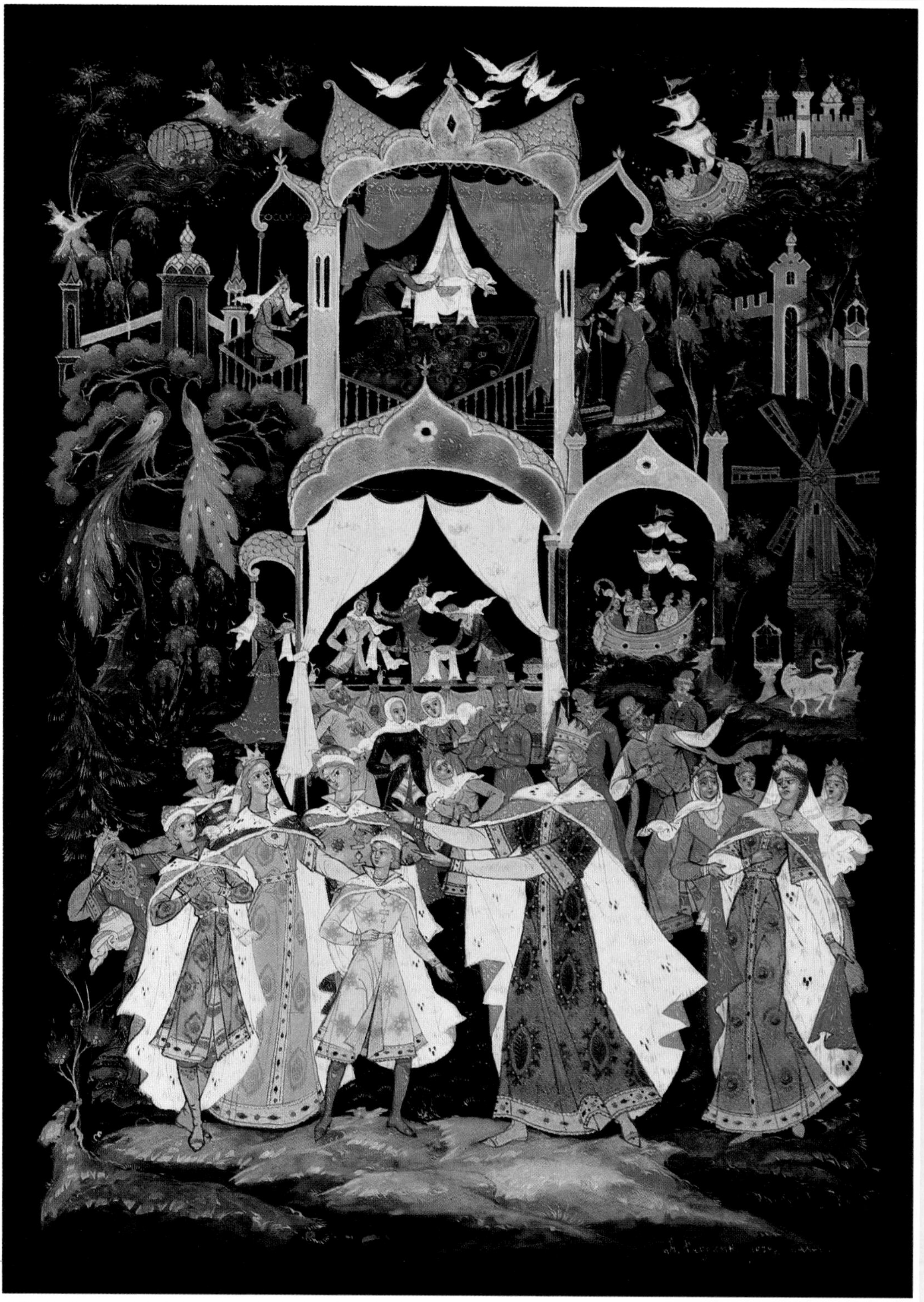

was born he turned out to be quite ordinary—with no gold, or silver, or moon and stars. When the prince learned this, he summoned his noblemen who deliberated and decreed thus: the princess and her child should be put in a barrel, sealed up and thrown into the sea.

So they put them in a barrel and threw it into the sea. The barrel floated farther and farther away and the princess's son grew not by the hour, but by the minute. At last the waves carried the barrel to an island, and it smashed open against the shore. The boy and his mother climbed out and looked about them for somewhere to build a shelter. They entered a dark wood, and the son spied a pouch lying on the path; picking it up he was delighted to find a flint and steel. Now they could make a fire. He struck the flint with the steel—and out sprang an axe and mallet. "What is your wish?" they cried. "Build us a palace. And make sure there is plenty to eat and drink." The axe chopped down trees and the mallet knocked in stakes; and in no time at all they had built a magnificent palace, the like of which did not grace a single realm: it was more beautiful than tongue could tell or pen could relate. And inside it was all the heart could desire.

Merchants sailing past the island marvelled at the magnificent palace and sailed on to the realm of Prince Ivan who by then had taken a second wife. No sooner had the ships brought their wares ashore than the merchants went to the palace with their news and gifts. "Hail, merchants," Prince Ivan greeted them. "You have sailed the seven seas and visited many lands. What tidings do you bring?" The merchants replied that in the middle of the ocean, on an island where a dense forest used to grow and robber bands roamed, and which could not be crossed by foot or horse, there now stood a palace like no other in the world. And in that palace lived a fair princess and her son.

Prince Ivan at once made ready to sail to the island: he wished to see the miracle for himself. But the wicked elder sister of the lost princess held him back. "That is no miracle," she said. "Now here's a true miracle for you: in the Thrice-Ten Kingdom beyond the Thrice-Nine Land is a verdant garden. And in that garden is a mill that grinds and winnows all by itself and sends the chaff flying a hundred versts. By the mill stands a golden pillar with a cage of gold hanging from it and a wise old cat walking round it. To the right he treads—a song to sing, to the left he springs—a yarn to spin."

The merchants set off home and on the way they visited the princess. She welcomed them gladly and entertained them most lavishly. The merchants told of how they had been to Prince Ivan, how he had wanted to see the island and how the elder sister had stopped him. The princess's son listened to all this and, as soon as the merchant ships had sailed away, he took out the pouch, struck the flint with the steel—and out sprang the axe and mallet. "What is your wish?" they cried. "By morning I want a verdant garden around our palace; and a mill in the garden that grinds and winnows all by itself and sends the chaff flying a hundred versts. By the mill there must be a golden pillar with a cage of gold hanging from it and a wise old cat walking round it." Next day the princess and her son awoke to find it all done as ordered: there was the garden, the mill and the golden pillar, with the wise old cat singing songs and spinning yarns. By and by, the merchants sailed past the island again and marvelled at the verdant garden. As soon as the princess's son spied the white sails, he turned himself into a fly, flew off and alighted on one of the ships.

The merchants sailed on to Prince Ivan's realm, dropped anchor, and hurried off to the palace with their news and gifts. Behind them flew the little fly. "Hail, merchants," the prince greeted them, "you have sailed the seven seas and visited many lands. What tidings do you bring?" The merchants replied, "In the middle of the ocean, on an island where a dense forest used to grow and robber bands roamed, and which could not be crossed by foot or horse, there now stands a palace like no other in the world. And in that palace lives a fair princess and her son. By the palace is a verdant garden. And in that garden is a mill that grinds and winnows all by itself and sends the chaff flying a hundred versts. By the mill stands a golden pillar with a cage of gold hanging from it and a wise old cat walking round it. To the right he treads—a song to sing, to the left he springs—a yarn to spin." Prince Ivan at once made ready to sail to the island: he wished to see the miracle for himself. But the wicked elder sister held him back. "That is no miracle," she said. "Now here's a true miracle for you: in the Thrice-Ten Kingdom beyond the Thrice-Nine Land is a golden pine in which birds of paradise sing regal songs." Thereupon the fly grew angry, bit his aunt upon the nose and buzzed out of the window.

The princess's son flew home, turned into a handsome young man, took out his pouch, struck the flint with the steel—and out sprang the axe and mallet. "What is your wish?" they cried. "By morning I want a golden pine to stand in our garden. And in its branches there must be birds of paradise singing regal songs." Next day the princess and her son awoke to find the pine-tree growing in the garden. The merchants sailed past the island again and marvelled at this wonder. They reached Prince Ivan's realm with the princess's son on board, this time as a mosquito. "Hail, merchants," Prince Ivan greeted them. "You have sailed the seven seas and visited many lands. What tidings do you bring?" The merchants replied, "In the middle of the ocean, on an island lives a beautiful princess with her son. By their palace is a verdant garden and in that garden is a mill that grinds and winnows all by itself and sends the chaff flying a hundred versts. By the mill is a golden pillar with a cage of gold hanging from it and a wise old cat walking round it. To the right he treads—a song to sing, to the left he springs—a yarn to spin. And in that garden is a golden pine in which birds of paradise sing regal songs." Prince Ivan at once made ready to sail to the island: he wished to see the miracle for himself. But the wicked elder sister held him back. "That is no miracle," she said. "Now here is a true miracle for

122

you: in the Thrice-Ten Kingdom beyond the Thrice-Nine Land there are three brothers—knee-high in silver, chest-high in gold, with the moon on their brow and stars about their sides." At that the mosquito grew angry, gave his aunt an even harder bite on her nose and buzzed out of the window. He flew home, turned into a handsome young man and told everything to his mother. "Oh," the princess cried, "those are my sons, your brothers." "Then I shall go and find them," he said.

By and by the princess's son came to the Thrice-Ten Kingdom. He looked about him and saw a house in a clearing. "I will go in and rest there," he thought. He entered to find a table laid ready: it held three loaves of consecrated bread and three bottles of wine. But there was not a soul to be seen! He broke a piece of bread from each loaf and ate it, then drank a mouthful from each bottle and hid behind the stove. Suddenly three doves flew in, struck the earth and turned into handsome young men—knee-high in silver, chest-high in gold, with the moon on their brow and stars about their sides. They came up to the table and saw that someone had eaten of their bread and drunk of their wine. And they said, "If a robber had broken in he would have taken everything; but this man has only taken a little. Evidently a good man has come to visit us." Hearing this talk, the youngest brother came out from behind the stove, saying, "Hail, brothers! Mother sends her greetings and bids you come to her." What happiness and rejoicing there was then! In a trice all four struck the ground, turned themselves into doves and flew home to their mother.

It was not long before the merchant ships sailed past the island again. The merchants looked at the island and marvelled. They reached Prince Ivan's realm, and hurried off to the palace with their news and gifts. "What tidings do you bring?" he asked, and they told him about the wonderful island. "On that island lives a beautiful princess with four sons. Three sons are more handsome than words can tell: knee-high in silver, chest-high in gold, with the moon on their brow, and stars about their sides. They walk about the gardens and light up the trees and flowers." Prince Ivan would not put off his journey a moment longer. He boarded a ship and sailed for the island. There he was met by his wife and four sons. They kissed and embraced and spoke of all that had come to pass. As soon as Prince Ivan learned how he had been tricked, he ordered the wicked elder sister to be shot. Leaving his second wife, he began to live again with the first, and they lived happily ever after.

Sister Alyonushka
and Brother Ivanushka

Once upon a time there lived a king and queen who had two children: the boy's name was Ivanushka, the girl's Alyonushka. Then the king and queen died; the children were left alone and decided to go out into the world and seek their fortune. They walked and walked until they came to a pond, with a herd of cows grazing nearby. "I am so thirsty," said Ivanushka. "Do not drink, little brother, or you will turn into a calf," said his sister. He heeded her words, and on they went until, after many versts, they came to a stream, with a drove of horses nearby. "Oh, sister, if only you knew how thirsty I am," said Ivanushka. "Do not drink, little brother, or you will turn into a foal." Ivanushka heeded her words, and on they went until they came to a lake, with a flock of sheep nearby. "Oh, sister," said Ivanushka, "I am so terribly thirsty." "Do not drink, little brother, or you will turn into a lamb." Ivanushka heeded her yet again, and on they went until they came to a river, with pigs feeding nearby. "Oh, sister," the boy cried, "I must have a drink or I will die of thirst." "Do not drink, little brother, or you will turn into a piglet." Once more the boy heeded his sister's words, and on they went until they saw a flock of goats grazing near a well. "Oh, sister, I must drink now," he cried. "Do not drink, little brother, or you will turn into a little goat." But this time he did not heed his sister's warning and drank some water. At once he changed into a goat, skipping around Alyonushka and bleating: "Maa-aa, maa-maa-aa."

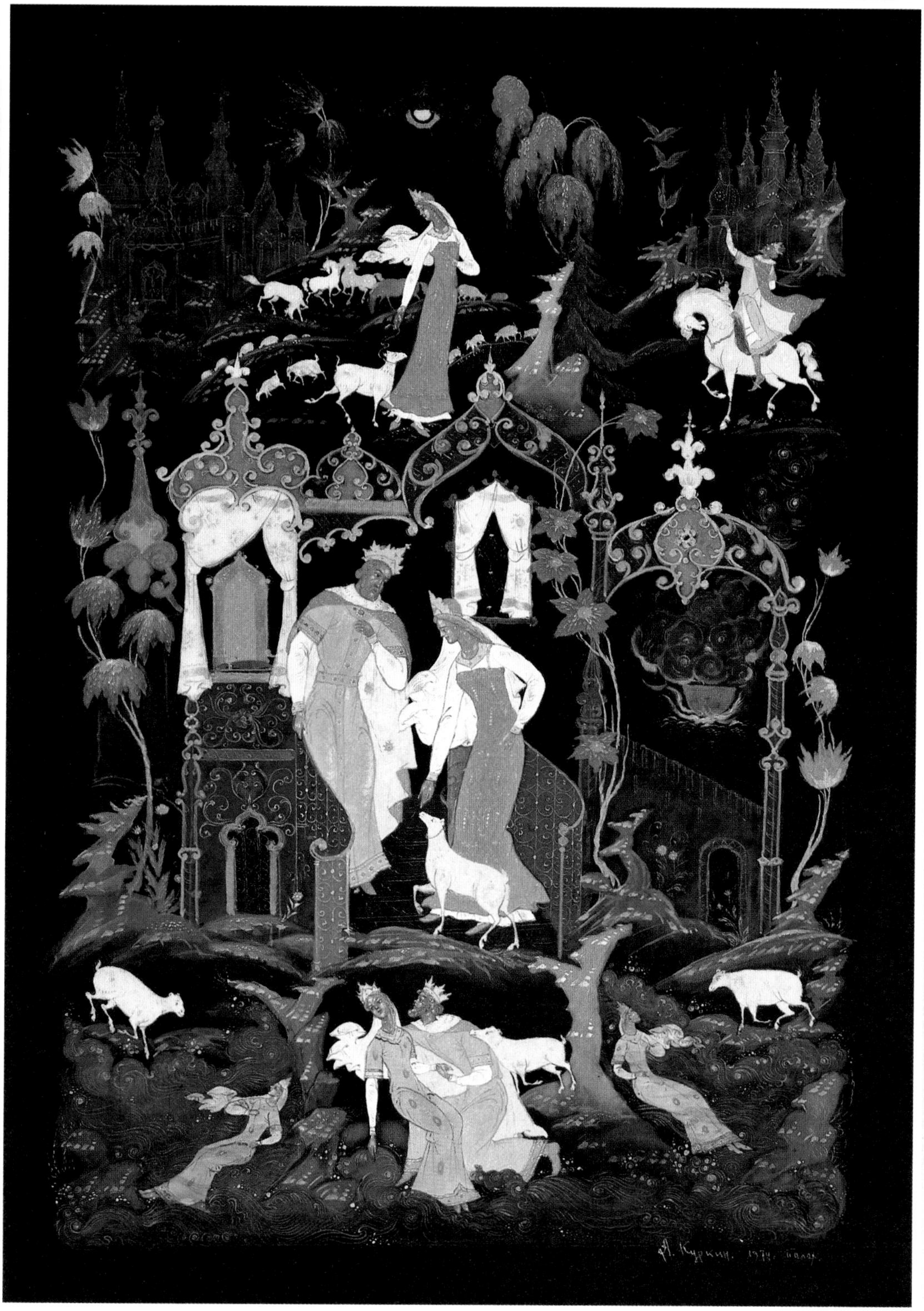
А. Куркин. 1974.

Alyonushka put a silk sash about his neck and led him along shedding bitter tears. The goat gamboled about until he strayed into the gardens of a certain king. The servants saw him and straightway reported to the king. "Your Majesty," they said, "there is a goat in our gardens, being led along by a fair young maid." The king bade them find out who she was. "I will tell you," said Alyonushka. "There was once a king and queen who died, leaving us children all alone. So I am a princess, and my brother here is a prince. He heeded not my words, drank water from the well and turned into a goat." The servants told this to the king. The king summoned Alyonushka and was so taken with her that he decided to marry her. The wedding took place and they began to live together. The little goat lived with them, gamboling in the gardens, and eating and drinking together with the king and queen.

One day the king went off hunting. While he was away a sorceress came and cast a spell on the queen: Alyonushka fell ill and grew thin and pale. Everything went sad in the king's gardens: the flowers began to fade, the trees to wilt and the grass to wither. When the king returned he asked Alyonushka: "Are you unwell?" "Yes," she replied. Next day he again went hunting. And as Alyonushka lay ailing at home, the sorceress came to her, saying, "I can make you well, if you like. Go to such-and-such a lake at sunset for so many days and drink the water there." The queen took her advice and, in the twilight, went down to the lake; but the sorceress was waiting for her: she seized the maid, tied a stone about her neck and tossed her into the water. Alyonushka sank to the bottom. The poor little goat ran up to the lake and wept bitterly. The sorceress made herself look like the queen and went to the palace.

When the king came home he was delighted to find the queen well again. They sat down to dine. "Where is your little goat?" he asked. "We don't need him here," she said. "I told them to keep him out; the place reeks of goat already!" Next day, when the king had gone hunting, the sorceress beat the goat mercilessly and threatened, "As soon as the king gets back, I'll ask him to slaughter you." When the king returned, the sorceress kept on at him to have the goat slaughtered. "I am sick and tired of him," she said. The king felt sorry for the goat, but there was nothing to be done; she nagged him so much that finally he agreed to have the goat killed. Seeing that steel knives were being sharpened, the kid ran sobbing to the king with a last request. "Sire, let me go down to the lake to take one last drink and rinse out my insides." The king gave him leave and the little goat ran down to the lake, stood at the water's edge and cried plaintively,

> "Alyonushka, my sister so dear,
> Swim back, swim back, to me here.
> The flames are rising,
> The pots are boiling,
> No more shall I see you, I fear."

And she answered him,

> "Ivanushka, my brother dear,
> A heavy stone does pull me down.
> A cruel snake has sucked my heart."

126

The goat wept and returned home. At midday he again begged the king: "Sire, let me go down to the lake to take one last drink and rinse out my insides." The king let him go. So the little goat ran down to the lake, crying plaintively,

"Alyonushka, my sister so dear,
Swim back, swim back, to me here.
The flames are rising,
The pots are boiling,
No more shall I see you, I fear."

And she answered him,

"Ivanushka, my brother dear,
A heavy stone does pull me down.
A cruel snake has sucked my heart."

The king began to wonder why the kid kept running down to the lake. The goat asked the king a third time: "Sire, let me go down to the lake to take one last drink and rinse out my insides." The king let him go, but followed behind unnoticed. As he came to the water's edge he heard the little goat calling to his sister,

"Alyonushka, my sister so dear,
Swim back, swim back, to me here.
The flames are rising,
The pots are boiling,
No more shall I see you, I fear."

And she answered him,

"Ivanushka, my brother dear,
A heavy stone does pull me down.
A cruel snake has sucked my heart."

Again the little goat began to call to his sister. This time she rose to the surface and appeared above the water. In a trice the king caught hold of her, tore the stone from her neck and carried her onto the shore, asking her how it had all happened. She told him everything. The king was overjoyed and so was the goat: he hopped and slapped, and everything in the gardens began to bud and blossom again. As for the sorceress, the king condemned her to death. A bonfire was made in the courtyard and she was burned upon it. After that the king and queen and the little goat began to live and prosper in peace and happiness, and to eat and drink together as before.

The Frog Princess

Long, long ago, in days of yore, there lived a king who had three sons, all of them grown to manhood. One day the king called them to him and said, "My sons, let each of you make a bow for himself and shoot an arrow. The maiden who brings your arrow back will be your bride; and he whose arrow is not returned will stay unwed." The eldest son shot an arrow and a prince's daughter brought it back. The middle son loosed an arrow and a general's daughter brought it back. But young Prince Ivan's arrow fell into a marsh and was brought back by a frog holding it between her teeth. The first two brothers were joyful and happy, but Prince Ivan was downcast and cried: "How can I live with a frog? Marrying is for a lifetime, it isn't like wading a stream or crossing a field!" He wept and wept but there was nothing for it: he had to marry the frog. All three couples were wed together according to the custom—the frog being held aloft on a platter.

Some time passed. One day the king wished to see which bride was the best needle-woman. So he ordered them to make him a shirt. Poor Prince Ivan was again downcast and cried: "How can my frog sew? I'll be a laughing stock." The frog only jumped across the floor croaking. But no sooner was Prince Ivan asleep than she went outside, cast off her skin and turned into a beautiful maiden, calling, "Maids and matrons, sew me a shirt!" The maids and matrons straightway brought a finely-embroidered shirt; she took it, folded it and placed it alongside Prince Ivan.

128

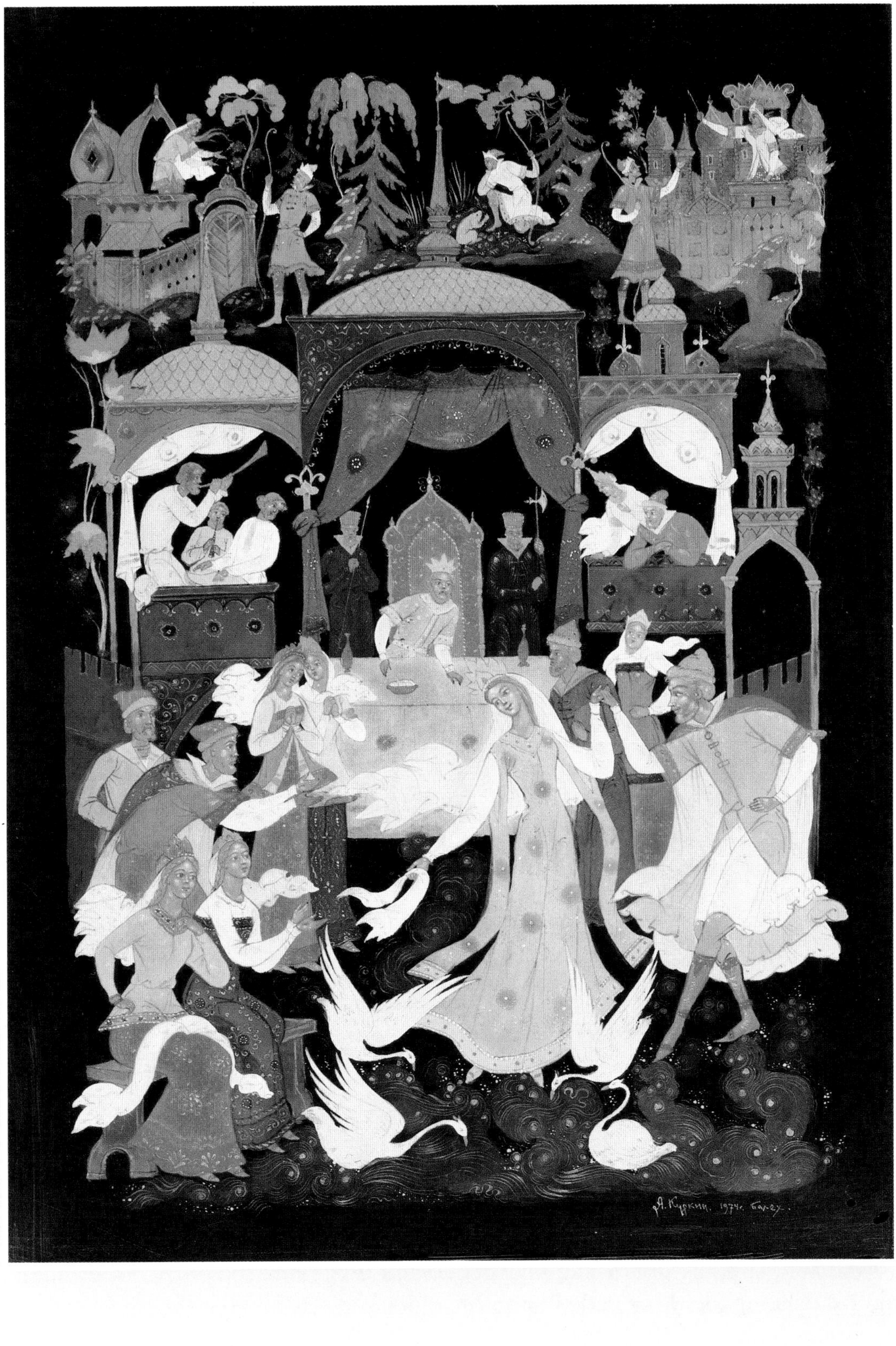
А. Куркин. 1974г. Палех.

Thereupon she turned back into a frog as if nothing had happened. In the morning Prince Ivan awoke and was overjoyed to find the shirt which he took forthwith to the king. The king gazed at it and said: "Now there's a shirt for you, fit to wear on holy days!" Then the middle brother brought a shirt, at which the king said, "This shirt is fit only for the bath-house!" And taking the eldest brother's shirt, he said, "And this one is fit only for a smoky peasant hut!" The king's sons went their separate ways, with the two eldest muttering among themselves, "We were surely wrong to mock at Prince Ivan's wife; she must be a cunning sorceress, not a frog."

Presently the king again issued a command: this time the daughters-in-law were each to bake a loaf of bread, and bring it to him to judge which bride was the best cook. The other two brides had made fun of the frog, but now they sent a chamber-maid to see how she would bake her loaf. The frog noticed the woman, so she kneaded some dough, rolled it out, made a hole in the stove and tipped the dough straight into the fire. The chambermaid ran to tell her mistresses, the royal brides, and they proceeded to do the same. But the crafty frog had tricked them; as soon as the woman had gone, she retrieved the dough, cleaned and mended the stove as if nothing had happened, then went out on to the porch, cast off her skin and called, "Maids and matrons, bake me a loaf of bread such as my dear father used to eat on Sundays and holidays." In an instant the maids and matrons brought the bread. She took it, placed it beside Prince Ivan, and turned into a frog again. In the morning Prince Ivan awoke, took the loaf of bread and gave it to his father. His father was receiving the loaves brought by the elder brothers: their wives had dropped the dough into the fire just as the frog had done, so their bread was black and lumpy. First the king took the eldest son's loaf, inspected it and despatched it to the kitchen; then he took the middle son's loaf and despatched it thither too. Then came Prince Ivan's turn: he presented his loaf to his father who looked at it and said, "Now this is bread fit to grace a holy day. It is not at all like the burnt offerings of my elder daughters-in-law!"

After that the king thought to hold a ball to see which of his sons' wives was the best dancer. All the guests and daughters-in-law assembled; everyone was there except Prince Ivan, who thought: "How can I go to the ball with a frog?" And the poor prince began to weep bitterly. "Do not cry, Prince Ivan," said the frog. "Go to the ball. I shall follow in an hour." Prince Ivan was somewhat cheered at the frog's words, and left for the ball. Then the frog cast off her skin and turned into a lovely maid dressed in finery. When she arrived at the ball, Prince Ivan was overjoyed, and the guests clapped their hands at the sight of such beauty. They began to eat and drink. But the frog-princess would eat and slip the bones into her sleeve, then drink and pour the dregs into her other sleeve. The elder brothers' wives saw this and followed suit, slipping bones into one sleeve and dregs into the other. When the time came for dancing, the king called upon his elder sons' wives but they insisted on the frog-princess dancing first. And she straightway took Prince Ivan's arm and came forward to dance. She danced and danced, whirling round and round, to the delight of all. When she shook her right sleeve, woods and lakes appeared; when she shook her left sleeve, all kinds of birds flew about. The guests were filled with wonder. When she finished dancing, everything disappeared. Then the wives of the two elder sons began to dance. They wished to do as the frog-princess had done, so they shook their right sleeves and bones flew out hitting folk about them; and when they shook their left sleeves, water splashed all over the onlookers. The king was most displeased and soon called an end to the dancing.

The ball was over. Prince Ivan rode off ahead of his wife, found the frogskin and burnt it. So when his wife returned and looked for the skin, it was nowhere to be seen. She lay down to sleep with Prince Ivan, but just before daybreak she said to him, "Oh, Prince Ivan, if only you had waited a little longer I would have been yours. Now God alone knows when we shall meet again. Farewell. If you wish to find me you must go beyond the Thrice-Nine Land to the Thrice-Ten Kingdom." And the frog-princess vanished.

A year went by, and Prince Ivan still pined for his wife. As a second year began, he made ready to leave, seeking first the blessing of his father and mother. He rode for a long way and eventually chanced upon a little hut facing the trees, with its back to him. "Little hut, little hut," he called. "Turn your face to me, please, and your back to the trees." The little hut did as he said and Prince Ivan entered. There before him sat an old woman, who cried, "Fie, Foh! There was neither sight nor sound of Russian bones, yet now they come marching in of their own free will! Whither go you, Prince Ivan?" "First give me food and drink and put me to bed, old woman, then ask your questions." So the old woman gave food and drink and put him to bed. Then Prince Ivan said to her, "Grannie, I have set out to rescue Yelena the Fair." "Oh, my child," the old woman said, "you've waited too long! At first she spoke of you often, but now she no longer remembers you. I haven't seen her for a long time. Go now to my middle sister, she knows more than me."

In the morning Prince Ivan set out, came to another little hut, and cried, "Little hut, little hut, turn your face to me, please, and your back to the trees." The little hut did as he said and Prince Ivan entered. There before him sat an old woman, who cried, "Fie, Foh! There was neither sight nor sound of Russian bones, yet now they come marching in of their own free will! Whither go you, Prince Ivan?" "I seek Yelena the Fair, Grannie," he replied. "Oh, Prince Ivan," the old woman said, "you've waited too long! She has begun to forget you and is to marry another. She is now living with my eldest sister; go there now, but beware: as you approach they will know it is you. Yelena will turn into a spindle, her dress will turn to gold. My sister will wind the gold thread around the spindle and put it into a box which she will lock. But you must find the key, open the box, break the spindle, toss the top over your shoulder and the bottom before you. Then she will appear."

Off went Prince Ivan, came to the old woman's hut, entered and saw her winding gold thread around a spindle; she then locked it in a box and hid the key. But Prince Ivan quickly found the key, opened the box, took out the spindle, broke it as he had been told, tossed the top over his shoulder and the bottom before him. All of a sudden, there was Yelena the Fair standing in front of him. "Oh, Prince Ivan," she sighed, "how long you were in coming! I almost wed another." And she told him that the other bridegroom would soon arrive. But, taking a magic carpet from the old woman, Yelena the Fair sat upon it and they soared up and away like birds. The bridegroom set off quickly in pursuit. He was clever and guessed that they had fled. He was within ten feet of them when they flew on the carpet into Rus. Just in time! He could not follow them there, so he turned back. But Prince Ivan and Yelena the Fair flew home to the rejoicing of all; and lived happily ever after.

The Potter

A potter was once driving along the road with his pots, dozing as he went. King Ivan overtook him, saying, "Safe journey!" The potter looked round. "Thank you, Sire," he said. "Were you dozing?" asked the king. "Yes, Your Majesty. Fear not him who sings songs, fear him who slumbers." "You're a bold one, potter," said the king. "I like fellows like you. Coachman, drive more slowly. Tell me, potter, how long have you plied your trade?" "Since a lad, and now I'm of middle age." "Do you earn enough to feed your children?" asked the king. "That I do, Your Royal Majesty. Yet I do not plough, nor do I reap or mow, nor can the frost kill my crops." "True, potter," said the king, "yet the world is not without evil." "Yes, Your Royal Majesty, there are three evils in the world." "And what might they be, potter?" "The first is a bad neighbour," said the potter; "the second is a bad wife, and the third is a bad head." "Tell me," said the king, "which is the worst evil?" "I can always escape from a bad neighbour," said the man. "So, too, can I from a bad wife as long as she stays with the children. But there's no escaping a bad head; it's with you always." "True enough, potter. You're a smart fellow. Listen, you stand by me, and I by you. When the geese come flying out of Russia, pluck them clean, plump and lean." "Done," said the potter. "They'll be as bald as a coot when I'm through with them." "Well, now, potter, stay a while and show me your pots."

The potter stopped and began to show his wares. The king looked and chose three earthenware pots. "Can you make me more of these?" "How many would you

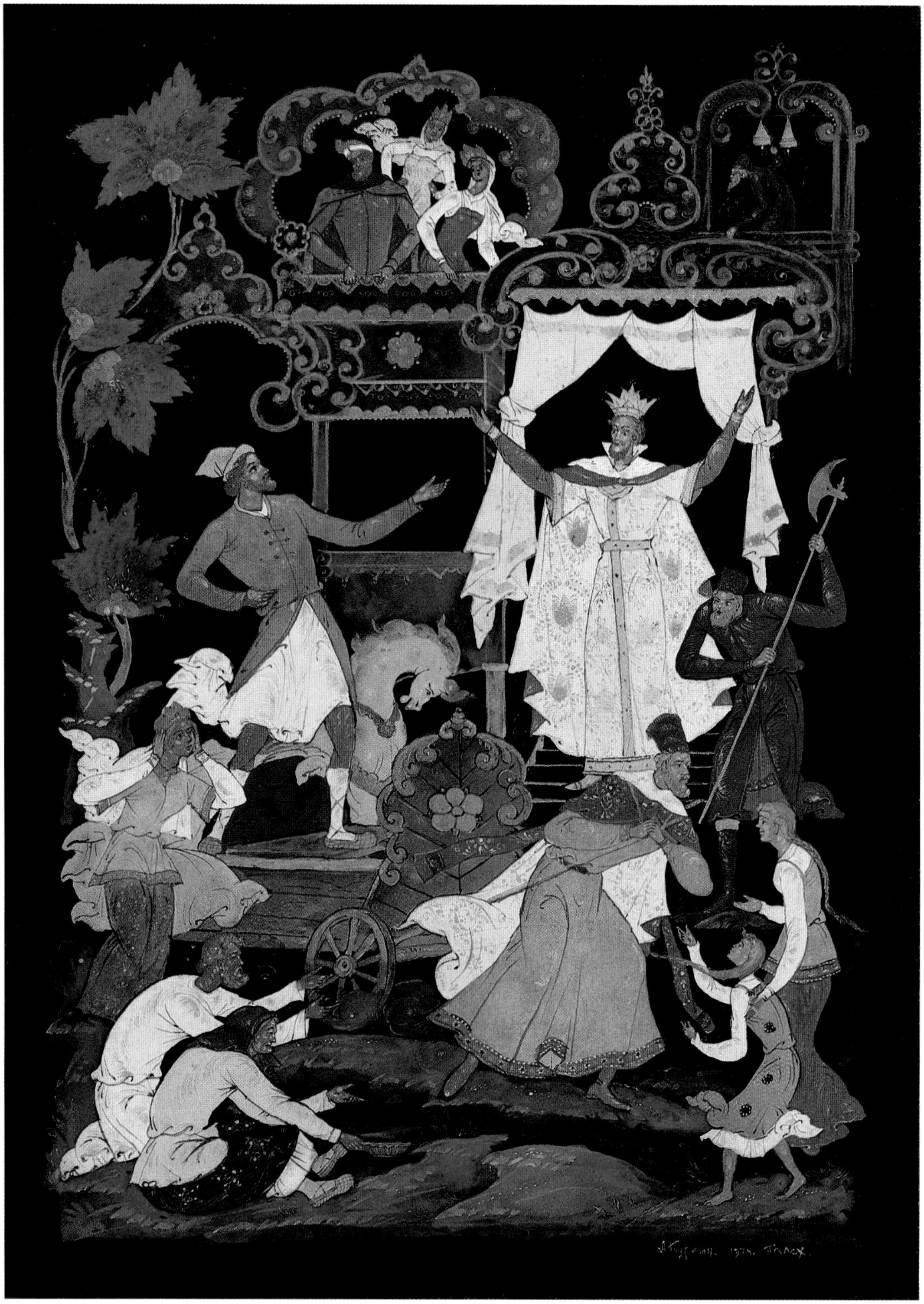
А. Куркин. 1974. Палех.

like, Your Majesty?" "About a dozen cartloads." "How much time will you give me?" "A month." "I can deliver them in a fortnight, right to the town. You stand by me, and I by you." "Thank you, potter." "And you, King, where will you be when I deliver the wares to town?" "I'll be staying at a merchant's house." The king arrived in town and gave orders that everyone was to use only earthenware pots at their parties: no silver, lead, copper or wood. The potter finished the royal order and brought his pots to town. In the market place a governor came up to him and said, "God be with you, potter." "Your humble servant." "Sell me all your pots." "I cannot; they have been ordered." "What does it matter? Take the money. You cannot be kept to the bargain if you received no payment in advance. Well, how much do you want?" "Fill each of my pots with coins." "You ask too much, potter." "Very well then, for every one filled with coins you will get two free. Agreed?" They settled on that. "You stand by me, and I by you." They began to pour coins in the pots and empty them, until the man ran out of money. But there were plenty of pots left. The governor, eager to get his hands on the goods, went home to fetch more money. Again they poured and poured, in and out, and again there were plenty of pots left and no money. "What are we to do now, potter?" asked the governor. "You didn't expect that, did you?" the potter said. "But I tell you what: pull me to that house over there and I'll give you both the pots and the money back."

The governor hummed and hawed: he was sorry for his money and sorry for himself. But there was nothing to be done, so he finally agreed. The horse was unharnessed, the potter sat in the cart and the governor began to pull him along.

The potter burst into song as the governor pulled and pulled. "Where am I to take you to?" he asked. "To that house over there," came the reply. The potter sang merrily striking a high note as they came to the house. The king heard him, ran out on to the porch and recognised the potter. "Ah, welcome, potter, I'm glad to see you." "Thank you, Your Royal Majesty." "What's that you are riding on?" "A bad head, Sire." "Well, you are a smart fellow, potter; you know how to sell your wares. Governor! Take off your uniform and boots. And you, potter, take off your caftan and bast shoes. Now put on each other's clothes. You knew how to sell your wares, potter! You worked little but pleased me much, whereas you, governor, knew not how to honour your governor's rank. Well, potter, did the geese come flying out of Russia?" "They did." "And did you pluck them clean, plump and lean?" "No, Your Majesty, I plucked them clean and fleeced them lean."

Wise Replies

A soldier had served full five and twenty years in his regiment without ever seeing the king in person. When he returned home he was asked about the king and he knew not what to say. So his relatives and friends began to taunt him, "You say you served five years and twenty and never saw the king!" He was so vexed that he decided to go and take a look at the king. When he arrived at the palace the king asked him, "What have you come for, soldier?" "It's like this, Your Royal Majesty, I served you and God full five and twenty years, yet I never saw you in person. So I've come to take a look." "Well, have a good look," said the king. The soldier walked around the king three times, inspecting him thoroughly. Finally the king asked, "Am I handsome?" "Yes, Sire." "And now, soldier," said the king, "tell me: is the sky far from the earth?" "It is so far that when they knock up there we can hear it down here." "And is the earth wide?" "The sun rises over there, and sets over here—that's how wide it is." "And is the earth deep?" "I once had a great-grand-dad who died ninety years ago; he was buried in the earth and has never come home. So it must be deep." Then the king sent the soldier to gaol, saying, "Keep your wits about you, soldier. I shall send you thirty geese and you must pluck a feather from each of them." "Very well," the soldier said.

Then the king summoned thirty rich merchants and put to them the same riddles as he had put to the soldier; they racked their brains but could not answer. So they

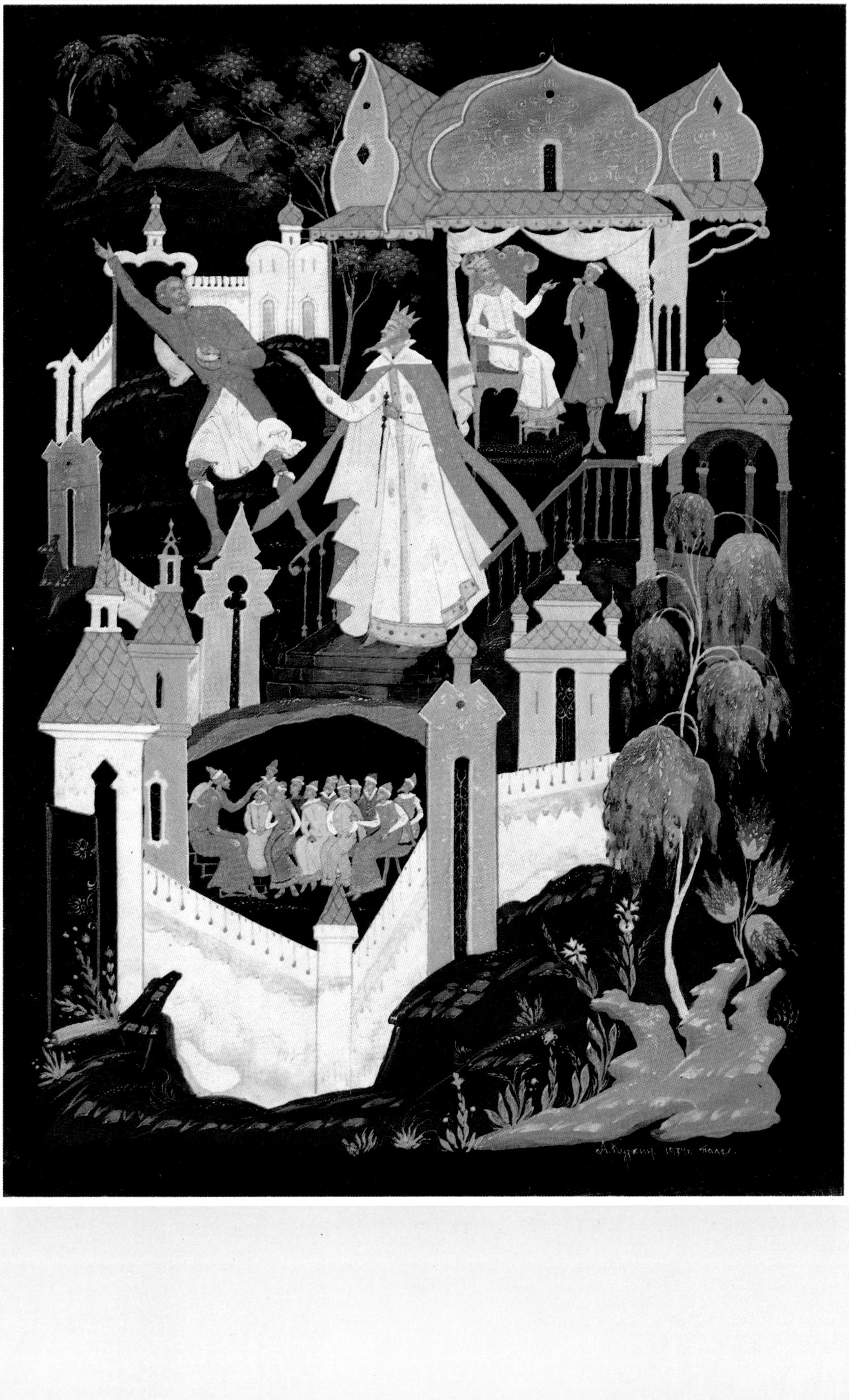

were sent to gaol as well. When the soldier heard their story, he said to them, "Each give me a thousand rubles and I will tell you the answers to the riddles." "Gladly, brother," they said. "Only tell us." The soldier took a thousand from each of them and told them how to solve the king's riddles. Two days later the king summoned the merchants and the soldier. He put the very same riddles to the merchants, and let them go as soon as they answered correctly. "Well, soldier," he said when the two of them were alone, "did you pluck a feather from each of them?" "I did, indeed, Your Majesty, and a golden one at that." "Is your home far?" "It's out of sight so it must be far." "Here is a thousand rubles for you. And God be with you." The soldier returned home and lived a life of carefree ease.

The Soldier and the King
in the Wood

In a certain realm, in a certain land there once lived a peasant who had two sons. One day the recruiting sergeant came and took the elder son for the army. The lad served his sovereign loyally and faithfully, and was fortunate enough to rise in a few years to the rank of general. At that time there was a new recruitment and it was his younger brother's lot to be chosen. His head was shaved and he was sent to the same regiment in which his brother was a general. The new soldier recognised the general, but was snubbed at once. His brother told him straight, "I don't know you and you don't know me!"

One day the soldier was standing guard in his sentry-box near the general's quarters; the general was giving a big dinner and many officers and gentlemen had arrived. Seeing them enjoying themselves while he had nothing, the soldier began to weep bitterly. The guests asked him, "Soldier, why are you crying?" "Who wouldn't cry?" he said. "My brother is making merry, yet he refuses to remember me." The guests told this to the general who flew into a rage. "Don't you believe him. He is talking nonsense!" He ordered his brother to be relieved of guard duty and given three hundred lashes for having dared to say he was related to the general. The soldier was so aggrieved that he put on his battledress and deserted the regiment.

By and by he came to a dense, dark forest where folk hardly ever went and began living there on berries and roots. Shortly after the king went hunting with a large retinue. They rode across a wide plain, set the hounds loose, blew on their horns and began to make sport. All of a sudden, from out of nowhere sprang a tall stately stag; it darted past the king, plunged into a river, swam across and disappeared into the forest. The king followed it across the river with his horse and galloped in pursuit, but soon lost track of it. The other hunters were left far behind. All around him was a dense, dark forest: the king did not know which way to go and there was no path in sight. He wandered about till evening and grew very weary. Suddenly he came upon the runaway soldier. "Good morrow," said the soldier. "What are you doing here?" "Well, it's like this," replied the king. "I went hunting and lost my way in the forest. Can you show me the path, brother?" "But who are you?" "A servant of the king." "Well, it is too dark now," the soldier said. "Come, you had better spend the night in the forest, and tomorrow I'll show you the way."

They went off to find a place to spend the night and shortly saw a little hut. "God has sent us shelter," said the soldier. "Let us go in." So they went inside and found an old woman sitting there. "Hello, Grannie." "Hello, soldier." "Give us something to eat and drink." "I would gladly have a bite to eat myself, but there's nothing in the house." "You lie, old hag," cried the soldier, rummaging in the oven and along the shelves. He soon found the old woman had plenty in stock: she was well-supplied with liquor and all manner of food. The soldier and the king sat down at table, had a good supper, then climbed up into the attic for the night. Said the soldier to the king, "God helps those who help themselves. Let one of us keep watch while the other rests." They drew lots and it fell to the king to keep guard. The soldier handed him his sharp sword, stationed him by the door, and warned the king not to fall asleep but to wake him at once if anything untoward happened. Then the soldier lay down to sleep, wondering whether his companion would make a good watchman. "He is not used to it. I'd better keep an eye on him, just in case."

The king stood on guard for a while, then his head began to nod. "Why are you nodding?" called the soldier. "Are you sleepy?" "No," replied the king. "Then watch out," the soldier said. The king stood there for another quarter of an hour, then again began to drowse. "Hey, friend, you're not sleeping, are you?" called the soldier. "No, certainly not," said the king. "If you do nod off, don't blame me for the consequences." The king stood for another fifteen minutes, then his legs gave way and he fell down asleep. At once the soldier jumped up, took his sword and began to give the king a good thrashing. "Is that the way to keep guard?" he shouted. "I served for ten years and was never forgiven a single mistake. They can't have taught

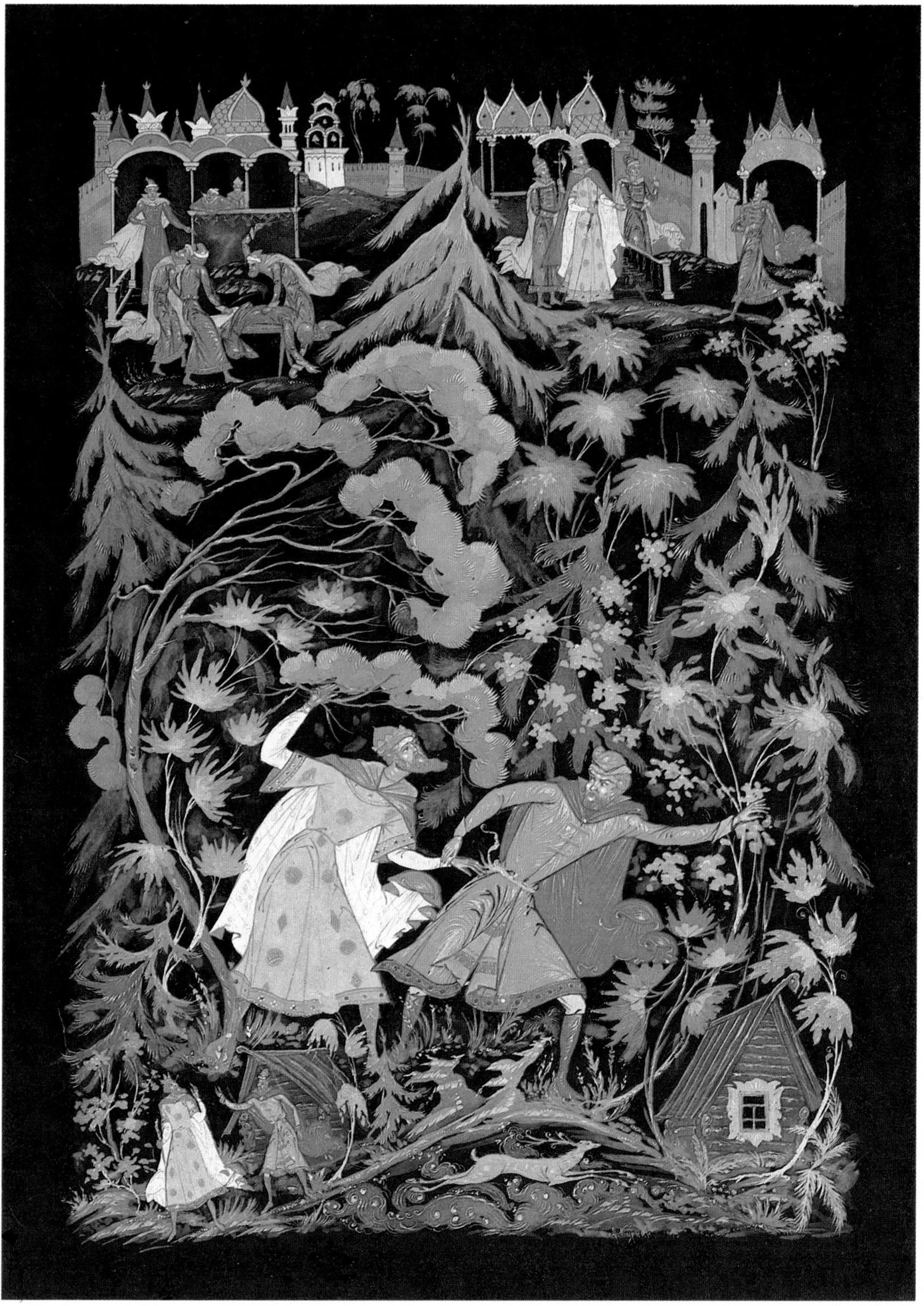

you anything. I let you off the first and second time, but the third time is too much. You'd better lie down to sleep. I'll keep watch myself."

The king lay down to sleep while the soldier stood guard. Suddenly robbers burst into the hut. The old woman welcomed them, saying, "We have guests." "That's all right, Grandma," they said. "We've been riding all night with no luck at all; and good fortune has entered our hut of its own free will. Let's have some supper first." "But our guests have eaten and drunk all there was." "Ho, what bold fellows! Where are they now?" "They climbed up to sleep in the attic." "Then I'll go up and take care of them," said one of the robbers. He took a big knife and climbed up the attic ladder; but no sooner had he stuck his head through the attic door than the soldier cut if off with his sword—and the head went rolling across the floor. Meanwhile the robbers wondered why their companion was taking so long. In the end they sent another of their number. But the soldier slew him too. Before long he had slain all the robbers.

At daybreak the king awoke and, seeing the dead bodies, asked, "Oh, soldier, what has happened?" The soldier told him all there was to tell. Then, climbing down from the attic and seeing the old woman, the soldier shouted at her, "Wait, you old hag! I'll cook your goose. So you keep a robbers' den here, do you! Hand over their money right away." The old woman opened up a chest full of gold and the soldier poured the gold into his knapsack, filled his pockets and told his companion to help himself. But the king said, "No, brother, I don't need it; our king has plenty of money as it is, and what is his will be ours." "Please yourself," said the soldier, and led the king out of the forest. When they came to the highway, the soldier said, "Follow the road and you'll reach the town in an hour." "Goodbye," said the king. "And thank you for your help. Come and see me and I'll make you a happy man." "How can you? I have run away from the army, and if I show my face in town that will be the end of me." "Don't you worry, soldier. I'm in the king's favour. If I tell him of your courage, he'll not only pardon you, he'll reward you too." "But where can I find you?" "Come straight to the palace." "Very well, I'll be there tomorrow."

The king took leave of the soldier and set off along the highway. He came to his capital city and straightway gave orders to all guards, watchmen and patrols to be on the alert: when a certain soldier appeared he was to be treated like a general. Next day, when the soldier appeared at the city gates, all the guards ran out and saluted him like a general. The soldier wondered what it was all about, asking in amazement, "Who are you saluting?" "We are saluting you, soldier," came the reply. Taking a handful of gold out of his knapsack, he gave some to the guards to buy vodka. He walked into the town, but wherever he appeared, the guards saluted him—he scarcely had time to tip them all. "What a gossip that servant of the king is!" he thought to himself. "He has told everyone I've plenty of money." When he arrived at the palace, he found the troops all assembled and the king waiting to meet him, wearing the same clothes as when hunting. Then the soldier realised with whom he had spent the night, and he was very frightened. "So it was the king," he thought. "And I thrashed him with the flat of my sword as if he was one of us!" But the king took his arm, thanked him before the assembled troops for saving his life and rewarded him with the rank of general. The elder brother was demoted to a simple soldier. That would teach him not to disown his own kith and kin!

The Wise Maiden

Two brothers were journeying along: one was poor, the other rich. Each had a horse: the poor one had a mare, the rich one a gelding. And they stopped for the night together. During the night the poor man's mare bore a foal which rolled under the rich man's cart. In the morning, the rich man woke up his brother and said, "Get up, brother. My cart bore a foal in the night." The brother rose and said, "How can a cart give birth to a foal? It was my mare that foaled." "If your mare really was his mother," said the rich man, "he would surely be beside her." They argued for a while and finally went to the judge to settle the affair. The rich man gave the judge some money, but the poor man had to rely on words.

Finally, the matter reached the king himself. He summoned both brothers before him and put four riddles to them: What is the strongest and swiftest thing in the world? What is the fattest thing in the world? What is the softest? And what is the sweetest? The king gave them three days to solve the riddles, telling them to return with their answers on the fourth day.

The rich man thought and thought, remembered his neighbour and went to seek her advice. She sat him down at the table, offered him food and drink and asked him why he was so downcast. "The king has set me four riddles, and given me three days only to solve them." "What are they, neighbour? Tell me." "Here is the first riddle: what is the strongest and swiftest thing in the world?" "That's easy. My

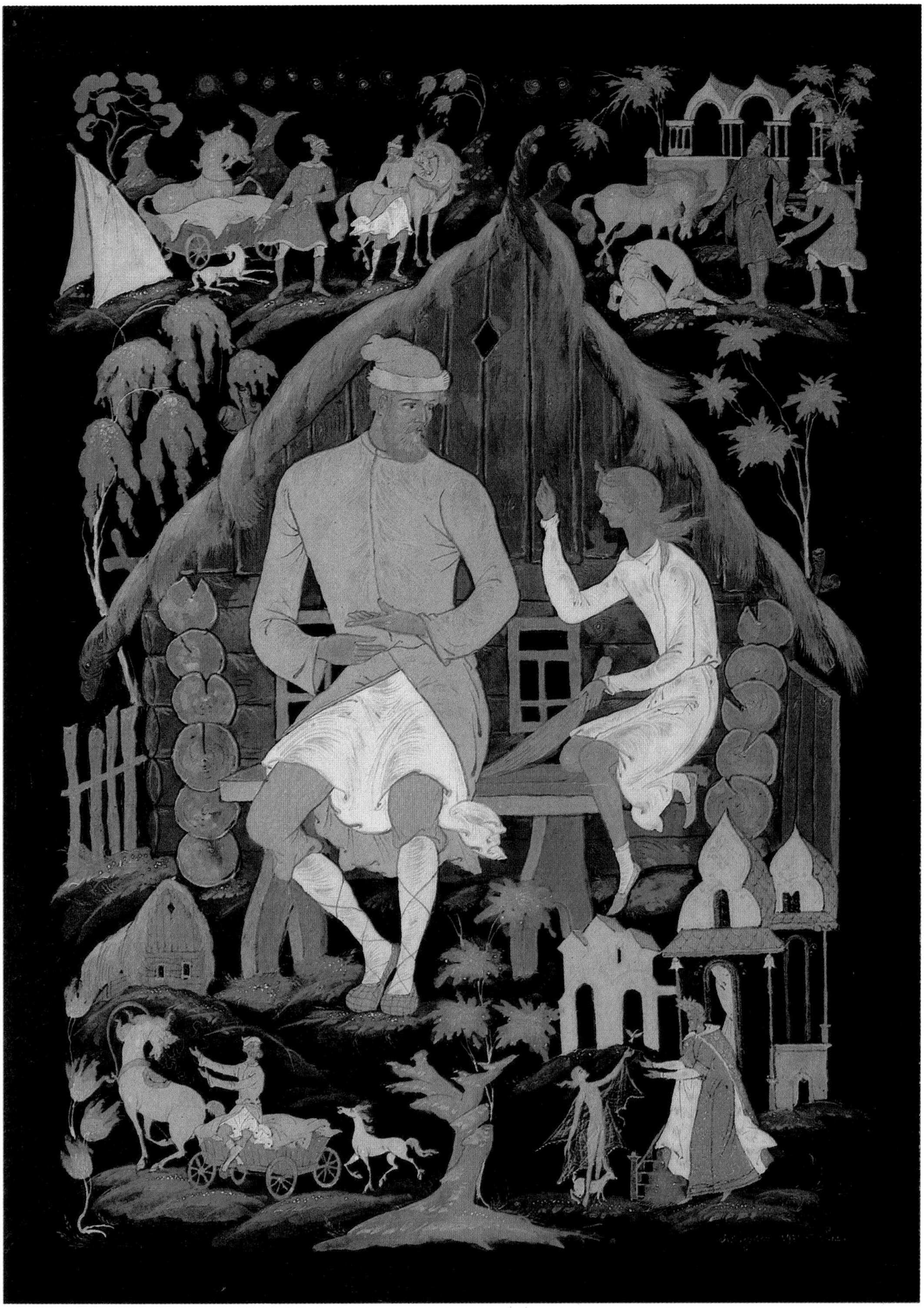

husband has a bay mare which is faster than anything in the world. If you lash her with a whip she will overtake a hare." "The second riddle is this: what is the fattest thing in the world?" "We have been feeding a spotted boar for the past two years, and he has become so fat he cannot stand on his own four feet." "The third riddle is: what is the softest thing in the world?" "Oh, everyone knows that: eiderdown! There's nothing softer." "And the fourth riddle is: what is the sweetest thing in the world?" "The sweetest thing," she said, "is my little grandson Ivanushka." "Oh thank you, neighbour. You have taught me good sense; I'll never forget that."

In the meantime, the poor brother shed bitter tears and went home. As he entered the house he was met by his seven-year-old daughter, his only child, who asked why he was sighing and shedding tears. "Who wouldn't sigh and shed tears? The king has set me four riddles which I will never solve." "Tell me what they are." "Very well, child. What is the strongest and swiftest thing in the world? What is the fattest, what is the softest and what is the sweetest?" "Go and tell the king this, Father. The strongest and swiftest thing in the world is the wind; the fattest is the earth, for it feeds everything that grows and lives; the softest is an arm, for whatever we lie on, we still put an arm beneath our head; and there is nothing sweeter in the world than sleep."

The two brothers, rich and poor, came before the king. The king heard their answers, then asked the poor man, "Did you make up those answers yourself or did someone help you?" "Your Royal Majesty," he said. "It was my seven-year-old daughter who helped me." "If your daughter is so wise," the king replied, "take her this silken thread. Let her weave a pretty towel for me by tomorrow morning." The poor man took the silken thread and went home sad and downcast. "Alas," he told his daughter. "The king has ordered you to weave a towel from this thread." "Grieve not, Father," said the little girl. She snapped off a twig from the besom, handed it to her father and told him, "Go to the king and tell him to find a craftsman who can make a loom from this twig, so that I can weave his towel." The poor man told this to the king. And the king, in return, gave him a hundred and fifty eggs, saying, "Give these to your daughter and tell her to hatch me a hundred and fifty chicks by tomorrow."

The poor man returned home even more sad and downcast than before. "Out of the frying pan, into the fire, my child." "Grieve not, Father," she answered. And she cooked the eggs and put them away for dinner and supper, then sent her father to the king. "Tell him that the chicks need one-day millet for feed. Let them plough a field, sow the millet, reap and thresh it all in a single day. Our chicks won't look at any other grain." The king listened to all this and said, "If your daughter is so wise, let her come to me tomorrow morning neither on foot nor on horseback, neither naked nor clothed, neither with a gift nor without one." "Oh dear," thought the poor man. "Even my daughter cannot solve such a hard riddle. We are surely lost."

"Grieve not, Father," said his daughter when she heard the task. "Go to the huntsmen and buy me a live hare and live quail." Her father did as she bid and brought the hare and quail.

Next morning, she took off her clothes, pulled a net over her, took the quail in her hand, sat upon the hare, and went off to the palace. The king met her at the palace gates. She bowed to him, saying, "Here is a little gift for you, Sire." And she handed him the quail. But as he stretched out his hand, the quail flapped its wings and flew away. "Very well," said the king, "you have done all I said. Now tell me this: your father is poor, so what do you live on?" "My Father catches fish on dry land, so he never needs bait for water. And I carry the fish in my skirt and cook soup." "You silly girl! When have fish ever lived on dry land? Fish swim in the sea!" "Are you so wise? When has a cart ever born a foal? Only mares give birth to foals!" The king awarded the foal to the poor man and took the girl into his palace. When she grew up he married her and she became queen.

The Sage

There was once a poor but sly peasant who was nicknamed Little Bug. One day he stole some linen from a dame and hid it in a sheaf of straw, then went about boasting that he had second sight. When the dame came to him to have her fortune told, Little Bug asked her, "What will you give me for my work?" "A pood of flour and a pound of butter." "Very well," he said. And he used his powers of second sight and told her where the linen was hidden. In two or three days the squire's stallion disappeared; Little Bug, the rascal, had led it away and tied it to a tree in the woods. So the squire sent for the peasant, who used his powers and said: "Go quickly and you will find the stallion in the woods tied to a tree." The stallion was fetched from the woods; the squire gave the peasant a hundred rubles and the man's fame began to spread about the realm. Then the king had the misfortune to lose his wedding ring; he looked here, there and everywhere—in vain. So he sent for the sage to be brought swiftly to the palace. And he was seized, bundled into a carriage and brought to the king.

"Now I'm for it," thought the man. "How can I find out what's happened to the ring? When the king gets angry he'll banish me to the end of the earth." "Welcome, my man," said the king. "Use your powers and tell me where my ring is. If you succeed I'll reward you with gold; if you fail, I shall chop off your head." Thereupon the peasant was led into a special room and given all night to use his powers and have the answer by morning.

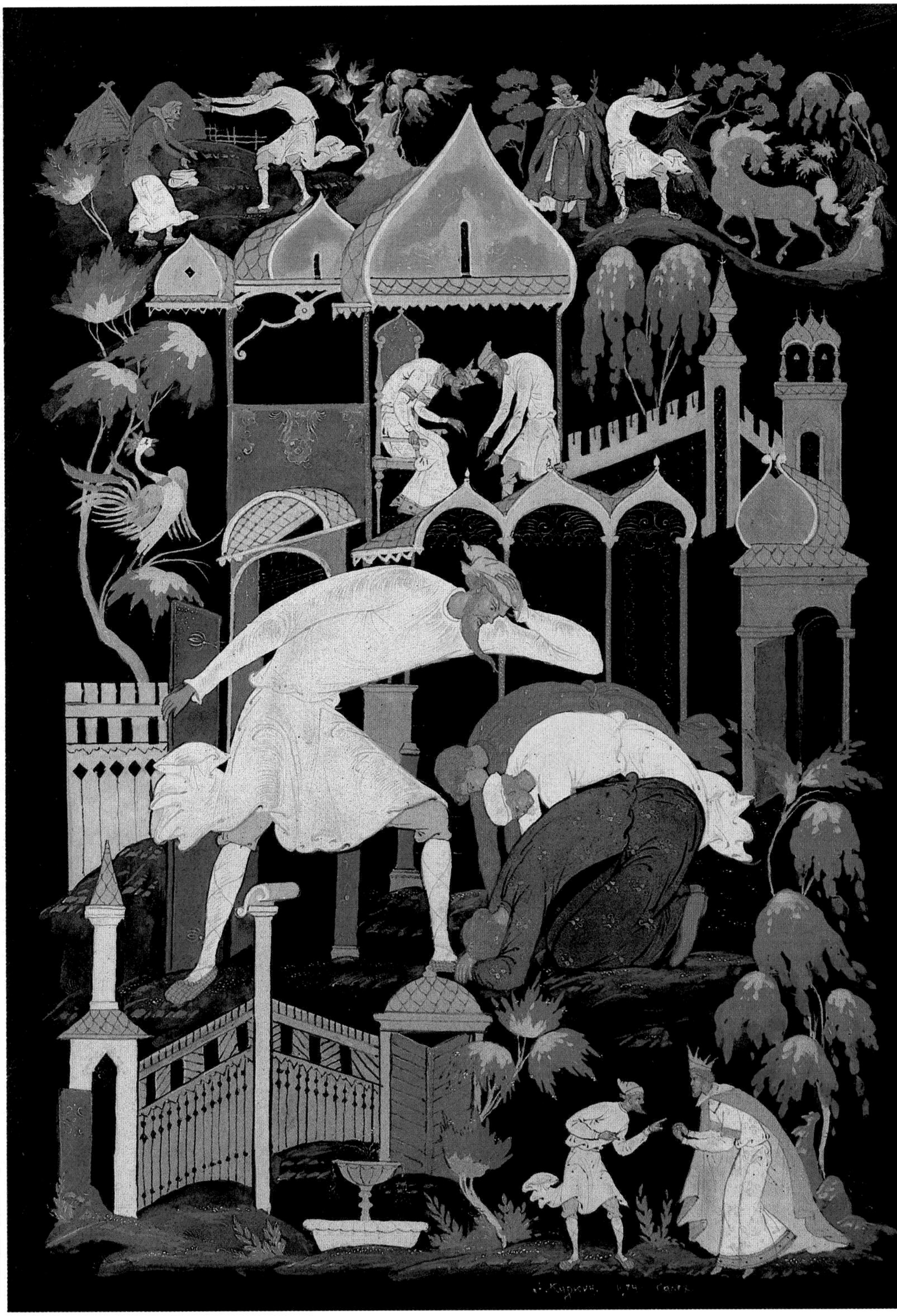

The peasant sat pondering in the room, "What answer can I give the king? I'd best wait till dead of night and make a dash for it; as soon as the third cock crows I'll be off."

The king's ring had been stolen by three servants: a lackey, a coachman and a cook. "Now, brothers," they said among themselves, "what if the sage finds us out? That will mean certain death for us... Let's listen at the door: if he keeps silent, we're safe, but if he finds us out, we'll have to beg him not to tell the king."

Off went the lackey to eavesdrop. Suddenly the first cock crowed and the peasant muttered, "Thank the Lord! That's one of them, two more to go." The lackey's heart fell and he rushed off to his companions. "Oh, brothers," he said. "He found me out. The moment I got to the door, he cried: 'That's one of them, two more to go!' " "Now let me listen," said the coachman. And he went to eavesdrop. Just then the second cock crowed, and the peasant muttered, "Thank the Lord. That's two of them, one more to go." "Oh dear, brothers," said the coachman to his cronies. "He's found me out too."

But the cook said, "If he finds me out, we'll have to go straight to him, fall on our knees and beg him not to give us away." So the cook went off to eavesdrop. Just then the third cock crowed; the peasant crossed himself, muttering, "Thank the Lord, that's all three of them!" And he made straight for the door to run away. But the thieves came up and fell on their knees, begging him, "Have mercy, do not tell the king. Here is the ring." "Very well, then, I forgive you."

Taking the ring, he lifted a floor-board and hid the ring under it. Next morning the king asked, "Well, peasant, how are things with you?" "I have the answer," he said. "Your ring rolled under this floor-board." With that the floor-board was raised and the ring found. The king rewarded the sage generously with gold, ordered the servants to give him food and drink aplenty, and himself went for a walk in the garden. As he was walking down the path, he saw a bug, picked it up and went back to the sage. "Now then, since you are a sage, tell me what's in my hand." The peasant took fright and said to himself, "Well, Little Bug, the king's got his hands on you now!" "Yes, yes, that is right," said the king. And he rewarded him even more richly and sent him home in style.

The Thief

There once lived an old man and woman who had a son named Ivan. They fed him until he grew big, then said to him, "Well, son, we've fed you till now; henceforth feed us to the end of our days." "Since you fed me till I grew big," replied Ivan, "feed me until I grow a moustache." So they fed him until he grew a moustache, then said, "Well, son, we've fed you until you grew a moustache; now feed us to the end of our days." "Oh, Father and Mother," replied their son, "since you fed me till I grew a moustache, feed me until I grow a beard." There was nothing for it: they gave him food and drink until he grew a beard; and then they said, "Well, son, we've fed you until you grew a beard; now feed us to the end of our days." "Since you fed me till I grew a beard, feed me until old age." The old man could bear it no longer and went to the squire to complain about his son.

The squire summoned Ivan, saying, "You idler, why don't you feed your father and mother?" "How can I feed them? Or are you telling me to steal? I never learned to work and now it's too late for me to learn." "I don't care," said the squire, "steal if you like, but feed your mother and father so that I hear no more complaints about you." Just then the squire was informed that his bath was ready and he went off to steam himself; it was nearly evening. The squire had his bath, came back and asked, "Hey, who's there? Hand me my slippers!" Quick as a flash Ivan took the squire's

151

boots, handed him the slippers, and went off with the boots under his arm. Once home he said, "Here, Father, take off your bast shoes and put on the squire's boots."

Next morning the squire discovered that his boots were missing and sent for Ivan. "Did you take my boots?" "I do not know and cannot tell, but it's my doing." "You rascal!" exclaimed the squire. "How dare you steal!" "But it was you, squire, who told me that you did not care as long as I fed my father and mother. I would not like to disobey your orders." "In that case," said the squire, "here's another order: go and steal my black ox from the plough. If you do, I'll give you a hundred rubles; if you don't, you'll get a hundred lashes." "As you say," replied Ivan.

Right away he made for the village, stole a rooster, plucked all its feathers and hastened to the field. He crept up to the edge of a furrow, picked up a clod of earth, put the rooster underneath it and hid behind some bushes. When the ploughmen went to plough a new furrow, they knocked against the clod of earth and thrust it aside. At once the plucked rooster jumped out and raced off across the ruts and hummocks. "What a miracle we've dug up!" cried the ploughmen, giving chase. When Ivan saw them running like madmen, he made quickly for the plough, cut the tail off one ox, stuck it in the mouth of a second, unharnessed the third and led it home.

The ploughmen chased and chased after the rooster, but failed to catch it. When they returned they found the black ox gone and the spotted ox without its tail. "Well, brothers," one said, "while we chased after the miracle, one ox ate another ox: it ate the black ox whole and bit off the spotted one's tail!" And they went to the squire with drooping heads. "Forgive us, Father, one ox ate another ox." "Oh, you stupid dolts," the squire railed at them, "whoever saw or heard of an ox eating another ox? Summon Ivan to me." The lad was summoned. "Did you steal the ox?" asked the squire. "I did, my lord." "What have you done with it?" "I slaughtered it; I sold the hide at the market and fed the meat to my father and mother." "Well done," said the squire. "Here's a hundred rubles. Now go and steal my favourite stallion which is kept behind six locks and three doors. If you succeed, I'll pay you two hundred rubles; if you fail, you'll get two hundred lashes." "Very well, my lord, I'll do my best."

Late that night Ivan crept into the squire's house. There was no one in the entrance hall, and he saw the squire's riding clothes hanging on a peg. Taking the overcoat and hat, he put them on, ran out onto the porch and shouted loudly to the coachmen and grooms, "Hey, lads, saddle up my favourite stallion and bring it here." The coachmen and grooms took him for their master, ran off to the stables, unlocked the six locks, opened the three doors and led the saddled stallion out to the porch in a trice. The thief mounted, lashed its flanks and was gone like the wind.

Next day the squire asked, "Well, how is my favourite stallion?" But the horse had disappeared the night before. He had to send for Ivan. "Was it you who stole

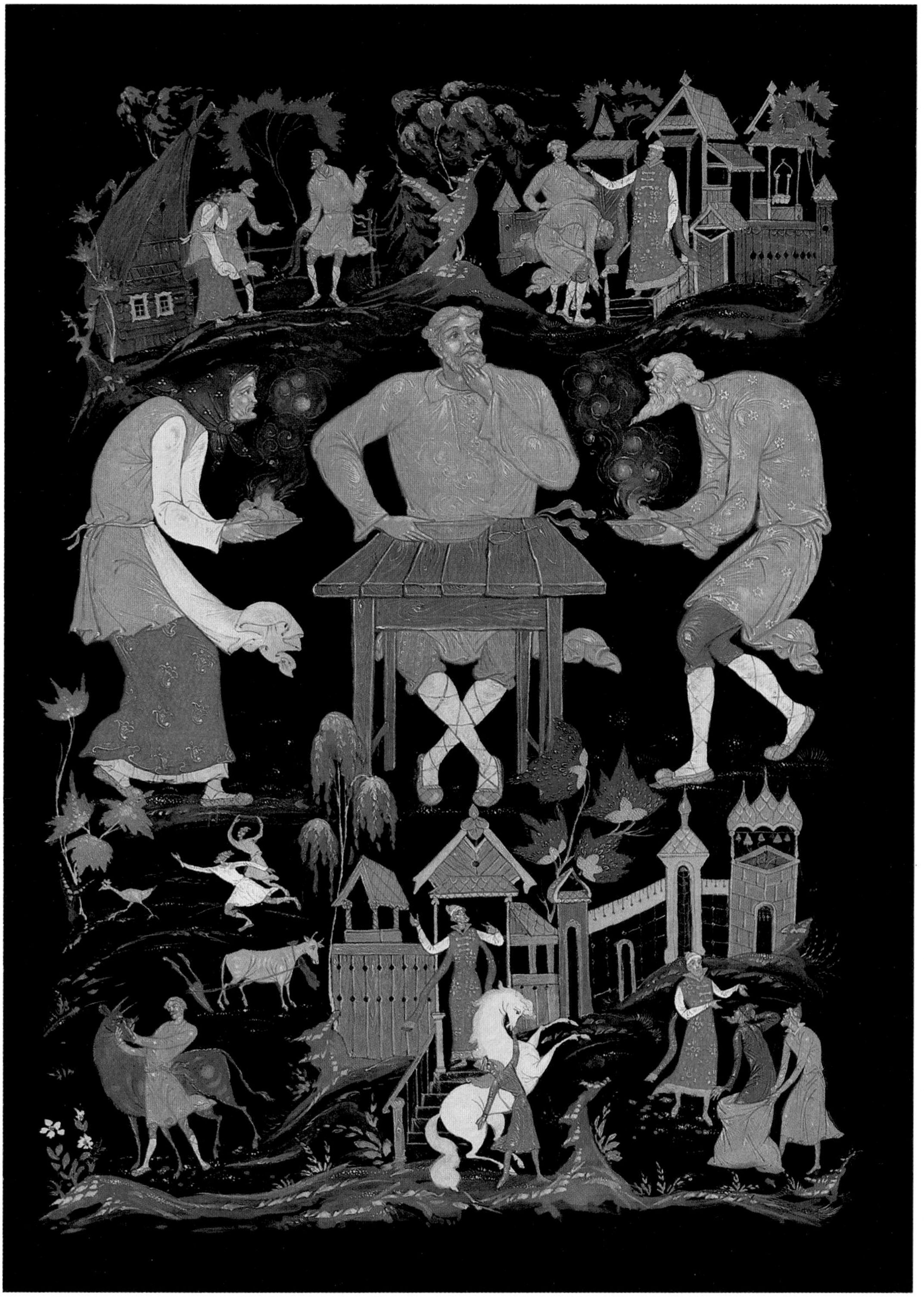

my stallion?" "It was indeed, squire." "Where is it now?" "I sold it to horse-traders." "You are lucky that I ordered you to steal it myself. Take your two hundred rubles. And now steal the holy hermit." "What do I get for my troubles, squire?" "What about three hundred rubles?" "That will do." "But what if you fail?" "That's up to you. Do what you will."

The squire then summoned the holy hermit and said to him, "Watch out: you had better pray all night long, don't dare to sleep. Ivan the thief has boasted he will carry you off." The holy man took fright, lost all desire to sleep and sat in his cell chanting prayers. On the stroke of midnight Ivan the thief came knocking at the window with a sack. "Who's there?" "An angel from heaven sent to bring you up to paradise alive. Climb into my sack." The holy man was stupid enough to climb into the sack, the thief tied him up, slung him over his shoulder and carried him off to the belfry. It was a long way. "Will we soon be there?" asked the holy man. "Wait and see," said Ivan. "At first the way is long and smooth, but at the end it's short and bumpy."

Ivan carried the sack upstairs, then let it roll down again. The holy man was badly bruised: he counted every step! "Oh, the angel spoke the truth," he said. "The first part of the journey is long and smooth, but the last part is short and bumpy. I never suffered so much even on earth." "Have patience, salvation is at hand," said Ivan. He lifted the sack, hung it on a fence near the gate, put two birch sticks as thick as a finger nearby, and wrote on the gate: "Whoever passes by and fails to hit this sack three times shall be cursed and sent to hell!" So everyone who passed by gave the sack three good whacks. The squire chanced to pass the gate and asked, "What is in that sack?" He ordered it to be taken down and untied. Out crawled the holy hermit... "How did you come to be in there? Didn't I tell you to watch out? I'm not sorry you were thrashed with sticks, but I'm sorry to have lost three hundred rubles because of you!"

The Crafty Peasant

There was once an old woman who had two sons. One died and the other went on a long journey. Three days later a soldier called at her house, asking her to let him spend the night there. "Come in, dear lad, where are you from?" "From the nether world, Grannie." "Ah, dear boy! My son has recently passed on; did you, perchance, see him?" "I did indeed: we shared the same room." "Well I never!" "He's tending cranes in the nether world." "Oh, my goodness! I hope it does not tire him too much." "It certainly does. You know that cranes are always wandering off among the sweet-briar, Grannie." "I hope he doesn't get his clothes torn." "He certainly does, tattered to pieces." "My dear boy, I have a length of linen and about ten rubles in money; will you take them to my son?" "Very well, Grannie." After a while the second son arrived home. "Greetings, Mother." "While you were gone, I had a visit from a man of the nether world, who told me about my dead son. They shared the same room. So I gave him linen and ten rubles to take to him." "If that's the case, Mother," said her son, "farewell. I'll go out into the world and if I find anyone more stupid than you I'll come back and support you. If not, I'll throw you out of the house." So saying he departed.

Coming to a village he stopped alongside the squire's yard and saw a sow waddling about with her piglets. He went down on his knees, bowing before the sow. The mistress was watching from a window and called to a serving girl, "Go and ask why that peasant is bowing." "Fellow," said the girl, "what are you doing on your knees bowing to a pig?" "Lassie," said the man, "go and tell the mistress that your spotted sow is my wife's sister; my son is to wed tomorrow and I am inviting her to the wedding. Ask your mistress's leave for the sow to be a guest at the wedding and her piglets to join the wedding procession." When the mistress heard this story, she told the girl, "What an oaf! Fancy inviting a sow to a wedding with piglets too. But never mind, let folk have a good laugh at him. Dress up the sow in my fur coat, and harness a brace of horses to the carriage; she must not go to the wedding on foot." So the carriage was prepared, the sow was placed in it with her piglets, and the peasant drove off with them.

The squire returned home from hunting. His wife greeted him, splitting her sides with laughter. "Upon my word, you should have been here to enjoy the fun. There was a peasant bowing to our sow. 'Your spotted sow is my wife's sister,' he said. And he invited her to his son's wedding, and her piglets to the wedding procession." "I know," said the squire, "you let her go." "That I did," she said. "I had her decked out in my fur coat and put in a carriage pulled by two fine horses." "But where was the peasant from?" "I've no idea, my dear." "Then it's not the peasant who's the oaf, it's you!" The squire flew into a rage at his wife's stupidity, saddled his fastest mare and set off in pursuit.

When the peasant heard the squire catching him up, he drove the horses and carriage into a dense forest and hid them there. Then he went back to the road, took off his hat, threw it upon the track and sat down beside it. "Hey, you," shouted the squire riding up. "Have you seen a peasant riding by with a brace of horses? He had a sow and some piglets in a carriage, too." "I certainly have," said the man. "He passed by long ago." "Which way did he go? How can I catch him?" "He's not far ahead, but there are many turnings. You'll only get lost. You probably don't know the road, do you?" "Then you go after him, brother. Catch the peasant for me." "No, I can't do that, squire, I've a falcon under my hat." "Never mind, I'll guard your falcon." "Don't let him escape. He's a rare bird. My master will skin me alive if he's lost." "How much is he worth?" asked the squire. "A good three hundred rubles." "Well, if I do let him escape, I'll pay up myself." "No, squire, that's what you say now, but I've no way of telling you'll keep your word." "So, you don't trust me, eh? Then here's three hundred rubles for you just in case." The peasant took the money and galloped off into the forest, while the squire stayed guarding the empty hat.

156

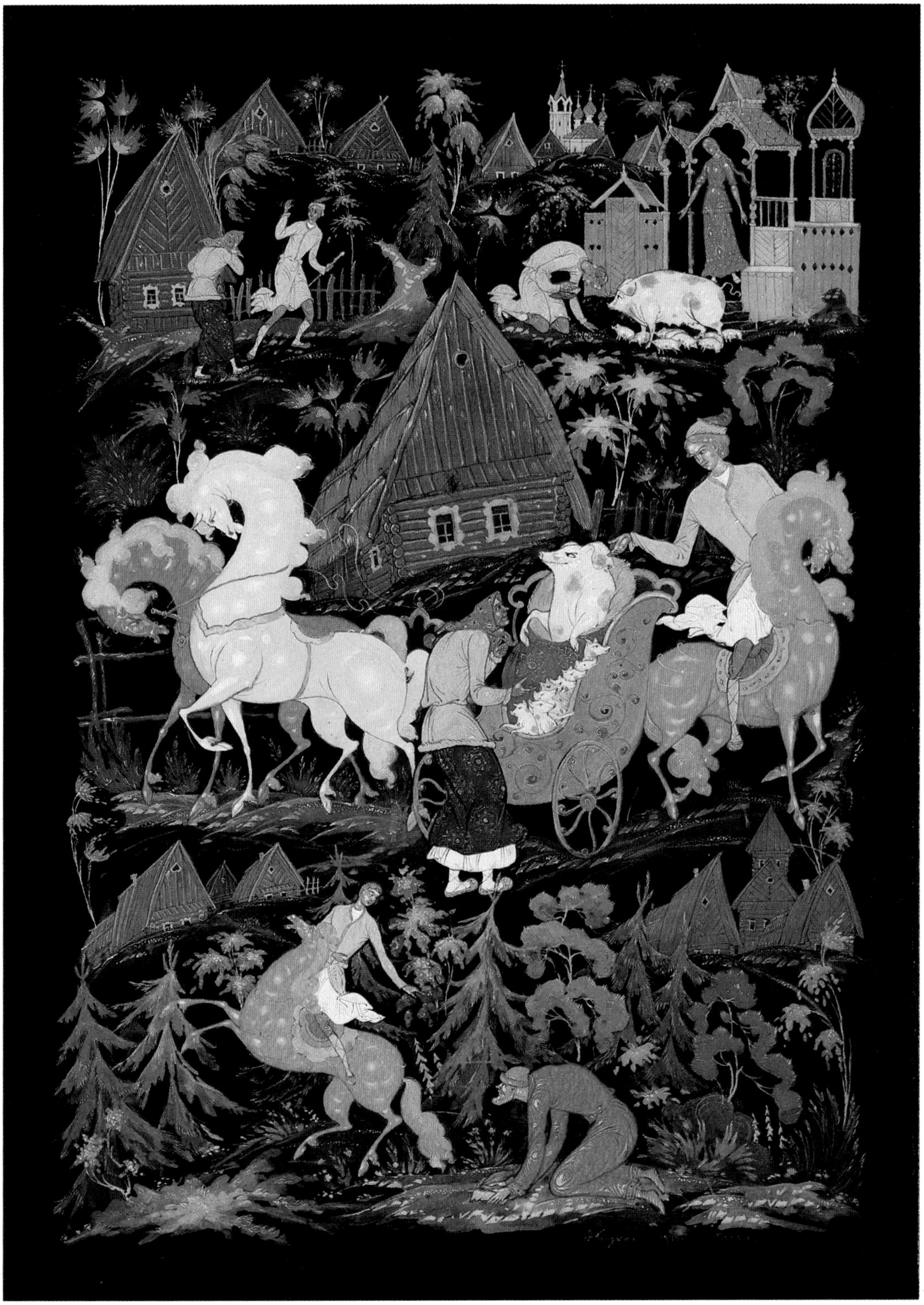

He had a long wait. The sun was already setting, but still the peasant did not return. "Perhaps I'd better look and see if there really is a falcon under this hat. If there is, the man'll be back; if not, there's no sense in waiting." He lifted the hat—and there was no falcon! "The scoundrel! That must have been the same peasant who tricked my wife!" Spitting with anger, the squire went back to his wife. The peasant had got home long ago. "Well, Mother," he said, "you can stay. There are folk more stupid than you in the world. I was given three horses and a carriage, three hundred rubles and a sow and piglets—all for nothing."

REQUEST TO READERS

Raduga Publishers would be glad to have your opinion of this book, its translation and design and any suggestions you may have for future publications.

Please send all your comments to 43, Sivtsev Vrazhek Lane, Moscow, Russia.

E-mail: raduga @ pol.ru

ББК 84.4Р
В67

Волшебное кольцо

В67   Народные русские сказки. Из собрания А. Н. Афанасьева (на английском языке) / Илл. А. Куркина. — М.: ОАО Издательство "Радуга", 1998. — 160 с., илл.

В книгу вошли тридцать три сказки, собранные знаменитым фольклористом XIX века А.Н. Афанасьевым.

В $\dfrac{4803010104 - 157}{030(03) - 98}$ без объявления

The text is printed according to the edition:
The Magic Ring. Russian Folk Tales.
Raduga Publishers, Moscow, 1985.

ИБ № 6980

Редактор *Н. Вергелис*
Художник *А. Куркин*
Оформление *В. Мирошниченко*
Художественный редактор *К. Баласанова*
Технический редактор *Е. Мишина*

Подписано в печать 30.11.98. Формат 84x108/16. Бумага мелован.
Гарнитура Таймс. Печать офсетная. Условн. печ. л. 16,8.
Уч.-изд. л. 14,75. Тираж 8 000 экз. Изд. № 8722.

Лицензия ЛР № 020846 от 23 декабря 1993 г.

ОАО Издательство «Радуга»
121839, Москва, пер. Сивцев Вражек, 43.

ОАО «Иван Федоров». 191119, Санкт-Петербург,
ул. Звенигородская, 11. Зак. 8289.

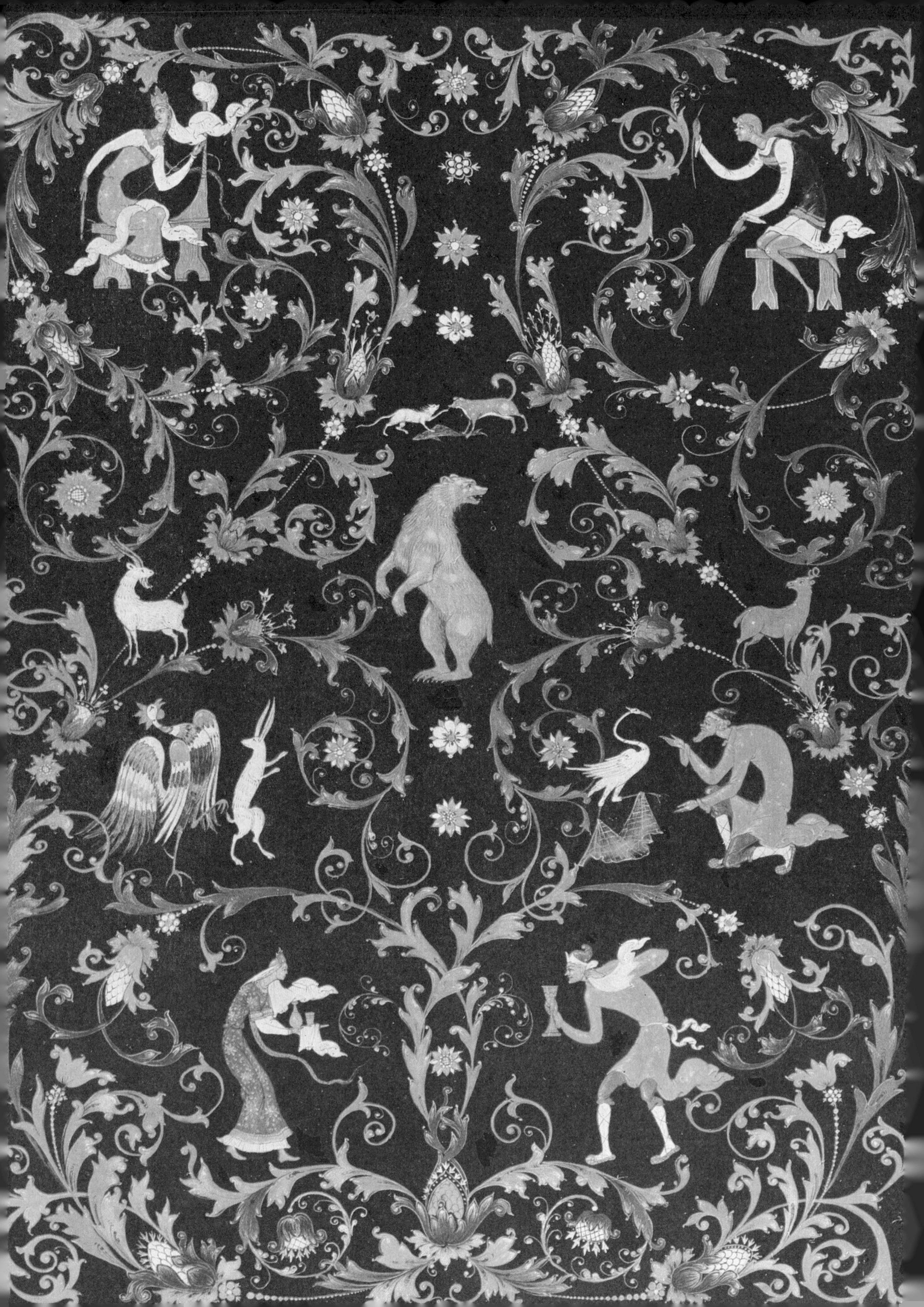